CLAIRE HIGHTON-STEVENSON

CLAIRE HIGHTON-STEVENSON

Copyright © 2024 Claire Highton-Stevenson
All rights reserved.
The Taste of Her
This is a work of fiction. Names, characters, businesses, places, events, locales, and incidents are either the products of the author's imagination or used in a fictitious manner. Any resemblance to actual persons, living or dead, or actual events is purely coincidental

Copyright © 2025 Claire Highton-Stevenson
All rights reserved.
Hot to the Touch
This is a work of fiction. Names, characters, businesses, places, events, locales, and incidents are either the products of the author's imagination or used in a fictitious manner. Any resemblance to actual persons, living or dead, or actual events is purely coincidental.

ISBN:9798304125307

DEDICATION

To those friends who come into your life later, but not late…They arrived perfectly on time.

Looking forward to more murder, mystery, comical, dinners with AADS.

And for those with more grammar skills than I…A huge thank you to Linda and Michelle.

CLAIRE HIGHTON-STEVENSON

AUTHOR'S NOTE

After 30 plus books I don't know what to say as an acknowledgement anymore, so I've switched to Author's note, where I can waffle.

And if you'd like to waffle more with me, you can find me on my new Patreon (Free) Site. Links at the end of the book.

For me, much of social media has now lost its charm. Overrun by ads and trolls and posts get lost in the either, arriving days after the event. But on Patreon, I have found a space where none of that happens. Where I can engage with my readers ad free. And you might be concerned that it's a Patreon page, because those are usually utilised to monetise. I'm not doing that. My profile will remain free to any reader who wishes to join in the conversation. The only thing I'm asking anyone to do, is buy books. Especially in these dark days when Amazon boycotts threaten out very existence.

Without you all, this isn't possible.

Thank you!

And if you ever find somebody, who you find Hot to the Touch, remember not everyone gets a second chance. Grab it when you get yours.

CLAIRE HIGHTON-STEVENSON

ONE

"What's it called?" Camille asked her friend of thirty-five years.

Rosie glanced up at her over the edge of her magazine and pushed her strawberry blonde hair away from her face. "You're going to need to be more specific if you want an actual answer, or were you being rhetorical?"

Camille sighed. "I mean when you get to that stage in life, and nothing makes sense anymore." She stared across the pool at the goddess sunning herself on the edge. Dark curls, now almost slick against her head, cascaded down her back, still wet from her last venture into the water. Even from across the pool, Camille could see the rivulets dripping down her arms and chest, running to the sanctuary of that flimsy bikini, never to be seen again as they nestled into an ample bosom. The tattooed arm was interesting, Camille mused, although she was too far away to see what the design was.

"Mid-life crisis?" Rosie answered.

Nodding, Camille reached for her drink. It was something colourful, with a ridiculous name and very alcoholic, but it tasted wonderful in this almost unbearable heat. "Yes."

"Why?" Rosie asked, despite her face being back behind her magazine.

"I think I'm having one."

Rosie closed the magazine slowly and placed it down onto the pile of books. All stacked neatly beside an oversized beach bag. One she'd filled with every possible thing they might need for an afternoon by the pool.

Camille was not the mid-life crisis kind of woman. At least, she hadn't been thus far in her life. There were no clues to suggest there could be an impromptu upsetting of her usual equilibrium. Camille Franklyn was no nonsense; tough as old boots.

Nothing could knock Camille off of her A-game.

"What's wrong?"

Camille let out a long, loud sigh and flopped back against her sun lounger, dragging her attention away from the goddess and back to her friend. She studied Rosie for a moment. Still in good shape - they both were for women entering their fifties. Her hair kept shorter than Camille liked to wear herself, a few greys sprouting but on the whole a nice-looking woman. Had she ever been attracted to Rosie? No. Why not?

"I just feel…different, like something is awakening in me that I didn't know existed, and it's throwing me off kilter."

"What thing?"

Camille was silent. Her cheeks would have reddened had it not been for the fact they were already sunburnt from yesterday. She instinctively pulled her hat lower.

"You know you can tell me anything?" Rosie offered, twisting around and planting her feet on the ground.

"Of course I can, I just… I don't know if I'm ready to tell myself it yet."

Rosie stood up. "Well now I am intrigued. And I need another drink. So do you. Same again?"

Camille nodded. "Yes, why not?" She watched her friend slide her flip-flops on and then click-clack her way towards the bar. That was when she felt it again.

Eyes on her.

She turned slowly back to look across the pool and found herself the subject of the dark-haired woman's attention.

It sent a shiver through her body. A sensation she recognised. A delicious feeling of instant attraction. But why?

She was Camille Franklyn. Fifty-two years old. A straight mother of two who had a successful business career in finance. Her body count wasn't high, but it was very male. And yet, the idea of this woman…this complete stranger sunbathing across from her…doing very imaginable things to her, had revealed something within her. Something she wasn't sure she knew what to do with.

Long, tanned legs shifted when the woman raised a hand to her sunglasses and lowered them down her nose just enough to make it obvious she was definitely looking at Camille. Her mouth twisted slowly into a smile that conveyed much more in the silence than words ever could.

"I decided to get something different," Rosie was saying as she closed in on the sun loungers with two glasses in her hand and a menu tucked under her arm. "Hungry?"

Camille took one last glance at the woman who was mysteriously captivating her before she craned her neck up towards Rosie. "No, not really." *'Not for food' anyway*, she said to herself.

"Oh. Well, I'll wait for you then." Rosie passed her the glass and then licked her finger where some of it had spilled onto her hand as she'd walked. "Who were you looking at?"

Camille turned her head slightly back to the other side of the pool and got herself comfortable again.

"My mid-life crisis."

TWO

"So, you're gay now? Is that what you're telling me?"

Camille rolled her eyes. "No, I am not telling you that I am gay. I'm simply saying that clearly there must be some dormant part of me that has those interests."

"Lesbian interests?" Rosie said with a smirk on her face that required a raise of a brow to accompany it.

Looking at herself in the hotel room mirror, Camille pursed her lips. She pulled her hair up. It was far too hot still, even with the evening breeze, to have it all hanging around her neck, despite how good her now sun-kissed her hair looked - a shade lighter than her natural honey blonde.

The ivory-coloured silk chemise over the flowy white cotton trousers made her tanned skin glow.

Was she a lesbian now?

"It's just a door that's opened. I haven't even stepped through it, I just..." She hooked an earring into her left ear. "Haven't you ever just wanted to try something different?"

Rosie sat down elegantly on the edge of the bed. "I try something different off the menu all the time. I've yet to want to try lady parts."

"Don't mock me," Camille said, smiling at her in the mirror as she fiddled to slide the second earring into her other lobe.

"I'm not. I'm intrigued, to be honest. Have you always had these thoughts?"

Camille considered it for the umpteenth time. "I've always found women attractive. I can see what it is about Julia Roberts that would make anyone want her. But no, I don't think I've ever considered actually dining out on *lady parts* before now." She turned around and checked her reflection from behind.

"Maybe you should then," Rosie said with a shrug. "I mean, everybody is doing it. Apparently late-in-life lesbians are all the rage if you take any notice of Tik Tok."

"Tsk, Tik Tok? You know I don't use social media."

"Well, if you did, you'd know by now that you can be anything and anyone you want. Including a rampaging later-in-life lesbian," Rosie said, yanking the door open and coming face to face with an older couple on their way down to dinner. She smiled at them both. "Evening."

When the other guests had disappeared around the corner, Camille and Rosie both burst into laughter.

"That will give them something to talk about over dinner," Camille said, catching her breath and calming herself.

"Maybe it will give them food for thought." Rosie grinned. "Speaking of food, do you want to share a paella one night before we go? They won't let me order one on my own."

"Of course. Just say when, I'm not fussy."

They took the stairs. It was only one floor down. Entering into the large dining room just as the couple from the hallway were being seated.

"Do you know what I think?" Rosie said, nudging Camille as they waited to be shown to a table.

"What?"

"We could..." she leaned closer, "have a 'what happens in Madeira stays in Madeira', kind of holiday."

Camille turned to her, eyes twinkling. "Are you suggesting we get laid?"

"I'm suggesting that if the opportunity for a holiday romance were to present itself in these last few nights here, then why not? We're both adults, and we have no significant others to worry about."

"I see what you're saying." Camille smiled as she considered it. Maybe this was the opportunity to scratch this new itch. Just as she thought it, she caught sight of something, or someone, moving in her peripheral vision.

It was her.

Sans the sunglasses and bikini, instead she was —wrapped—was the only word Camille could think of, in a white dress that clung to every curve of her body. Her tanned skin highlighted even more against the whiteness of the cloth. The tattoo was more evident – bright colours that swirled from the top of her arm to her wrist.

Their eyes met, and there was that smile again.

It said, yes.

It was a smile of permission. To approach. To talk. To...who knew what else.

"Good evening. May I see you to your table?" A man's voice jolted Camille from her thoughts. She pulled her eyes away to acknowledge him and ignored the look her friend was giving her. She could read that too. It was

Rosie's 'I see what you're looking at.' kind of face.

"Oh, shut up," Camille said, passing Rosie to follow the younger man to their table.

"What happens in Madeira…" Rosie sung out behind her, chuckling to herself when she glanced back and noticed the woman still watching Camille.

THREE

"So, you've never even thought about it? Not even once?" Camille asked Rosie as they ate. She tried to focus on the medium-rare steak and perfectly fried chips, and not glance too often towards the woman now sitting at the bar, openly staring at her.

"Nope," Rosie said. "I mean, don't get me wrong, men are generally pigs and finding a decent one to date is extraordinarily difficult at times. But I like them, and their boy parts, and everything those boy parts do."

"Well, so do I," Camille agreed. "On the whole, sometimes…"

"Sounds like you're not as sure as you thought you were."

Camille looked from Rosie to the woman on the stool. "No… I… I was married for twenty years. Of course I enjoyed—"

"You divorced him because you stopped having sex."

"We stopped being intimate-full stop-and he found another outlet for that," Camille said, sipping her cocktail.

"Hm hm."

"What does that mean?"

Rosie chuckled. "It means, maybe, with your new-found dormant fantasies—"

"They're not fantasies." Camille scoffed and swallowed the last mouthful of her drink.

"Then what would you call them?"

The woman on the stool paid for a second drink with her card, without taking her eyes off Camille. She licked her lips and then dragged the lower one between her teeth, and it took everything Camille had to turn away.

Rosie turned to look back at whatever was keeping Camille so focused.

"Ah, the woman from the pool. She's hot, I'll give you that."

"She's too young. But I can enjoy looking at her."

Rosie grinned. "I'm betting she's over thirty, and that's—"

"Far too young," Camille insisted.

"Pfft. I might agree if we were at home and this was a long-term option, but…" She waved to the waiter and indicated the bill. "We're in Madeira, and you are a free woman."

The waiter slid the bill onto the table.

"I have a headache," Rosie said.

"Oh, well, let's get back to the room and—"

Rosie rolled her eyes and took the bill. "No, I'm going to go back to the room and lie down quietly in the dark, and you…" She stood up. "You're going to finish your drink, and then go over there and talk to her."

"I am not," Camille said, quite defiantly.

"Oh, you bloody well are," Rosie said firmly. "Find out if this is just a fantasy, or something you really want."

"What if—"

"If what?" Rosie sat back down again.

"I've never…with a woman, you know."

Rosie laughed. "How many men have gone down on you?"

"Enough. I didn't keep count."

"My point is, you know what you liked and didn't like, what did it for you and what didn't…"

"Of course, but it's not—"

"It is. It's just communication. And in all honesty…" Rosie glanced back at the woman. "She doesn't strike me as a newbie." She stood back up, covered Camille's hand with her own and squeezed. "Find out…and Camille?"

"Yes?"

"Enjoy it."

FOUR

Camille finished her drink. For a full minute, she sat at the table and watched as the other woman waved over the bartender and signalled, "Two."

Standing, Camille made a decision. It was now or never. Rosie was right. This was an opportunity she'd be foolish not to take, wasn't it?

She'd regret it. The 'what ifs,' and the never knowing.

Confidently, she walked towards the bar.

Towards the possibilities of something new.

The woman smiled knowingly as she approached.

"I did wonder if you might follow your friend and leave," the woman said, using her index finger to push a crystal tumbler towards Camille. Its contents a large ice ball, almost the size of the glass, swimming in clear liquid. "Tequila, how it should be drunk. Slowly, so you can taste it and enjoy it."

Her voice was sultry, a hint of an accent, maybe French, definitely not Spanish, but it was there, and it was subtle, sexy.

"Are you going to join me?" she asked and looked towards the stool. "I'm Leila." She held her hand out. Long fingers, short nails painted a bright yellow.

"Camille."

As their hands touched, and fingers gripped,

Leila's thumb rubbed slowly against Camille's skin.

"Camille? That's beautiful. It suits you."

"You're very charming." Camille rested her arm along the bar and cupped the glass in her palm, mirroring Leila.

Leila smiled slowly. "I like women. I think they should be treated the right way, and if you hadn't noticed, I like you."

"Oh, I noticed," Camille answered, captivated now she was much closer. Brown eyes. She'd guessed that herself earlier, but it was nice to have confirmation. "You're difficult not to notice."

Leila laughed. "I think only interested parties' notice. Men mostly. I'm flattered but..." She shrugged. Her fingertips reached out and touched Camille's hand again.

"How old are you?" Camille asked, feeling the heat surge her body and ignite her.

"My age won't matter if you spend the night with me."

"What makes you think I want to do that?"

Leila let her eyes roam Camille. "Sweetie, you've wanted that from the moment you laid your eyes on me three days ago." Her other palm landed gently on Camille's knee. "Tell me I'm wrong."

Camille said nothing. She didn't have to. Her eyes said it all.

"So, I think we should enjoy this tequila, and you can decide if you want to come to my room or regret missing out on this moment for the rest of your life."

Camille laughed at Leila's brazen confidence, and

yet, felt at ease with it.

"You really do think highly of yourself, don't you?"

"Camille, I am very confident in the strong possibility that we will spend an extremely pleasurable night together. And that scares you a little bit."

"Am I that obvious?"

Leila pushed her finger and thumb together. "Just a little." She smiled knowingly.

Lifting her drink to her lips, Camille admitted, "I've never done this before."

"A one-night stand? Holiday romance? Been with a woman?"

"Yes. All of that…" Camille nodded. "I was married, had two children and then when that ended, I was single for a while before I dated a few men. Short relationships mingled in there somewhere…but never a woman, or anything so forbidden."

"I'm going to be honest, Camille, there's something about you that just turns me on. I'm attracted to you, and I'd like to fuck you, but if it's not something—"

"I want that," Camille cut in. Just the words, and the way Leila's mouth moved when she said it, caused an instant arrow of desire that hit hard. "I'm just…"

"Nervous?"

"Yes. Is that silly?"

Leila reached for the glass and took it from her. Then she took her hand and stepped off the stool, urging Camille to follow. "In the morning, you will think so, yes."

FIVE

Leila Ortez stepped inside and crossed the room to open the patio doors that led to the balcony. A refreshing breeze instantly cooled the warm space. She stepped outside and leaned against the metal rail that edged the balcony wall, taking in the view of the town further down the coast, all lit up and twinkling in the night sky. Music from the outside bar below drifted up to be heard from the balcony.

She turned and stared back into the room, at the woman who had followed her in. Camille stood just inside the closed door, hands clasped together in front of her. Nervous, yes, but confident enough to be here.

"Do you want to leave?" Leila asked.

"No," Camille replied, but didn't move.

The curtains billowed as a gust of wind caught them. Leila smiled and casually stepped back inside, watched intently by her guest.

She liked that.

Complete attention.

Leaning down, she flicked the switch to the bedside lamp and let the small bulb illuminate. She then turned to face Camille, reaching up and behind her own neck to loosen the clasp that held her dress up.

Undone, the material fell to the floor and pooled at her feet, leaving her naked.

She said nothing, enjoying the way thoughts moved across Camille's face.

Curiosity, a little fear, intrigue.

Slowly, she stepped towards Camille.

Her lips curled upwards again when she stood in front of the older woman. Leaning forward, she knew that Camille was thinking she would kiss her. Instead, she reached past and flicked off the main light.

"Do you like what you see, Camille?" she whispered seductively against Camille's ear before moving away and affording her the opportunity to look some more.

Camille visibly swallowed before she nodded and stuttered, "Y-yes."

"That's good, it's a start, yes?"

"Do you want me to get undressed?" Camille asked with such a hint of hesitation that Leila felt the thrill of it.

A woman like this, confident, demure and capable, now not quite so sure of herself and the situation she'd found herself in.

"Do you want to get undressed?" Leila asked, dragging her index finger down Camille's neck.

"I—" Camille closed her eyes and gathered her thoughts, and without a word, she turned and pulled her ponytail to one side.

Leila didn't need any instruction to understand the silent plea: undress me.

Assured fingers reached for the tiny button and expertly flicked it back through the safety of the loop that held it secure. When she took hold of the zip, she moved closer. Camille pressed up against the back of the door.

The zip lowered, and then Leila's hand moved to the base of Camille's spine, sliding under the material and around until she could slip beneath the band of her trousers and underwear.

"What will I find?" she whispered once more against Camille's ear.

"I uh—" Camille gasped when deft fingers parted her and slid effortlessly against her clit. "God, that's—"

"Wet." Leila chuckled, slowly circling the already engorged bundle of nerves. "I like that, Camille."

"Hm hm."

"You like that, don't you?"

Camille nodded, biting her lip. "Yes," she finally got out just before Leila's fingertip slid lower. "Oh, God."

"I will lead until you decide otherwise, Camille. You understand that, right?"

"Yes."

"Good." Her fingers withdrew, and she smiled to herself at the small groan Camille emitted at the loss. "Don't worry, I'll be back there any minute, but right now..." She stepped back and turned Camille around. "I want to see you naked."

SIX

In that moment, Camille had a thought about her life. There was no element of it where she wasn't in control. Even in her marriage, she had taken the lead. At work she was very much the ball-crushing Ice Queen who took no shit from anyone and got things done. And yet, here she was allowing a complete stranger to dominate her.

And Leila was right.

It made her wet.

She could feel her clit pounding between her thighs, desperate to be touched and played with and tortured if need be. Not painfully. *She wasn't into that, was she?*

No. Tortured…as in teased. Taken to the brink and held back from it – pushed to her limits. What were her limits? Why was she only considering that now?

Camille's eyes scanned the naked form in front of her. Perfect breasts, perky and tanned. That was a surprise. She hadn't been topless around the pool.

Dark nipples, hard and erect.

Camille scanned lower and understood she was being presented with this moment to do so, but it wouldn't last long. Leila looked ready to devour her.

"Take it off, Camille," Leila said, a little impatiently. "Unless you've changed your mind."

"No, I haven't, I just... I wanted to look at you."

Leila grinned. "You'll have plenty of time for that."

Without further ado, Camille raised the hem of her chemise and lifted it off over her head. Just as quickly, she pushed her trousers to the floor.

"All of it." Leila's instructions sent another shot of arousal directly to her clit.

When she was almost naked, the tattooed arm of her soon to be new lover, slid around her. A warm palm eased slowly upward until it reached the underside of her breast.

Camille held eye contact as she reached behind her back and unclipped her bra. When it loosened, Camille brought her arms up instinctively to cover her breasts.

Leila moved closer and took her hands, pulling them away until they dropped to her sides.

"I'm going to say this once, and once only." Her hands raised and took hold of Camille's face. "You are beautiful as you are. Do not hide from me, but more importantly, do not hide from yourself." Her palms slid away from Camille's cheeks. Taking hold of the straps to her bra, Leila pulled them away from Camille's shoulders until her breasts were uncovered. "See, so beautiful, don't you think?"

Camille was unsure what she thought about anything anymore, but she wasn't going to argue with the gorgeous creature who was able to turn every nerve ending into a flickering spark, ready to combust at any moment, while also liquifying her insides, and turning her legs to jelly.

"Yes." Camille gasped as she looked down at the

fingers rolling her nipple gently between them. She couldn't remember a time when she had ever been this turned on, and she could do nothing to stop the groan of approval that escaped because of the sensation the movement was creating.

"Shall we continue?" Leila asked. Her other hand sliding down Camille's hip, stopping at the band around her waist where her lace knickers sat snugly against her skin.

"Yes," Camille answered. Her hands moved by their own volition to grab at the material and pushed it away from her skin as though it was the cause of her body's discomfort, the lace now itching against her sensitive flesh.

She needed them gone.

She needed Leila's attention on her.

With the underwear wrapped around her knees, she watched as Leila stepped forward, eyes held. Camille cried out when those fingertips plunged once more between her folds and firmly pressed against her.

"Now, we play. Okay?" Leila smirked, circling her clit expertly. "Now, we play."

SEVEN

She was led.

Leila held her hand and walked backwards until the bed hit the back of her calves and she smiled once more. She sat herself down, perched on the edge. Her knees parting to reveal herself completely to Camille's gaze.

"On to your knees please, Camille."

Heart pounding, Camille did as she was asked and found her eyeline now with a very different view. Unable to look away, she felt almost indecent as she studied Leila's pussy.

God, did she just call it that? She'd never used that word in her life, and yet, here she was, and her brain could only react. There was no chance to consider or plan, just a reaction.

"Come closer," Leila instructed, her thighs parting further. "You see how wet you make me?"

Camille could see.

It was obvious. The evidence was right there. Hairless, wet, and puffy outer lips and the tiniest bud of her clitoris poking out through the slim gap that had opened with the movement.

"Inhale, Camille. Breathe me in. Allow all of your senses to enjoy this."

Closing her eyes, Camille breathed deeply. A

unique, sweet, spicy aroma filled her nostrils – not unlike her own scent she considered.

She felt her hands being taken. Her eyes remained closed as she continued to breathe and enjoy the way her brain was altering its thought patterns, reminding her over and over that she was naked, in a room with another naked woman, using words like pussy and enjoying the scent Leila's pussy radiated.

Her palms were placed down onto warm flesh, Leila's thighs if she were to guess.

"Explore," Leila said quietly. "Let your fingertips roam my body."

"I want to touch you," Camille admitted.

"You are touching me."

"No, I—not…I want to touch you." Her eyes opened, and she found Leila's eyes locked on her. "Your…I want to touch your…"

"Say it," Leila urged. "What do you want to touch, Camille?"

It was one thing using words in her head. Saying them aloud, however…

Leila leaned forward, her mouth against Camille's ear.

"Pussy?"

"Yes."

Leila took her hand once more and pulled it between her legs, until Camille could feel the heat against her fingertips, but not touch.

"Say it. Tell me." Their eyes locked once more.

"I want to touch…your pussy," Camille said in

barely a whisper, still shocked at herself that she would even think such language.

"Own it, Camille. Don't shy away when you are so close."

She was right. Camille knew that. In any other area of her life, she wouldn't be embarrassed or afraid to ask for what she needed. God, usually she just demanded it, so why was this different?

"Pussy." She spoke more confidently. "I want your pussy."

Without another word her fingers were thrust against the damp, soft skin.

"You only need to ask."

Everything else was instinctual, and when Leila brought her hand up and slid her fingers into Camille's hair, firmly encouraging her forward, Camille breathed deeper and went with it.

Her face fell between firm, warm thighs. Her nose and mouth pressed against the soft flesh just long enough to appreciate it.

"Use your tongue. Kiss it," Leila urged, her hips rising to meet Camille's mouth. The fingers in her hair tightened. Finally, Camille pressed her lips more firmly and moved them in a way that yielded soft mewls of delight. Every sound and taste encouraged more enthusiasm.

Camille's tongue slid forward and lapped at Leila's engorged clitoris.

Leila cried out, "Yes, like that!" Her body jolting with the pleasurable sensations Camille was creating.

Elated, Camille plunged deeper. Wanting to

experience more.

    The world of sapphic sex had not just opened a door to Camille Franklyn, it had blown it wide open, and there was no way she was turning back now.

EIGHT

Rosie was showered and dressed, reading the hotel's brochures offering excursions and entertainment, when the door to their room opened slowly.

"The wanderer returns." She smiled lazily as Camille entered the room and fell back against the now closed door. The usually elegant and put together woman she had known all these years looked like she'd been mauled by a wild animal. Her hair was unbrushed and pulled roughly back into a ponytail, her make-up was smeared, and she had several marks around her collarbone that looked conspicuously like love bites. As for her clothes, well, they'd need ironing at the very least.

"Judging from the state of you, and the fact that it is almost 10am, I'm going to hazard a guess that someone had a good night?"

"I'm not sure I have the words for what that was," Camille admitted.

She looked as though she were in shock - a happy shock, at least.

"That good, eh?" Rosie chuckled.

"I said, and did, things I'd never have imagined in my wildest fantasies… I don't know who I am anymore." Camille finally pushed off from the door and closed the short distance to sit on her bed. "Maybe I am gay now…"

Rosie raised one brow. "Do you need a drink? I know it's early but…"

"No. I need a shower though." She stood back up again and grabbed her towel. "I'll meet you down by the pool?"

"I can wait for you here if you want to talk about it?"

Camille smiled at her old friend. "I will talk about it, but right now, I think I still need to process it, and-" She sniffed herself. "Jesus I smell like sex."

Rosie guffawed. "I thought that was a myth."

"So did I, but now, I know different." She pushed the bathroom door open. "I'll be down the minute I'm showered.

"Alright, I'll order us up some late breakfast."

"Yes, that would be lovely," Camille said, the sudden thought of food creating a loud rumble from her tummy even Rosie heard. "I am starving."

"Worked up an appetite, clearly," Rosie teased and picked up her bag, slinging it over her shoulder. "I'll try and grab some good loungers but no doubt they'll all be gone now."

"Do your best. We'll make do with whatever you get."

Camille closed the door, and Rosie found herself grinning as she left the room and headed down to the pool.

There were two loungers free, so Rosie nabbed them before anyone else had a chance to sneak past her.

Laying her towel out on one for herself, she placed

her bag down onto the other to let everyone else know it was being used by someone else.

She found her magazines, and her phone. Checking it for messages before arranging everything on the small table between the beds. And then she put her umbrella up and sat back ready to read and enjoy the peace and quiet.

That was when she noticed *her*.

The woman Camille was dumbstruck over had just sat at one of the tables where breakfast was still being served.

Rosie watched her from behind her sunglasses and magazine. The woman looked composed, assured, confident as she settled into the chair and smiled up at the waiter who filled her glass with cool, iced water. Calmly sitting back, relaxed, sipping her water as she glanced around casually, never stopping in one spot for long before she moved on to stare elsewhere.

When the waiter reappeared, the handsome one she'd spotted on their first day here, the woman said something to him, *"Probably her order,"* Rosie thought. But the woman paid him no more interest once he'd stopped writing and walked away. Instead, she glanced around again, and it became obvious, she was now staring at Rosie or was it the empty lounger next to her?

Lifting her magazine just a little more, Rosie hid the grin that had appeared on her own face. *"Camille Franklyn, you really are surprising,"* she laughed to herself.

"Can I get you anything?"

A deep accented voice said, loudly enough that Rosie looked up. The handsome waiter now smiled down at her. "There's still time for breakfast, or if you prefer, a cold drink?"

"Ah, that would be most excellent. Could I please order a plate of pastries for two. And you'd better make that two orange juices as well, thank you..." she read his name badge, "Pedro."

"My pleasure." He winked and held her gaze for just a little longer than most people did. Long enough it made her blush a little. "I'll be right back. Enjoy the sun."

"I will..." she said, watching him walk away, his tight white trousers hugging a rather exceptional backside.

When she looked up again, she noticed Camille making her way around the edge of the pool. Hair still wet and brushed back off her face, sunglasses on, and a brightly coloured sarong wrapped around her hips. She looked like Sharon Stone, elegant and demure, with her bag hanging off of one shoulder.

"Breakfast will be here any moment," Rosie said when Camille reached the sun loungers. "And just so you're aware, your...woman is across the pool at a table, looking for you."

"Is she?"

Rosie quickly glanced. "Yes, and staring right at you."

"I'd best give her something to look at then." Camille grinned and untied the sarong to reveal a new bikini. Neon pink might just be the brightest swimwear around the pool.

"Does she have a name?" Rosie asked. "I can't keep thinking of her as, '*your woman.*'"

Camille chuckled. "I quite like it. But yes, it's Leila."

She hung the sarong over the arms of the sunshade and then eased herself down onto the lounger.

Only then, did she make the pretence of casually looking around until she found Leila. She waved with a quick and flirty wiggle of her fingers, and then turned back to Rosie.

"So, I take it that you have answered your question?" Rosie said.

"Yes, but now I have more questions."

"Like?"

Camille laughed. "Like how much I enjoyed being told what to do."

"That's not been the case before, with men?"

"God no," Camille scoffed. "Mostly they're all too intimidated. Half the time, if I wanted to get off, I'd have to be very clear on what I wanted, otherwise…" She waggled two fingers at Rosie.

"More information than I need," Rosie chuckled. "But don't stop. I love facts and information." She ceased talking to Camille and twisted quickly towards the approaching Pedro. "Thank you so much," she gushed when he arrived beside her lounger. "You're so kind."

"My pleasure. It's no problem," he said, placing the plate piled with French pastries down onto the small table. "And two orange juices."

"Fabulous." Rosie reached into her purse, pulled out a five-euro note, and held it out to him. He took it, along with her hand.

"Thank you."

When it appeared Pedro wasn't leaving, Camille coughed gently and smiled up at him. "Thank you."

"Of course. Anytime," he said, before turning back to Rosie and smiling some more, and then he walked away, with Rosie gawping after him.

"So…what happens in Madeira…?"

Rosie blushed. "What? Oh, Pedro? God…no, I mean…really? You think?"

"Oh, yeah, I think."

Rosie stared after him. "He is cute."

"Sure is. You should go for it."

"Maybe I will…" Rosie turned back and picked up a pastry. "Lover Girl's still looking."

"So she is," Camille answered. Sitting back, she picked up her orange juice and drank down half the glass. "I wonder how long she's here for."

"You didn't ask?"

"Was a tad busy with other things." Camille's barely there smile curled her lips on one side of her mouth. "Anyway, it's a holiday fling. We talked about what we needed to talk about…"

"Uh huh, I bet you did. I should have taken a photo of you this morning. I don't think I've ever seen you look so…"

"Be very careful with what you say next." Camille laughed.

"Dishevelled. Undone. Come apart. Shagged." Rosie laughed with her.

Camille stared across at Leila. "Yes, well, I might just let it happen again."

"I think you should." Rosie licked her fingers clean and stood up. "Think I'll go for a dip and give Leila an opportunity to come over."

"Hm, you do that."

NINE

Leila watched as Camille's friend stood and then walked towards the pool. Taking the stairs down, she stopped on the second one, clearly feeling the chill of it, but she didn't get out and return to her lounger.

With her drink finished, Camille laid back and bent one leg, allowing her knees to fall open – an invitation, Leila hoped, because Camille then lowered her glasses and stared straight across the pool at her.

Leila felt the excitement flood her system. Older women like Camille did that to her. All in control, until she had them where she wanted, and suddenly, they were doing things they never thought they would. Good things, exciting things, but nonetheless, things they'd never expected.

Camille had been exactly how Leila had read her – Confident and alluring, in a quiet kind of way, but definitely no shrinking wallflower. No, Camille knew what she wanted, and in her day-to-day life, would take it. With men it would have been the same, but not with Leila.

Last night had been so far out of Camille's comfort zone, she had allowed herself to be led, dominated even, until finally, she'd understood what she wanted, and then…Leila sighed at the memory. The tables had flipped and the real Camille came out to play.

Now, Leila wanted her even more. Three more nights until she went home and back to the mundane job that paid her a terrible wage and bored her to tears. Three more nights to potentially spend with Camille.

It would be worth it – she already knew that. And then, they'd never see each other again.

Camille would just be a pleasant memory Leila would think about from time to time. Someone she could draw on for a fantasy when alone time was all she had.

She chuckled to herself, and wondered if Camille knew just how many people probably got off thinking about her.

Leila got up and effortlessly swept around the pool until she was standing beside Camille. She sat on the edge of the lounger before Camille even realised she was there.

"Good morning." she said, raking her fingertips down the length of Camille's arm.

"Did we not say that earlier before I left?" Camille answered. Her eyes hidden by the sunglasses.

"Yes, we did. Right after I sank to my knees and—"

Camille sat up, her fingers moving instantly to press against Leila's lips to shush her. "Do not humiliate me."

"I wasn't," Leila said, somewhat caught between scolded and turned on. "Would you like me to leave?"

"I didn't say that." Camille softened a little, and got quieter as she leaned closer. "But don't think that because I let you fuck me all night, you can announce it to the entire world, do you understand me?"

"Of course," Leila replied, feeling reprimanded. "I'll leave you to enjoy the day. You know where to find me."

"Leila, I didn't—" But it was too late. Leila was already walking away. And she didn't turn to look back either.

"Well, that didn't look good," Rosie said from the pool. She'd swum up to the edge and was now resting her forearms along the side.

Camille breathed deeply. At home, in work, she wouldn't have cared what anyone thought of her. But something about Leila pulled at her emotionally.

"I'll be back, don't let anyone steal my spot."

"Yes, ma'am," Rosie said in a fake American accent, chuckling as Camille pulled her sarong free and began wrapping it around her as she stalked back towards the hotel. "Chasing girls. Who'd have thunk it?"

TEN

Camille knocked on the hotel room door and waited. She was about to knock again when the door opened, and Leila stood in front of her naked.

"I—" She was startled, not expecting Leila to be so undressed. But it was perfect, and exactly what she wanted, wasn't it? It was why she was here, to see her again – to scratch the itch that now permanently bothered her.

"If you're going to be rude to me and treat me like a cheap slut, then I guess I should dress accordingly," Leila said, before turning and walking away, leaving the door open.

Camille went inside and closed the door, instantly reminded of the previous night and earlier that morning. The bed was still unmade, but at least the odour of sex had gone with the doors to the balcony now open again.

"I don't like being caught unaware," Camille said.

"That's not an apology," Leila remarked, barely looking at her as she poured some water from a bottle.

"You think I owe you an apology? Because I put my boundaries in place?"

Leila swigged down half the glass before placing it onto the small counter. "You don't get invited to fuck me all night and then treat me like I'm an embarrassment to you."

"You're a holiday fling, Leila, we're not dating. I don't want the world to know—"

"That you eat pussy, and like it?" Leila glared at her. "You don't want the world to know you like eating my pussy, no?"

"That's not fair—"

"Get out," Leila said calmly.

"What?"

"I said leave. Get out. If I am embarrassing to you outside of this room, then you don't get to stay in it. Get out."

"I don't want to get out," Camille countered.

"Oh? What do you want? To sneak up here and get your rocks off before you scuttle off back downstairs and pretend you're someone you're not?"

"Yes, I thought that was the agree—"

"No, I offered you that last night," Leila said. "Today is a different matter. Today's offer is not last night's."

Camille ran a hand over her head. "I don't understand, this is—" She bit her bottom lip. "I'm sorry. I clearly misread the message, and I got it wrong, okay? I'm sorry if I hurt your feelings—"

"Not *if*." Leila stopped her. "Not *if* you did something. I already told you, you did. So, *if* is not an apology. *If* is an excuse. *If* is manipulation."

Camille felt her nostrils flare. This woman was both annoyingly frustrating and sexy as hell. Nobody ever spoke to her like this. Never had she been called out by anyone in the way Leila was doing. It both pissed her off and turned her on.

Three steps. That was all it took before she was standing right in front of Leila, almost nose to nose.

"I'm sorry that I hurt you."

"Go on."

"For fuck's sake, Leila, what do you want from me?"

"Respect. You want my body, you damn well respect me."

What the hell was happening here? Camille couldn't get her head straight. It was all just so intoxicating; the way this woman looked at her, spoke to her, the way she smelled so good.

She didn't think about it. Her body just acted. Knees bent, and before she knew it, she was on them. The cool tile against her skin, looking at Leila's navel, and inhaling her aroma once more, propelling Camille into action.

She bent forward and placed a firm kiss against Leila's stomach, looking up at her through hooded eyes.

"I'm sorry I hurt you. Let me make amends." Her eyes closed and lowered, and she felt a hand on her head.

"How are you going to make amends?"

"I'll—"

"Not words, Camille. Show me."

Camille reached for her.

Both palms wrapping around taut thighs, as she positioned herself, ready to do whatever it took to make Leila happy.

Her palms moved around to the front of Leila's thighs, her thumbs stretching to open her up and expose her clit to Camille's eager tongue.

"Good. That's nice," Leila encouraged. The muscles in her legs tensing beneath Camille's touch. "I like that. Don't stop."

Camille did as she was told, working her tongue around Leila's clit in tight circles, sucking on the third pass before starting all over again.

The hand on her head tightened its grip, pulling more firmly to hold her in place. She didn't mind. It made her wet – she knew that much. When Leila's hips began to move in earnest, Camille almost came herself when Leila said, "Flatten your tongue." And the moment she did, her hair was pulled, and she was held still as Leila rode her mouth.

The only way she could breathe was through her nostrils and they were squashed against Leila's mons. Only the scent of her filled the air around Camille, and just when she thought she might never breathe properly again, she felt her lover shudder and groan and push her away.

"On the bed," Leila said, staggering toward it, her legs like jelly. She fell onto her back, still panting. "Come." She patted the bed beside her and, Camille rose up from her position and came towards the supine body. "You know where I want you."

Camille whimpered. She'd been forgiven.

Now, it was her turn.

ELEVEN

"Won't your friend be wondering where you are?" Leila said, rolling onto her side to face Camille.

"Rosie knows where I am," Camille stated.

Leila sat up. "You told her? And yet you get pissy with me about being discreet."

Camille turned to look at her. There was a sheen of sweat across Leila's brow from the heat and exertion. "She's been my friend for the best part of thirty-five years. I trust her implicitly, and she already knows my secrets - as I know hers. Strangers around the pool are a different matter entirely."

"Strangers you'll never see again," Leila huffed.

"Why is it so important to you to be seen with me? Why can this not just be—"

"Your dirty little secret?"

Camille shrugged. "Yes, if you want."

"Because I don't want. I know my value, and I don't need you to validate me, but I won't hide who I am. I won't make myself soft and pliable for the world."

Opening up, Camille said, "When I go home, this will be nothing more than an exciting memory. A moment in time where I dined off the menu and not a la carte. I'm not gay. I was curious, and you were willing, and that means we both got what we needed from it."

"So curious, you came back for more." Leila

smirked.

"I did, yes. And I've three more nights left of my stay here to continue that, if you want to. Or we can call it quits now and say our goodbyes and you can stop leering at me across the pool."

"Will you have dinner with me?"

"No," Camille said firmly. "I'm here with my friend, and though she is more than accepting of my disappearing off for the night, I won't just drop her and leave her to dine by herself."

"I suppose that is fair."

Camille swung her legs off the side of the bed and got up. Looking down at Leila, she knew she would not enjoy being told they wouldn't see each other again, but boundaries were boundaries, and she needed them more than ever right now.

"So, will I see you tonight?" Camille asked, picking up her sarong and bikini top from the floor, she began to get dressed.

"Ten o'clock," Leila said, rolling onto her stomach. "Don't keep me waiting."

Camille rolled her eyes. The demand from anyone else would get them a short, sharp retort that would leave them in no doubt who was in control.

"I'll see you at ten." Camille tied the sarong and walked towards the door. "Thank you, Leila. I do appreciate you."

"You appreciate my mouth on your pussy, but I'll take your gratitude."

Camille's fist landed softly against the door. She would not bite. "I'll see you later."

"Yes, you will." Leila chuckled as the door closed with a soft click. She picked up her phone and called the first number on the list, holding it to her ear until it was answered. "You know you said, get under someone to get over her?"

The voice on the other end of the call said, "Yes."

"Well, I did, and now I might just have another problem."

"What?"

"I like her. But this is just fun for her."

"It's supposed to be just fun for you too."

Leila rolled over. "I know, but…God, she's just perfect…everything about her."

"Well, just enjoy it, and remember you come home soon and then you can focus on getting that dream job you've been hankering after for months. Get a tan, get laid, and come home."

"Yes, Bestie." She giggled. "I'll see you at the airport. Don't be late."

"I'm never late."

TWELVE

Rosie looked positively glowing when Camille returned.

"Have fun?" Rosie asked, grinning.

Camille pressed her lips together but couldn't hide the smile. "I did and… I have a date later."

"Oh, that's good because…" Rosie leaned in. "You were right, Pedro has invited me to dinner later."

"Dinner? Well, that's…" Camille smiled. "This holiday is quickly turning into a very relaxing experience."

"Isn't it just?" Rosie chuckled. "You don't mind, do you?"

"Not at all. I think we both agreed what the rules are now."

"Yes, and he is dreamy." Rosie giggled. "And I haven't had a…you know, in months, so…if you're going to be busy all night, can I bring him back to ours?"

Camille laughed. "Just keep it to your own bed."

"Of course." Rosie laughed too. "Drinks?"

"Yes, absolutely, I'll get them. Something fruity?"

Rosie nodded and settled back to enjoy the sun while Camille got up and walked back around the pool to where the bar was.

She made her order and then turned to people

watch while she waited. *Who was she kidding?* She was looking for Leila. She knew that much. Whether she wanted to admit it or not, the younger woman had gotten under her skin a little.

The sound of the barman shaking alcohol and ice distracted her for a moment, but when she looked around again, she noticed her.

Leila stood to one side of the bar, talking, smiling, and laughing with another woman. Camille watched as the woman reached out and touched Leila's arm. Something about it made Camille twitch with jealousy.

"I'll be right back for those," she said to the bartender, pointing to the empty glasses.

With confident feet, she moved through the seating area, and within seconds, she found herself standing beside Leila and the woman who had no place being this interesting.

"Leila, may I speak with you?" Camille asked, smiling at the woman's expression when she noticed how Camille touched Leila's arm and let it linger.

Leila turned. "Camille, of course. Excuse me for a moment," she said, turning to the woman and waiting for her to walk away. "What can I do for you?"

"I uh…my plans later have changed, and I thought maybe you'd like to join me for dinner."

"Dinner," she said leisurely. "Well, that is a change." A smile appeared, gradually. "And you want to have dinner with me, in front of everyone else."

Camille gazed towards the woman, now moving away from them, before answering, "Yes."

Leila stepped closer. "Because you want to have dinner with me…" She let her finger dance down

Camille's arm. "Or was the invite because you saw that woman speaking to me, and you have a sudden surge of jealousy?"

Camille sighed. How the hell did this woman read her so easily when nobody else dared?

"Do you want to have dinner with me, or not? Because I can find something else to do, and I am quite adept at eating by myself."

Leila's eyes lit up and she licked her lips. "You know, it's quite sexy when you go all Ice Queen."

"I can just go." Camille turned to leave but stopped when she felt the soft hand on her arm.

"Yes, I would like to have dinner with you," Leila confirmed, clearly not wanting to push her luck too far.

"Good. Then I'll meet you here at seven."

Leila paused. "We're eating here? At the hotel?"

"Is there somewhere else you would prefer?" Camille asked, turning back to face her.

"No, here is lovely, I just thought you wanted your dirty little secret kept…secret."

Camille breathed deeply. "Well, as you said, 'strangers I won't see again,' right?"

Leila's smile widened. "Yes, completely right."

"So, I'll see you at seven. Sharp," Camille said, feeling a little more in control of things than she did earlier.

THIRTEEN

"Right, so, I'll be gone all night but expect me to be back in time for breakfast. Which means young Pedro needs to be gone," Camille instructed as she organised her handbag.

"Got it. I think I can manage that. I mean, he might not want to stay at all, or he might want to leave straight after, or he might not—"

"Rosie!" Camille said sharply. "Get it together. He's asked you to dinner. He's a waiter and you're a tourist. He's not looking to wine and dine you and not get something else out of it, so get in the shower and make sure you shave anything pertinent, and then…" She leaned in and kissed Rosie's cheek. "Do as you told me – enjoy it."

"Yes." Rosie smiled sheepishly. "You're right. I guess I'm just a little bit nervous."

At the door, Camille stopped and turned back to her friend. "Then let him lead." She went to leave and then stopped and closed the door again. "Unless he's selfish, in which case be demanding. Trust me, you'll be happier for it."

"I'm not like you, Camille."

"And how am I?"

"You know, more…aggressive, insistent, refusing to accept anything that doesn't work for you." Rosie waved her hands at her. "I mean, look at you."

Camille had dressed to impress. She knew that. But she was appreciative that at least Rosie had noticed.

Rosie's smile turned a little sad. "I wish I was more like you."

"Sometimes, I wish I were more like you," Camille admitted.

"Really?"

"Really. Now, get yourself into that little black dress I know you packed, and have a good time."

Rosie laughed. "Okay, why don't we both try and be a little more like each other and see how that pans out."

"Hm. I'll do my best." Camille smiled, and this time when she opened the door, she left the room.

Stepping into the restaurant, Camille fully expected to be the first to arrive. To her surprise, Leila was already sitting at the bar, looking all relaxed in another white dress, fingering a short glass filled with ice, and Camille assumed, Tequila.

It took a moment before Leila felt herself being watched and she turned to find Camille walking towards her.

"I'm impressed," Camille said, placing her bag onto the bar. She took Leila's glass from her and drank the contents.

"You're impressed I'm here on time, or that I turned up at all?" Leila inquired with a slight tilt of her head. She waved at the bartender and indicated "two" with her fingers, just like she'd done the previous night.

"Well, if I'm honest, I'm still confused by you," Camille admitted.

Leila chuckled. "Of course you are, I don't follow your rules."

"My rules?" Camille said, raising one perfectly plucked brow. "And what are my rules?"

Leila ran a finger over her own bottom lip as she considered the question. She paused long enough for the barman to place two drinks in front of her.

Camille took one and waited.

"I know women like you...I'm very much attracted to women like you. I know what you want... what you desire."

"And that is?"

"Okay, let me know how well I do." Leila smiled and sipped her drink. "You work somewhere where you're in charge. You're the boss in some capacity or another. Total control. You're a perfectionist. You expect, no, you demand, respect. Everyone tiptoes around you. Nobody wants to poke the bear and have her lash out at them, punish them. You enjoy it, the way they scuttle around after you...but you don't respect them...because you think they are..." She paused. "Weak. And yet, it makes you feel powerful."

Camille stiffened, yet said nothing, but she took a sip of her drink and didn't take her eyes from Leila's.

"It must be exhausting always having to be so... limited." Leila finished her analysis.

"So, what is it that I desire?" Camille asked, putting her glass down. "If I'm such a control freak..."

"That's easy." Leila smiled. "But I don't think you've worked it out yet."

Camille thought about the men she'd slept with over the years. "I've had several sexual relationships, all of which have required a certain level of—"

"You slept with men, right? Men who, ultimately were intimidated by you. Men who didn't know what to do with you unless you told them."

Again, Camille said nothing, but it rankled just how close to the truth Leila was.

"You see, I'm not afraid to tell you what I want, and to take it, Camille. You don't intimidate me. You can be here, or you can leave. I'm good with whichever you choose to do. But you won't leave…"

"No? Why not?"

"Because for once, you're getting what you desire…"

"Which is?"

"You like it that, for once, you can let go, and just… be a good girl, as long as nobody else knows. You like your secrets. It all makes you feel powerful…just in a different way."

"Your table is ready, if you'd like to follow me." The waiter placed their drinks onto a tray and led them both towards a table in the corner that overlooked the pool. "Is this table to your liking?"

She was about to launch into all the reasons it wasn't a good table, when she heard Rosie's voice in her head reminding her she should try and be a little more 'Rosie.' And Rosie would not complain about a table.

"Yes, thank you." She smiled and took a seat. "This

will be fine," she said, more to herself than anyone else.

When the waiter left them alone, Leila laughed.

"That took everything not to say you wanted a different table, didn't it?"

"I don't know what you mean," Camille said, picking up the linen napkin and laying it casually across her lap.

"It's all just fucking hot," Leila said, checking her out openly. "This air of indifference, and yet, beneath the surface, it's all bubbling away ready to erupt. Maybe we should just skip dinner and—"

"Maybe, you should do less analysing of me."

"But you fascinate me."

It didn't go unnoticed how much those words hit Camille and woke her up. She was used to people being interested in her, but this was different. She liked this younger woman's attention.

"You're wrong about one thing," Camille said, looking her young lover dead in the eye.

"Oh, do share." Leila smiled coyly. "I want to know everything about you."

"I don't enjoy it – the way people are around me. I want them to grow some balls. To be the best version of themselves." She pursed her lips as she considered something else. "If they choose to tiptoe around me, then I will push them, and if that means they scuttle, so be it."

"Why would you not want to soften your image?"

"I don't know," she admitted. "Maybe it's just the way it is. I'm comfortable with my life as it is."

"That's fair, I suppose." Leila watched her as she

sipped her drink. "You're not in your comfort zone now though, are you?"

"No, I'm not." She exhaled. She needed a change of subject. "Tell me about you. You're accent, French?"

"Oui." Leila giggled. "My father is English but has a Spanish mother. My mother is Moroccan. I was born in Rabat. So, I spoke French and English at home. When I was fourteen, we moved to England. That's my home now."

"So, you speak French fluently?"

"And Spanish, and Arabic, and of course, English."

"Very exotic," Camille said. "Now I understand how you have such an amazing skin tone too."

"The perks of good genes." Leila winked. "I could probably get by in Portuguese and Italian, but that might be me trying to impress you."

"I'm having dinner with you. You already impressed me." Camille gave a wry smile.

"You are English – of course you are – but which part?"

"South."

Leila chuckled. "You don't give anything away, do you?"

"I said you impressed me. But if you mean, I am private, then yes. I like to keep my secrets. Isn't that what you said?" Camille smiled and felt herself relax a little. "Maybe you intimidate me a little?"

"Moi?" Leila scoffed. "How?"

"Because you're so at ease with yourself, with what you like and want, and that's very…attractive."

"Thank you."

Camille picked up her menu. "So, what are you going to have?"

The wine was beginning to take effect, and Camille found her inhibitions loosening as they ate the last morsels of their dinner.

Leila had insisted on dessert, which had meant one last glass to finish the bottle.

"Are you alright?" Leila reached out across the table and took Camille's hand. "You look a little...warm."

"The wine, that last glass I think hit..." She giggled, and instantly stopped herself. "Probably one too many."

"I see." Leila smiled. "You know, it's okay."

"What is?"

"Laughing, finding humour and letting someone else see it."

"I laugh," Camille said defensively, "when something is funny. My being drunk is—"

"Funny?"

"Maybe." She smiled and allowed herself to relax again. *"What would Rosie do?"* "I find you quite disarming."

"Really, well, that's good to know under the circumstances. And I kind of like it...getting under your skin is..." She straightened in her seat. "Shall we go back to my room?"

"I'd like that, yes," Camille answered. The bill arrived and she signed it, signalling it could be added to her room bill.

"I could have paid for that," Leila said, watching Camille stand.

Camille shrugged. "Does it matter?"

Leila pushed her chair back and stood up. "No. I suppose it doesn't."

"Shall we go then?"

FOURTEEN

Leila opened the door, stood back, and allowed Camille to pass her and enter into the darkness of the room first.

Following her in, she closed the door quietly and then moved quickly to switch on a bedside lamp.

"So, what did you want to do tonight?" she asked Camille as she took one earring, and then the other, out.

"I—" Camille looked a little embarrassed. "I'm happy to let you lead. I mean, after all, you know what you're doing and seem to innately understand what I like…"

Leila remained silent, and continued to remove her jewellery, but her eyes, curious and alive, didn't leave Camille's face.

"You're just going to stare at me?" Camille said when she couldn't take the silence any longer, but she didn't stop watching as Leila's dress dropped to the floor.

Leila posed, white lace underwear and tanned skin. By Camille's expression, she knew the look was a winner.

"You're staring at me," Leila teased in return.

"Well, I'm sure that was the intention the minute you undressed."

"Maybe…but I am wondering…are you remaining clothed? Because I'm quite happy to work around it." She moved closer. "But I'd prefer not to."

Camille said nothing, her chest heaving as Leila stepped up and stood right in front of her. The aroma of her perfume filled the air when she leaned into Camille's ear, and whispered.

"Be a good girl and take it all off for me." She ran her fingertip down Camille's neck. "That little shiver that just ran down your spine…that's how you're entire body is going to feel when…"

"When?"

Leila chuckled. "When you grow some balls and show me the better version of yourself."

"Fuck, Leila, that's…"

"What you need," Leila said, pulling back to stare into those eyes again.

"Yes," Camille gasped out.

"So, take it all off and show me," Leila responded. She sat down onto the bed and shuffled back until she could lean against the pillows.

"Can I?" Camille looked around for her bag and reached inside for her phone. "Music, I'd like…I have a playlist."

"For stripping? I'm impressed."

Camille laughed. "No, but…it's…I put it together for an intimate liaison that didn't happen and…"

Leila smiled at her. "Sure, put it on."

Camille fiddled with the app and then placed the phone on the nearest surface. Tinny music played quietly, and she grabbed the phone again. "Sorry, volume. I always have it off." With the music louder, she put the phone back down again and took a moment.

"In your own time, Camille," Leila said, recognising the song. *I feel it coming* by The Weekend. It was a sexy song, and Leila nodded along as she watched Camille begin to sway and find her rhythm.

Her hips moved first and then her arms. She began to sway, eyes closing as she felt the music and let it guide her soul with the movements. Her arms raised higher and twirled around one another.

Her hands slid around the back of her neck, and up into her hair, before finding the button she needed to undo so she could slide the zip down, and let gravity deal with the dress.

It fell.

The material landing around her feet as her hands moved down her body and caressed her skin. Camille's fingertips danced along her collarbone and then cupped her breasts and squeezed.

That was the moment. Leila witnessed it happen and grinned. The moment Camille stepped out of her comfort zone and found the place that she was meant to be.

Her eyes opened and locked onto Leila. Her hips rolling and thrusting. If asked, Leila would admit it was hard to decide which part of the show she should pay most attention to. Which was why, she hadn't noticed Camille loosen her bra, until it was flung across the bed at her.

"Paying attention?"

"God, yes. You're a goddess," Leila answered, moving for the first time to crawl to the end of the bed. "Come to me."

The music played on as Camille edged her way onto the bed. Mirroring each other, Leila reached out and slid an arm around Camille's waist, pulling her closer as their lips met, and a ferocious need swelled up inside.

Leila's tongue tasted her. The essence of wine and a good meal, but something more, something akin to soft fruit, a mellowing of her soul. Languidly, her tongue searched the depths of Camille's mouth, burrowing beneath her tongue and slowly swirling.

Soft moans of pleasure and anticipation filled the silence between the notes as The Weekend continued to sing his soulful lyrics.

Leila's fingers edged Camille's underwear lower, until they were halfway down her thighs and Leila could slip her hand into the gap and pleasure her.

The moment between them had switched from holiday fling, of just sex and exploration, to something deeper. Something they both sensed meant more.

She pulled away from the kiss and watched Camille's face as, finally, she stopped the aching tease of the woman's hardening clit and penetrated her being. Fingers slid easily inside of her and hooked instantly to find the one nerve ending that would send Camille over the edge.

Her face contorted, focused on every movement Leila made. It was sexy and turned Leila on even more. To know she alone held this woman's pleasure, literally, in her hands.

The look of joy, and then peace, that came across Camille's face, when Leila finally pushed her over, was something Leila would remember forever.

FIFTEEN

"That was different," Camille said when, finally, Leila collapsed beside her. Easing herself up the bed, she reached for the aircon remote and turned it up.

"Was it?" Leila said, still lying on her front, her head turned towards Camille. She extended her arm, and with tender fingertips, she traced a line along Camille's torso, chuckling when Camille shivered at the touch. "Still turned on?"

Exhaling to control her reaction, Camille slid lower and turned onto her side.

One hand slipped beneath the pillow.

"How do you know?" she asked. When Leila looked confused, she added, "About me – how do you know what I need when we barely know one another, and men I have dated for months, have never worked it out?"

"Ah, well, firstly, I think being a woman gives me an advantage. Women think differently to men when it comes to sex. We have the same equipment, so I am fully aware of how it all works…" She leaned in and rubbed her nose against Camille's before gently kissing her mouth once more. "And…you're really not that difficult to read."

"I don't know one other person who would say that about me."

"That's because they are not inclined to." Leila smiled and moved closer, sliding her leg between

Camille's. "When you sleep with men, you've already accepted they only care about one thing, and it will be on you to produce anything different. You'll have to guide them."

"I suppose, yes."

"But me, I'm interested. My goal isn't how quickly I can get off – it's how long I can make your pleasure last, and what buttons I need to push to create an environment where you…" she rolled them both until she hovered over Camille once more, her hand disappearing back between Camille's legs, "can lose yourself and let go."

"I see. Well, when you put it like that, it all sounds so simple." Camille smiled into the kiss that followed.

"So, that's how I know."

Camille yawned. "Sorry."

"No, I take it as a compliment." Leila laughed and rolled back to the mattress. "We should sleep, unless you're sneaking out and leaving?"

"Rosie is potentially having her own holiday fling, so…can I stay?"

Leila sat up and grinned over her shoulder. "I suppose so. I can hardly see a lady sleeping in the hall, can I?" She stood up and walked naked towards the bathroom. "I need a shower. Are you joining me?"

"I don't know. Are you going to fuck me in there too?"

"Maybe," she called back, just as the water began to run. "Or maybe not." She poked her head around the door. "Come and find out."

Camille sighed, then yawned again, but Leila was

right. They both needed to shower.

The room was already steaming up despite the heat of the night. Leila was already under the water, shampooing her hair, when Camille stepped in behind her.

"Don't think about it, just let yourself react," Leila said without turning. Camille closed her eyes and imagined what she would want if someone were joining her, and then she knew.

She glanced around and found what she wanted. Squeezing shower gel into her hands, she confidently reached for Leila and began to move the soap all over her lovers body. Camille's touch wound around Leila's hips and up her torso to caress her breasts. Camille leaned against her, kissing the soft skin of her shoulder. The scent of her shampoo filled Camille's nostrils as she breathed her in.

Kissing her neck, Camille moaned when Leila's hand reached back and into her hair, holding her in place. Both of them wet, and soapy, as they moved against one another.

Camille pressed herself against Leila's rounded backside, aware that despite the multiple orgasms she'd already enjoyed, and how tired she felt, her body was reacting again.

"God, I can't get enough of you," she groaned when Leila twisted around.

"We have awoken the dormant beast." Leila turned them until Camille was beneath the flow of water. She picked up the shampoo. "Let me take care of you, just for tonight. Don't fight it."

Camille laughed. "I will try, but no promises."

"That's all I ask." She smiled and began to massage the shampoo into Camille's hair.

"That feels so good, actually," Camille said, relaxing into the touch.

"I think that's the point." Leila grinned. "By the time I'm finished with you, baby, you won't want to let me go."

"This isn't *Pretty Woman*." Camille turned, her hair still full of suds. "I will let you go."

"We'll see," Leila said, holding her stare.

SIXTEEN

Camille rolled over into the empty space. Her eyes opened slowly and became accustomed to the sunshine now lighting up the room. She stretched and enjoyed the cool breeze that rolled across her torso, her bare breasts, nipples puckering instantly, along with thousands of goosebumps across her skin.

"Oh, you're awake." Leila grinned from the balcony. She was dressed in a long white T-shirt she'd pulled down enough to sit on. "I ordered breakfast."

Yawning, Camille got up and stood naked as she tried to work out where her clothes had ended up.

"Grab one of my T-shirts out of that drawer." Leila stared at her.

"I should get going," Camille started to argue.

"Or you could put on a T-shirt and come sit out here with me and enjoy some breakfast." Leila picked up a small pastry and bit into it.

Without saying anything, Camille opened the drawer and took the top shirt, and put it on. "Happy?"

Leila turned to look at her again. "Very. You would be too if you started to live the life you actually want to."

"I am living the life I want to," Camille said, strolling out onto the balcony. It looked over the pool area and part of the restaurant.

"Uh huh, and yet, anytime you have an option

to leave…you choose to stay, despite arguing why you should go."

Camille pulled a chair out, then pulled the T-shirt lower so she could sit down. "You know you can be very annoying."

Leila laughed. "Because I'm right and you hate having to agree with me."

"Maybe." Camille smiled and plucked a mini croissant from the plate. "I find you…captivating, I guess."

Sitting back, Leila stared at her. "I like that."

"I'm sure you do… I'm sure that it's reciprocated too."

"I mean, you're okay." Leila smiled. "Are you coming back tonight?"

"I don't know. I need to speak with my friend and see how things went for her and whether she's expecting me to entertain her later."

"I think Pedro will keep her busy."

Camille eyed her carefully. "How do you know about Pedro?"

Leila tapped her nose. "I know a lot of things. I make it my business." She laughed. "I spend my day people-watching. I saw the way she looked at him, and I know he likes to enjoy available older women. It didn't take much to point him her way."

"You engineered Pedro taking Rosie out, in order to have me to yourself for the night?"

Leila nodded. "Hm hm."

"I don't know whether I'm angry with you or

flattered," Camille admitted.

Leaning forward, Leila slid her palm up the inside of Camille's thigh. "We both know how much you enjoyed it."

Camille squeezed her legs together to stop any further exploration of her enjoyment. "And we both know I'm not going to let you fuck me on the balcony in view of everyone."

Leila chuckled. "So, tonight then, and I'll fuck you every way I want to."

"Are you always this crude?" Camille asked, pouring a glass of freshly squeezed orange juice. She brough the cup to her lips as she sat down.

Leila watched Camille sit back in her chair, intently staring at her. "Yes. I say what I want. Then there are no miscommunications." She reached for her own cup, and grimaced when she realised it was empty. "Anyway, I think it arouses you in a way you haven't considered before. Maybe when men are crude it's been a turn off, but a woman…" She smiled like a wolf that had cornered its prey. "You want her to fuck you and play with you, and as we've discovered, to dominate you a little and demand your respect."

Camille remained quiet.

"But if you'd prefer, I can be more polite and let you guess what I want." Leila glanced at her with a smile playing on her lips, as she filled her coffee cup again.

"Don't change for anyone," Camille said.

SEVENTEEN

Camille sauntered down the corridor trying not to look as though she were just returning from a sexually explosive tryst, but she wasn't sure she was carrying it off when the outfit she had on was clearly evening wear.

Her thoughts dissipated, however, when Pedro passed her and smiled in a way that said they both knew something about the other.

When she came to her room, she slid the card into the slot and stepped inside.

Rosie was singing in the shower.

"I'm back," she called through the door. "Leave it running when you're done."

"Oh," Rosie stifled a giggle, "sorry was just—"

"Singing, yes, I can hear. No need to ask if you had a good night?"

The door opened and a flushed-faced Rosie stood, wrapped in a towel, grinning at her.

"God, he was...experienced." Rosie blushed. "It's been a long time since a man sorted me out like that, I can tell you." She moved past Camille. "You don't mind if I see him again tonight, do you? Only...we don't have long left and..."

"I get the gist. Of course not, I'll make myself scarce and you can..." She looked at the crumpled bed sheets on one bed and the neat, untouched bed that was her own. "Enjoy yourself. We only live once, right?"

"Yes, thank you for being so understanding." Rosie smiled like she'd just woken up on Christmas morning to a box filled with her favourite things.

Camille walked into the bathroom. "We're both being understanding, aren't we?"

"I guess we are, yes." Rosie laughed. "Did you want to get some breakfast?"

"You go ahead, I've already eaten. I'm going to grab a shower and then make the most of the day around the pool."

"Okay, I'll meet you down there. It's pretty quiet. Most people have gone on that boat trip."

"Great. Get us the good beds then." She closed the door and quickly stripped off, looking at herself in the steamed up mirror. "What have you done?"

She looked the same. And yet, she felt like a different person. Something had awoken, she was sure of that. Something she wouldn't be able to put back in the bottle.

Closing her eyes didn't help. A matinee of the previous night's exploration played constantly, repeating certain scenes so often she could almost feel Leila's hands on her. The way her fingertips danced over Camille's skin, had been tantalising. And her mouth – Camille released the breath she'd been holding – her hot mouth. So soft and wet and warm. Teeth that nibbled and bit. And a tongue that toyed with her. "Sweet Jesus," she whispered, suddenly aware her hand was between her legs. Fingers expertly worked her clitoris until she felt the frenzy of orgasm start to peak.

She watched herself – the way her facial muscles

tensed and grimaced with every touch that took her closer to release. "You want her, admit it," she said to herself. "Why can't you admit it?" The voice in her head answered back, *Because then where would you be?*

Grunting, fingers moving faster and harder, she needed more. She needed something, someone inside her. Imagination was all she had. She thought of Roger, the last man she'd been intimate with. Thought of his pulsing member and how she'd liked it at first, but all her mind would let her see was Leila. It was Leila she wanted inside of her, deep inside of her, thrusting and pistoning her hips until Camille was filled with nothing else but her.

"Jesus." She slammed her other fist into her mouth. Unsure whether Rosie had left or not, she couldn't cry out.

Faster, her fingers moved until she hit that spot, and then it was all she had in her to tense and relax her muscles and edge it ever closer, fingers slowly eking out every last pulse of pleasure until finally, she was spent.

"See you down by the pool," Rosie called out.

EIGHTEEN

The evening came around faster than Camille could have hoped. She'd spent the day sunning herself and was quite pleased with the tan she'd been building. Her skin felt sun-kissed, and now, she wanted something else kissed.

"Do you have any toys?" she asked Leila the moment the door opened and she entered the room she'd slept in these past two nights.

Leila chuckled. "You mean sex toys?"

"Obviously," Camille said, frowning at her. "What else would I mean?"

"What kind of toy did you want?"

Camille stepped closer, until they were face to face. "You keep saying you've fucked me. Well you haven't…and I want you to."

For a moment, Leila watched Camille's face. Her eyes slowly scanned Camille's beautiful face. From her eyes…down to her mouth, and those kissable lips. Before retreating slowly back to her eyes again as Leila considered the request. "You mean a strap-on?"

"If that's what you call it, yes, I want that."

"Why?" Leila asked without any judgment, though Camille felt judged.

"Look, you said I needed to speak my needs, and I need—"

"A penis?"

"No," Camille said firmly. "No, not that. I need you, but in *that way*."

For the first time since meeting her, Leila looked unsure of herself and she glanced away.

"What? What is it?" Camille said quickly. She stepped closer again, and placed a gentle hand against Leila's cheek. "Why are you looking so…deflated?"

"Because you've asked for the one thing I can't give you." Leila smiled sadly. "I didn't think I'd be enjoying this kind of holiday when I packed, and despite my bravado, I'm really not one for having to explain to airport security—"

"Yes, I get it." Camille chuckled at the thought. "It's fine, it was just an idea—"

"It was a good idea – one that I am now kicking myself I won't get to enjoy with you." Her head tilted as she considered something. "I think I would enjoy many things with you, Camille. Maybe we can swap numbers and hook up when we get home?"

Camille smiled at the idea. "It's a lovely thought but… I'm not ready to bring anything like this into my real world. This has been…wonderful, but it is all it can ever be."

"I don't believe that, but I will accept it," Leila responded, leaning into kiss her.

The kiss was different. There was something else attached to it; something Camille had never considered ever happening to her. She felt an attraction that went way beyond a holiday fling.

"Shall we eat?" she said quickly, before Leila could take things any further. "I thought we could go off-site and try the local restaurant on the corner. It's had rave reviews."

"Sure, let's do that." She untied the robe and let it drop to the floor. "I just need to get dressed."

Camille sat down on the edge of the bed and leaned back on her palms. "Okay, you do that."

"Okay." Leila laughed. "I'm not sure I've ever been watched getting dressed – it's usually the other way around."

"Well, there's a first time for everything." Camille smirked up at her. "Carry on."

Choosing underwear from the drawer, Leila turned to look at Camille. "You know, if you want to go out to eat, you need to stop looking like you want to eat me."

"I do want to do that," Camille admitted with a devilish smile and a gentle bite of her lip. It was impossible to look at Leila in any other way. "And I will, once we've been out and had dinner."

Sliding her underwear up tanned thighs, Leila took her time, enjoying the way Camille watched her.

"How about, just for tonight, you do one thing for me?" she asked when Camille's line of sight finally moved up to her face.

"What would that be?"

Leila stepped forward, planting her feet on either side of Camille's legs, slowly easing herself down until she was straddling her thighs. Her bare breasts were mere inches away from Camille's open mouth, and the captivated stare on her lover's face.

"Just for tonight, you pretend we are lovers, on

holiday together. Touch me in public, show me off, let the world see you for who you are, for one night."

Camille swallowed.

It really wasn't a difficult task. Showing Leila off to the world was the very least she deserved. But could she do it? Could she out herself, even for one night, in a world full of strangers?

"Alright."

Leila smiled into a kiss. "Thank you."

NINETEEN

As they stepped out of the hotel and onto the main street, Leila slipped her hand into Camille's. Squeezing gently, she stared up at her through dark sunglasses.

"Relax," Leila said when Camille stiffened. "I promise you; nobody will care."

"That's easier said than—" Camille took a deep breath and let her shoulders sag. The restaurant was no more than a few hundred feet away. She could hold someone's hand.

Lost in her thoughts, she was suddenly brought back to reality when Leila stopped walking and tugged her to one side. "Look at this, Darling," she said, pointing to a small necklace. "Isn't it beautiful?"

She was still hearing the endearment of *Darling* repeat in her head. Only when Leila let go of her hand, slid her arms up and over Camille's shoulders, pressing herself against her, did she realise Leila was speaking to her.

"It would look beautiful on you," Leila said. "Don't you think?"

Camille glanced around quickly. Only the man in the shop was watching, eagerly hoping they'd buy the piece. "Are you intending to manhandle me in public the entire evening?"

Leila grinned. "If you were my real lover, I would be doing a lot more."

Stifling the urge to pull away, Camille glanced down at the necklace again, and the small price tag next to it. It was cheap – not something she would buy at all, not for herself, and certainly not for a lover. Next to it, however, was a much larger piece; a solid silver locket with a small engraved heart and a ruby in the centre.

"I think this one would suit you," Camille said, taking Leila's hand and leading her into the shop. Before Leila could speak, they were inside, and Camille pointed to the locket. "May I see it?"

"Sí, sí," he said, grinning like the proverbial cat, as his eyes went back and forth between the women. Unlocking the cabinet, he slid the glass to one side and reached in for the necklace. "Is silver and ruby," telling her what she already knew. "You try?" He indicated his neck and Camille smiled at him.

"Gracias," she said, taking it from him and turning to Leila.

"What are you doing?" Leila asked, confused.

"Hold your hair up and turn around," Camille instructed, as she unclasped the chain. When Leila turned and lifted her hair, Camille placed the chain around her neck and secured it. "There, let me see."

It nestled beautifully, midway down her chest, glinting against the light.

"Do you like it?" Camille asked.

"Yes, it's beautiful but—"

"We'll take it," Camille said to the man behind the counter, already producing her card to pay for it.

"Camille, no…I didn't—I was just playing, you don't have to buy me…this is too much." Her fingers held it like it were the most precious thing she'd ever had.

Without so much as a glance, Camille's finger raised and pressed against Leila's mouth. "Shh." She finished the transaction and then turned to Leila. "I want to buy it for you; there's no ulterior motive. I'm already sleeping with you."

Leila laughed. "That is true."

They both thanked the man and left the shop. Outside, it was Camille who reached for her hand this time and led the way. "I am ravenous," she said, looking at Leila, who was still fingering the locket.

They were seated, with nothing more than a smile and a menu each. The waitress, like many at the resort, was a teenager earning extra money by working in the family restaurant. All she cared about was the potential tip and not getting in trouble with her parents.

It was a square table. Most couples sat opposite one another, but Leila had other ideas and took the seat that would place her on Camille's right.

With wine ordered, Camille chuckled to herself.

"What are you laughing at?" Leila asked, her hand still on the locket.

"You." Camille smiled warmly. She placed the menu down, and with her elbow on the table, she rested her chin in her palm and continued to look at Leila. "Has nobody ever bought you a gift before?"

"Yes, many times," Leila said, now conscious she was still touching the necklace. "But this was so... unexpected. Two days ago, I barely thought you'd even speak to me and now, here I am, enjoying dinners and receiving gifts, and I suppose, it makes me wonder what it would be like in another world where you and I could continue this."

"Ah, I see." Camille couldn't deny she had thought something similar, but the reality was, this *relationship* wasn't real. "In another world, maybe I'm not this person you're enjoying dinner with, and maybe you're not the same either. Being here, in this paradise, it allows other parts of us to be set free." Her smile widened. She'd certainly freed herself these past few days with Leila.

"I am glad you have found those parts of you." Leila returned the smile and held up a glass. "To more nights, and many more orgasms."

TWENTY

"Fuck, do not stop," Camille pleaded. She would beg if need be, but right now Leila's mouth and tongue had her on the precipice.

Leila's earlier, thrusting penetration had been so powerful, so everything she'd needed, that her entire body had shifted with the movement. Now, her head and one shoulder hung precariously off the side of the bed. Only her hands gripping the sheets, and Leila's embrace, stopped her from falling further.

The blood rushed around Camille's body made everything tingle.

Soft lips wrapped around Camille's clit, sucking insistently, and all Camille could do was tighten her thighs and hold her lover's head in place.

"Just like that, yes, God yes." She felt her body begin to shudder and quake, as every sinew in her body tightened and released, over and over, forcing her towards the orgasmic explosion ahead, and back again. "Don't stop—" And then she was there – at the precipice. Howling out and not caring who else heard her.

Aftershocks rocked her body as Leila gently licked and nuzzled, and waited for Camille's thighs to unlock just enough that she could glance up and grin.

"Yes." Camille breathed heavily, raising her head enough to look down her torso at her. "You can own that shit-eating grin...fuck...that was—" Her legs fell open, and Leila sat up. She wrapped her arms around Camille's thighs and pulled her back onto the bed, crawling up her body.

"You enjoyed that too much, I think." Leila laughed and snuggled against her.

For a moment, Camille thought she might be right. How would any man, moving forward, ever come close to this?

"I liked it a lot," she agreed, kissing the top of Leila's head. "I liked it a lot."

"Mm, I think we should sleep." Leila sighed, contented. She turned her head slightly and met Camille's mouth with her own. "You like how you taste on me?"

It was the first time Camille had acknowledged that. They'd kissed before when her wetness had smeared Leila's lips, but she'd never recognised it for what it was.

"Yes," she finally said, leaning into kiss her again. This time, she focused on the taste of herself. Leila smiled as their lips met. Understanding Camille had had another awakening.

"You taste so good," Leila said. "I'm going to miss it."

Camille laughed and rolled until they were face to face.

"You'll forget me the moment you're home and a pretty face comes along and piques your interest."

"Maybe, but I'll never forget Camille, my holiday fling."

"Well, I would hope not. I do, at least, like to think

I am memorable."

Leila's eyes closed slowly and opened again, tiredness creeping in. "I wish…" And then they closed once more and she drifted off.

Camille let her sleep. But quietly, she wished too.

TWENTY-ONE

She couldn't fathom the last time she'd woken wrapped in arms and legs and not felt suffocated by it, but this morning, when Camille's eyes opened, and she realised Leila was entwined, she found herself smiling. A sense of peace fell over her, and she closed her eyes again and allowed herself a moment to just enjoy it.

The reality was far from this idyllic bliss they'd created these last few days. Tomorrow, neither of them would be here. Camille's flight was at 11.35 a.m., and that meant being at the airport three hours earlier and leaving the hotel at seven.

"What time is your flight tomorrow?" she asked when it was clear Leila was awake and enjoying the moment, just as much as she was.

Leila stretched and yawned. "Too early. Eleven something."

"To Heathrow?"

"Yep, then a long drive home. You?"

"I think we're on the same flight," Camille answered, twisting around until they were completly face to face. "Where do you live?"

"Currently, Northampton."

"Currently?"

"Well, I am looking for a new job, and if I find the one that I will love, then I am prepared to move."

"I see."

"Where do you live?" Leila ventured to ask again.

"I live in Woodington. It's a largish town near Bath Street."

"Hm, that's nearer Gatwick. Why didn't you fly from there?"

Camille shrugged. "Because I let Rosie organise the trip." She pulled her closer. "See, I don't always need to be in control."

Leila laughed and kissed her. "Visit me when we get back, or I'll come to you."

"You know my answer to that," Camille said. "It wouldn't be the same."

"Maybe you are right, but still, you don't want to find out?"

Camille looked away.

It was one thing being this free on an island where she knew no one. Going home would be a different matter, wouldn't it?

"You are a beautiful, bright, and sexy woman, Leila. You have your entire life ahead of you," Camille said.

Leila was about to break in and speak but Camille held her hand up.

"Please, let me finish." Camille waited a moment and got her thoughts together. "I have enjoyed every moment I've spent with you; I've learned things about myself I didn't know I wanted to learn, and for that, I am grateful, and I will always look back fondly and remember this experience with you."

"You don't have to say anything more, I get it." Leila smiled sadly and touched the locket. "And I will have this as a reminder of you and what could have been."

"Yes, you will, and lots of wonderful memories of the time we shared together."

Leila squeezed her arm around Camille's waist. "But we have tonight, right? One last hurrah?"

"We will have some time tonight, yes. I'd like that very much." She kissed Leila slowly. "You've given me more than I could have dreamed of. Before you, I hadn't even dreamt it." She chuckled before becoming very serious. "I won't forget you."

"I'm glad that maybe I've helped you to find a little piece of yourself that was hidden."

TWENTY-TWO

Rosie was still asleep when Camille made it back to their room. A sense of sadness lingered at the corners of her mind she couldn't quite shake yet.

She showered and dressed for the day. A planned shopping trip into town to pick up some last-minute things that they would just have to have. As she sat on the balcony drinking a strong black coffee, waiting for Rosie to return to the land of the living, her mind drifted to Leila; something it had been doing quite a lot these past few days.

In another life, another world, maybe it would have all been so easy to allow this dalliance to spill over into her reality once they were back in England. But Camille Franklyn, at home, wasn't the Camille she was here, and she doubted very much Leila would even like her.

She heard what people said about her, not that she cared what they thought. She wasn't there to win friends. She was their boss; her job was to manage them, and she did that quite effectively. She didn't need to go for drinks after work or be invited to weddings and birthday parties.

'She'd heard: *The Ice Queen, Elsa, F and F,* which she'd discovered stood for *Frozen and Frigid.*' She'd laughed at that one; at least it was imaginative.

Rosie had asked once, "*Why don't you just fire them? You are the owner of the company after all.*"

"Because I get more satisfaction letting them make me lots of money. They're good at their jobs, it's why I employed them. I don't need them to like me."

And when she got back to the office, all of this adventure into the world of sapphic love, would fade into the distance, and she would be back to her old life and that was okay.

She heard a groan from inside the room and chuckled.

"Good night?" she called out.

The responding grunt implied it was, and she continued to sip her coffee quietly until she heard the rustling of bed sheets, followed by soft shuffling of bare feet on the cool tile.

"God, I feel like death," Rosie said, pulling on her sunglasses and sitting down in the only other chair. "Pedro took me dancing."

"Wow, that's energetic." Camille smiled. "The bedroom antics not enough exercise then?"

"Oh, there were plenty of bedroom acrobatics." She rubbed at her neck subconsciously as she leaned closer. "He held me upside down and ate me out."

Camille's brow raised.

"He called it 'The Snake.'" She poured a cup of coffee from the cafetiere. "I've ordered a book for when we get home. He was telling me about all manner of things and when he did 'The Superman,' well, let's just…I may need to date a younger man more often."

"It's certainly been an experience, this holiday. Maybe we should make it an annual occurrence," Camille said, with just a hint of a smile curling her lips.

"Are you going to date women when you get back?" Rosie asked. It was a fair question.

"I don't think so," Camille answered.

"Why not? You've looked, dare I say it, happy, since you've been dallying with Leila."

She had looked happy. She was aware of that herself, but this wasn't real, was it? This was a break from reality.

"Holiday romances are supposed to make you happy, that's the point of them. Then you go back to reality and life kicks back in and you find yourself—" She heard Leila's words in her head. *"Maybe I've helped you to find a little piece of yourself that was hidden."*

Rosie nodded. "I suppose so."

"Anyway, we have this afternoon to head into town, unless you've arranged something with Pedro?"

"No, I told him I'd see him tonight after we have our last dinner together."

Camille smiled at that. "Yes, I've told Leila the same. I thought it might be prudent to pack everything now, so we don't have to rush in the morning?"

"That sounds like a good idea. I'll quickly grab a shower and we can do that, and then venture into town for some lunch and shopping, before we say our goodbyes."

"Yes," Camille said, feeling a wave of sadness hit her like a tsunami. "I think that will work."

The checkerboard town square was awash with

tourists and locals alike, everyone leisurely enjoying the warm weather and the opportunity to wander aimlessly.

Cobblestone streets, lined with buildings dating back to another time, and cafés and restaurants, made Funchal a perfect place to grab lunch and coffee.

"I didn't realise there would be quite so many hills." Rosie laughed when they'd finally sat down.

"Certainly getting our steps up today." Camille smiled at her. "I imagine most of the locals are very fit."

"You'd have to be. Thank God Woodington is flat."

Camille turned her face to the sun. "I will miss it here, but I do miss the routine of home."

"I don't. I'd move here, or somewhere equally hot. I could work remotely and just put my feet up."

"And ravish more Pedros." Camille smiled across at her. "You should, if that's what you want to do."

"Maybe I will. For now, I'm content to just book a long weekend every couple of months, until he's bored of me."

Camille put her cup down. "Really? You're going to keep seeing him?"

Rosie nodded. "Yes. I think so. He asked if I will come back. He's so charming and respectful—"

"'The Snake' isn't respectful." Camille laughed.

"Okay, fine, he's respectful out of the bedroom, but quite frankly, I like him tossing me around like a ragdoll and giving me multiple orgasms all night."

"You'll get bored."

"And when I do, I'll stop and grow old gracefully, but right now, I'm fifty-one and I'm not dead yet."

"I'm pleased for you, I really am." Camille drank the last of her coffee. "Shall we finish off and then head back?"

TWENTY-THREE

The paella was one of the best Camille had ever eaten, and dinner with Rosie had been fun and enjoyable as they both wound down their holiday and worked out how they would navigate the next few hours.

They had a taxi booked for the following morning and agreed to both be back in the room by 6.30 a.m. for a quick shower and change, and then they would head off. Until then, they had several hours to enjoy with their respective flings.

It was just before 10 p.m. that night when she knocked gently on Leila's door.

It was hard not to smile when the door opened and Leila stood in the doorway, dressed in red this time. Her hair loose, a look that her hairdresser would describe as a little windswept, as though she'd stepped out of the ocean and the sun had dried it.

"You look—divine." Camille gushed a little, feeling the sensation of attraction tumble in her lower regions. Had she ever had that reaction to any man? Maybe Tom, her ex-husband, when they'd first met, and he'd swept her off her feet. She definitely had not felt the same by the time the marriage was over, and he'd left. Since then, it had just been a series of void-fillers if she were honest. Always nice guys— willing guys, but nothing special.

"Come in." Leila held the door for her. "I had a bottle of wine sent up. I thought maybe we could share it and—"

"I'd like that," Camille said quickly. Right now, she'd like anything this woman offered. "On the balcony?"

"Yes, it's a lovely warm night."

The bottle sat in a wine cooler alongside two stemmed glasses, a small bowl of salted, smoked almonds, and a trio of olives with capers.

"I know you've probably eaten but I figured a few snacks are always good, no?" Leila smiled and stepped closer. She grazed Camille's lips with her own, and wasn't told to stop, despite the fact that anyone could see them. "Did you miss me?" Leila smiled into the kiss. Slow and tender, their lips moved together, until Leila's tongue slid past Camille's and into her mouth, circumnavigating the space.

Camille let out a soft groan, one of want and need. And Leila smiled again, this time as she pulled away and broke the kiss.

"I'll take that as a 'yes.'" Leila picked up the bottle and poured two glasses, handing one to Camille. "To new experiences and future ones."

The glasses chinked and they watched each other take a sip. The wine was cool and crisp and just fruity enough.

"I want to know more about you, Camille," Leila said, taking one of the chairs.

"Like what?"

"Oh, so many things." Leila sipped some more, "Like…are you married?"

Camille scoffed. "No, God, no, not anymore."

"But you were?"

"I was, yes, a long time ago now. I've been divorced almost a decade. Tom decided his future lies elsewhere."

Leila sat forward, with all the alertness of a lioness ready to go into battle. "He cheated on you?"

Nodding slowly, Camille said, "Yes, and then he married her."

"And what about your children?"

"I have two boys. Marcus and Tobias. They've grown and flown the nest. Families of their own now."

"So, you're a grandmother?"

Camille smiled at the idea. She'd quite like that one day. "No, not yet, but I'm hopeful." She sipped her wine and then studied Leila. "My turn. You never did tell me your age."

Leila laughed. "You didn't tell me your age either. I don't think it matters. Numbers are…" She shrugged. "Life experience, maturity, humour; these are things we should use to decide if someone is for us, no?"

"Maybe. Still, I'm curious."

"I'm older than you think." Leila smiled. "How old do you think I am?" She turned her face one way, and then other, grinning as Camille considered it.

"When I first saw you from across the pool, I thought you were late twenties, but now, I think early thirties, maybe, thirty-two."

"I will take that." Leila laughed. "I'm thirty-nine."

"You are not!" Camille gasped. "Your skin is fabulous."

"Good genes, remember?" She continued to chuckle. "So, I thought you were in your forties. And I still think that."

"Well, I'll take that." Camille held her glass up. "I'm fifty-two."

Leila sat back and stared at her. "Wow, well, then I must repay the compliment and tell you that you are looking good for it."

"Thank you, I rely on monthly facials and drinking a lot of water." She smiled, but it faded when she placed her glass down. "Leila, I want to ask you something."

"Go ahead, I am an open book."

"Yes, you are, and I do love that about you, but it's more of a request. Leila, tonight, I want something that I have no right asking of you and I completely understand if you say no—"

"What is it? If I can give you it, I will."

Camille sighed. "Yes, I know you would and that's why it's so difficult to ask."

Leila sat forward and reached for her hand. "Camille, just ask."

"I want to—I would like to experience something with you. I love all the fucking and toying with me and all of that, but I'd like to—" she swallowed quickly and let out a shuddering breath before staring into Leila's eyes and saying, "Make love to me…and then…hold me until we have to leave?"

TWENTY-FOUR

Successive men had tried and failed to inspire a sense of romance between the sheets with Camille Franklyn. She'd always put it down to her icy exterior and the need to be in control of everything, including her intimate engagements. But the biggest lesson she had learned these past few nights, was that she'd just been choosing the wrong gender to provide her satisfaction.

Leila didn't falter, didn't miss a beat. She swept Camille up in a whirlwind of sensuality that had her falling over herself to climb into bed with Leila.

But tonight would be different.

"Where's your phone?" Leila asked. "Put your sexy playlist on."

Camille reached into her bag and fiddled with the phone until the music played loudly enough to be enjoyable, without being intrusive.

"It's the soundtrack to *Fifty Shades*," she said quickly, shaking her head at the ridiculousness of it.

"It works, and that's what matters, don't you think?" Leila said, stepping in and sliding her arms up and over Camille's shoulders, hips swaying gently. "Dance with me."

She pressed her body closer and let her fingers slide into Camille's hair, massaging her scalp as her hips continued to move and entice.

Growing in confidence, Camille slid her arms around Leila's waist and let her palms rest on the curve of her backside.

"Okay?" Leila asked, just as she grazed her lips against Camille's. "Just relax and let it all go."

Leila's palms slid back down Camille's chest, and then she turned and took Camille's hands in her own, cradling them across her body while she swayed and pressed her backside against Camille. Guiding Camille's movements to follow her own; moving them together slowly and deliberately.

When Leila felt Camille relax into it, and the beat of the music changed, she slid one of her arms up and back into Camille's hair, directing her head and guiding their mouths together once more.

The kiss was gradual, easing into a soft, tender caress of lips and tongue. Only when Camille's fingers squeezed and tightened did she break away, keeping hold of Camille's hand, leading her towards the bed.

"You are beautiful, and I will show you just how much," Leila said, sinking to her knees. Her palms stroked Camille's calf and lowered to slip her shoe from her foot.

With delicate fingers and seductive movements, Leila took her time, enjoying and pleasuring every inch of Camille's body, as she divested her of her slacks and underwear.

"You smell so good," Leila said, looking up at her with big brown eyes that told Camille she wasn't lying. "So good," she repeated, as she kissed a line from Camille's hip to her navel.

Camille swallowed and allowed herself to enjoy

it; to give this woman the control over her body, to let herself make love.

Leila stood back up and kissed her again on the lips. A little more urgency, but still slow and tender, as their mouths met fully and tongues engaged in the dance once more. Deft fingers unbuttoned the blouse and pushed it off Camille's shoulders. Instantly, her hands unclipped the bra, and when it fell loose, she pulled it free.

"So beautiful," she whispered, bending to kiss one nipple, and then the other.

Camille moaned softly at the pleasurable sensations her body was feeling. Everything felt so heightened already. Had she really never experienced this with anyone, not even Tom? She pushed those thoughts from her mind and focused back on the mouth currently clamped around her nipple, teeth and tongue teasing it stiff.

"Leila." Camille moaned, her hand rising to rest at the back of her lover's head. "Please. I need…" she swallowed, "together," she finally managed.

Leila stood to her full height and grinned. "Okay, my love." She led Camille to the bed. "Get comfy." She quickly stripped out of her clothing and stood to one side, smiling down at Camille, who now lay on her back, one leg bent, the other pulled aside, exposing herself.

Camille had never been like this with anyone, she considered, as she watched Leila climb onto the bed, one knee at a time.

"I want to make this about you, but I understand the need to share the experience." Leila crawled into the space between Camille's thighs and glanced down, smiling to herself. "So wet." She said it as though it were praise, and nothing to ever feel ashamed about.

"For you," Camille responded, reaching out for her. "I'm wet, for you, because of you."

"This pleases me." Leila giggled as she lowered herself until she lay against Camille's torso, her thigh resting against Camille's wetness. Adding pressure, she straddled herself across Camille's thigh, and slowly, she moved, creating a delicious friction for them both. When the rhythm was just right, and Camille's hips were rising and falling in unison with her own, she lowered further, and this time, the kiss conveyed everything they couldn't, or wouldn't, say.

TWENTY-FIVE

Camille wheeled her case down to the hotel reception and handed in their keys while Rosie said her goodbyes to Pedro.

"Did you enjoy your stay?" the woman at the desk asked, smiling far too brightly for this early hour, Camille thought.

"Yes, thank you. It's been…" She noticed Leila appear further along the desk, handing her own keys over. "A beautiful experience."

"We are so pleased. And hopefully we will see you again."

"Yes, maybe so," Camille said, unable to take her eyes off of Leila. They shared a smile. A shy, sorrowful smile.

"Your taxi will be outside, ready to take you to the airport as soon as you are organised."

"Okay, thank you." Camille finally turned back to the desk clerk. It was then, that she caught sight of Rosie, walking towards her. Her friends eyes wet and ready to release emotions Camille wasn't sure she could deal with right now. "Everything alright?"

"Yes, I just… you know." She laughed at herself. "It's been fun, hasn't it? I'm sad to go."

"It has," Camille answered. "The taxi is waiting."

She didn't wait for Rosie to give any opinion on

that before she took off, wheeling her case towards the exit Leila had just left through. Slowing her step, she didn't want to keep bumping into her and make this any more difficult than it already felt.

She was cross with herself about that. A fling, that's all it was, she kept reminding herself, but her mind would just wander back to the woman who'd awoken her to so many new possibilities.

"Here we go," Rosie said, pointing at a man with a moustache, waving them over. Rosie headed off and started talking to him as he loaded her case into the large boot. Camille caught Leila climbing into a taxi ahead of them. "Camille, are you coming?" Rosie shouted, already half into the back of the car.

"Yes, of course. There's no rush. We have plenty of time." She handed over her case and smiled at the driver.

"You'll probably see her at the airport," Rosie said, trying to be helpful.

Rolling her eyes for the first time in days, Camille felt the icy shroud begin to fall over her. "We said our goodbyes earlier."

"Oh, well..." Rosie pulled her seatbelt across and locked it into place. "Still, it might be nice to spend another few minutes—"

"I don't think so," Camille said with an icy edge. "It's not something I need to think about any further." She yanked the seatbelt and became frustrated when it stuck. She had to yank it twice more before she could lock it.

"Are you alright?" Rosie said quietly. The driver climbed into the car and said something neither of them heard properly.

"I'm fine, Rosie, I'm just ready to get home. And I'm tired and hungry." She spoke as though that would excuse her bad mood. She turned towards the window and looked out as the taxi pulled into traffic and the journey home began.

The airport was relatively small compared with most international airports Camille had been in. On the flight in, she hadn't really noticed as they were too eager to grab their cases and get to the hotel. Now, they had almost two hours to wait, having got through baggage handoff and security.

"Coffee?" Rosie asked, though she grimaced when she looked at the queue for it. One small kiosk was open.

"Please, and anything to eat, I really don't care what."

Rosie smiled at her friend. "I'll see what I can do. Why don't you see if you can find us somewhere to park our backsides?"

"Will do."

With Rosie's attention elsewhere, Camille finally took a deep breath and released it. She needed to focus, remain calm, and just sit it out until they could board the plane.

She tried to think if she could remember Leila on the plane on the way out, and if so, where she'd been sitting, because she was sure she would have noticed her. Maybe she'd come out the week before? She did have a great tan, Camille thought, before shaking her head free of any thoughts involving Leila.

There were two seats free in the corner and she moved quickly to nab them and settled down into one, placing her bag onto the spare seat to save it for Rosie.

Glancing up, she saw her friend in the queue, waving at her and miming something, but Camille had no clue what it meant. She couldn't imagine it being anything bad, so she just nodded and smiled. That seemed to work when she received a thumbs up.

She closed her eyes and let her head fall back against the wall.

"Camille."

Opening her eyes slowly, she sat up straight the instant Leila came into focus.

"Leila, are you alright?"

"Yes, I just— I wanted to…I know we said that this was it, but if I leave now, knowing that I didn't do everything I could—" She held out a folded piece of paper. "My number. It's up to you if you decide to use it or not, but I wanted to at least give you it so I don't live with any 'what ifs.'"

Camille reached out tentatively and took the paper from her. She didn't open it.

"We had fun, Leila," Camille said. "I'll cherish that."

"Yes." Leila nodded. "Goodbye, Camille."

She watched as Leila turned and walked away and out of sight. Glancing down at the paper in her hand, she considered it. Could they be something more?

Rosie was walking towards her carrying paper bags and coffee cups. She quickly shoved the piece of paper into the front pocket of her bag.

"Was that?" Rosie said, jutting her chin over her shoulder. "Leila?"

"Yes." Camille reached for the coffees. "I am ravenous."

TWENTY-SIX

The plane landed with a soft jolt and everyone around her began to unclip seatbelts and start to rummage in bags and chatter about innocuous things, like how far they had to go to get home.

Rosie stretched and yawned. "That was a good flight."

"You slept for most of it." Camille chuckled. "To be fair, I think I did too."

"At least we won't need a nap when we get home."

"Nap? We're not that old yet," Camille gasped.

Rosie nudged her. "You speak for yourself."

The plane had taxied into a gate and people around them began to stand and stretch and grab their bags from the overhead lockers.

"I never understood why everyone does that. You can't go anywhere." Camille moaned when someone's bag swung down and almost hit her.

"I know. Just sit it out and be the last off, then when you get to baggage, the wait isn't so long."

"Exactly." Camille nodded. She reached into her pocket and pulled out a packet of sweets. "Wine gum?"

"Don't mind if I do," Rosie said, plucking a green one out.

"I don't like those ones," Camille said, pulling a

face at it.

"I'm not the biggest fan but I'm not going to put it back."

The aeroplane doors opened, and people began to shuffle forward. Camille kept her eyes forward, but she couldn't miss the perfectly wrapped backside that slipped past.

"I'm glad you met her," Rosie said, noticing Leila too. "I think she's been good for you."

"Hm, yes, but now we're home and that door is closed."

"Oh Camille, don't be so stubborn." Rosie laughed.

Camille turned a little. "We both know that I'm not stubborn, I'm determined, and what happens in Madeira, stays in Madeira, right?"

Rosie saluted. "Yes, you're quite right, all…" She zipped her mouth dramatically.

The last of the stragglers made their way past them, so they stood up and collected their things, edging their way down the aisle and off of the plane.

"I've had a great time," Camille said. "Thank you for coming with me."

"Like I'd miss a week in the sun." Rosie laughed. "Shall we book another trip for the spring?"

"Back there?"

"Yes," Rosie said as they wandered along.

"Are you going to be spending the entire time shagging Pedro?"

"Quite possibly," Rosie admitted with a huge grin. "Is that a 'no' then?"

"It's a 'let's wait and see.'"

"But you're not saying 'no.'" Rosie pushed playfully.

"No, I'm not saying 'no.'"

"Good, because I already booked the room again," Rosie admitted.

"Rosie!" Camille laughed. "What if I can't do those dates?"

Rosie shrugged. "Then I guess it will be just me going. And you can explore your new lesbian side somewhere else."

"Ha, the chances of finding another hot young thing wanting to entertain me are very slim. I've got more chance of finding a Pedro." She shook her head at the idea and continued to laugh. It was funny how quickly things could change, she thought.

"Well, that's not all bad, is it?" Rosie said, looking earnestly at her.

Camille considered it. "I don't think I know anymore."

"You've got until March to work it out." Rosie laughed just as they entered the baggage hall.

Glancing around quickly, Camille didn't see her. She wasn't sure if she was grateful for that, or disappointed, but the one thing she knew without a doubt, was she would never forget those nights with Leila.

Hot to the touch

CLAIRE HIGHTON-STEVENSON

CLAIRE HIGHTON-STEVENSON

ONE

Since getting home from Madeira, everything had quickly changed for Leila Ortez.

A series of events had all fallen into place, and despite her despondency at not hearing from Camille, she couldn't deny she was feeling the joy of life, in full effect.

Job applications had gone out, and she'd interviewed for dozens, but only one had stood out from the moment she'd read the application's summary of the position.

It had everything. Opportunity for promotion. Working within a small team. Utilising all her skills. A very competitive wage, with extremely generous bonuses, holiday, and sick pay.

And best of all, it was in Woodington.

Not that she had known that when she'd originally applied. It wouldn't have mattered where the office was located; she wanted the job and was prepared to move almost anywhere.

So, discovering it was based in the very town Camille said she lived, felt like fate had stepped in. Because if she were completely honest, she was not over Camille.

A fling didn't leave her feeling like she'd met the woman of her dreams. Hook-ups would usually be fun and exciting, and both parties would be cool with walking away.

And Leila was not cool with it.

Deep down, she was pretty sure Camille hadn't been cool with it either, but she was at least honest about the fact she wouldn't contact Leila.

An impromptu meeting on the streets of Woodington while shopping or grabbing a coffee though, really would be coincidental, a matter of kismet, wouldn't it?

Accepting the offer had taken barely a second's thought, unlike the constant daydreaming of Camille, naked, writhing and begging, in her bed. So, it was really good when her flat went on the market and sold within a week.

Leila hadn't had time to think about anything other than packing and organising before she was on her way to start a new chapter in her life.

It had all been so fast.

"Paddy, be careful," Leila's best friend, Kristen, shouted at her boyfriend and his pal Jeff as they lugged boxes from the van into the lift.

A woman came down the stairs and glared at them all.

"Other people want to use that," she complained as she walked towards the exit.

"So sorry," Leila called out after her. "Last time, promise."

The woman all but snarled, and Kristen gave her the finger once the crabby neighbour's back was turned.

"Miserable cow." She looked around. "I hope all your neighbours are not like that."

"I'm sure they're all delightful. Maybe she's just having a bad day." Leila smiled and moved out of the way, as Jeff and Paddy struggled in with a chest of drawers.

"Right, that's it," Paddy said. "Kris, move the van so we don't get a ticket."

"Sure thing, Loverboy, " she cooed. "I'll grab us all some coffees, too."

"Welcome to Woodington." Paddy grinned as the doors closed, and Leila's life moved upwards.

TWO

It had taken Camille Franklyn two months before frustration had kicked in and meant she had braved the idea of going out and finding a bar to meet another woman.

Pushing all thoughts of her holiday fling, with the delightful, and much younger, Leila, from her mind, she'd even attempted to date men again, refusing to give into the idea that maybe she was something other than straight.

That plan had not gone well.

Several failed endeavours ensued, and she'd understood quite quickly she wasn't remotely interested in the idea of taking things further than dinner or drinks, and yet, she had the itch of arousal that needed scratching.

A need that pulsed between her thighs and had her sliding her hand into the warmth of her underwear far too often than she would like to admit.

But taking matters into her own hands wasn't enough.

Nothing she did was sufficient to quiet the active part of her brain that remembered just how much she had enjoyed the pleasure of sex with a woman. *With Leila*, the reminder came again.

Despite the reticence to investigate any further, and the lies she'd so clearly been telling herself about who she was and what her exploration had been about, she found herself booking a hotel in the neighbouring town of Bath Street.

And on a quiet, but wet, Wednesday evening after work,

she'd tied her hair back and slipped into a pair of comfortable jeans. Deciding casual was the way forward, she bought a new shirt, added heels and a raincoat, and bundled herself into all of it to avoid the cold.

Adding some light makeup, she felt very good about herself and the possibilities that lay ahead.

She walked inside confidently, considering she'd never frequented a gay bar before, and didn't consider herself a gay woman. In fact, Imposter Syndrome might have been a better label for how she was feeling much of the time lately.

Everything had been so much easier in the heat of Madeira. She could be herself without the watching eyes of her world, the corporate world, where she had a reputation to maintain. More personally, it was a world where she didn't have to think about Tom, and her failed marriage, and all the other failed relationship attempts since. Or what her sons would think, or her friends.

Because it made no sense to her. How had she maintained the life she had, without ever doubting herself, or who she was?

Until now.

Until Leila.

That was the reason why she'd finally given in and decided to find out. Was it just Leila, or was there more to it? Was it a mid-life crisis, or was there more to her sexual identity she might be forced to navigate?

She'd chosen the bar closest to her hotel. A more upbeat, younger and hipper crowd, she guessed, looking at the faces and clothing choices. She moved around the room relatively unnoticed as she took it all in. Was it okay to smile at someone, or go over uninvited? She had no clue how any of this worked.

There were so many new rules of engagement to steer

around. This wasn't a world she knew anything about. The question *what are you doing?* ran through her mind about as often as thoughts about Leila did.

Unfortunately, her expectations for gay bars were solely founded on what she'd seen on TV and in movies. Back when she was married, they'd socialised a lot in pubs and clubs. But nothing really like this, and once the boys were born and the business took off, Camille didn't have time for cavorting in bars, not that she'd ever cavorted previously.

Except with Leila, the reminder again came. God, how she had shamelessly romped with that woman.

Loud music cut through her overthinking, not anything she recognised, but the beat of it rhythmically moved through her body, urging her hips to sway, and her foot to tap, as she waited patiently at the bar.

Finally, she was served by a woman less than half her age and sporting multicoloured hair, and rings in places Camille didn't think should have rings.

She smiled and shut off her judgement. This was not her world, or was it? If it were to become her world, she considered she would need to readjust so much of her thinking.

Her drink arrived, as colourful as the bartender's hair, and very exotic looking.

Another little reminder of the holiday, and of the woman she had so casually brushed aside, once the holiday was over. At least, Leila would probably have seen things that way. She couldn't have been further from the truth.

She'd be a liar if she said she hadn't considered something more between them. But a secret long-distance romance was not a relationship Camille wanted to enter into, nor would it be fair to Leila.

Leila would never allow herself to be kept in the shadows. She deserved to be flaunted. Leila needed someone who was proud to stand beside her and not someone, like Camille, who would shy away from anyone ever knowing they were intimate together.

Camille did the one thing Camille Franklyn knew to do. Something she had learned a long time ago: she shut down her emotions and moved on.

She went home and pushed it all down and away.

Her ability to not let emotion get in the way of a decision was her superpower; it was why her business was so successful. And she'd been rewarded over and over again. Contract after contract, she'd built her little empire, putting investors in contact with companies looking for investment.

And since Tom had left, she'd done the same thing within her personal relationships, too. She dated men she had no emotional attachment to other than she liked them as people and enjoyed their companionship to a certain extent. Her plan worked, as they were happy to be kept at arm's reach, and didn't become clingy or needy of her time.

But Leila had been different.

Leila had opened something within Camille that she was struggling to shut down. Camille's biggest fear now was just how much of herself she might lose if she allowed Leila into her life.

Leila had gotten under Camille's skin and burrowed in so deeply Camille didn't honestly know she was there for the most part. Hidden within her subconscious until something was said, or a song played, or a scent wafted past and suddenly, there Leila was, back inside her mind, in her thoughts, reminding her instantly that out there, somewhere, was a woman with the power to bring Camille Franklyn to her knees.

Literally, and figuratively.

Sipping her drink through one of those horrible paper straws, Camille moved casually around, bumping into people as they bustled their way to the bar or the dance floor, checking out several women who piqued her interest and gave her the once over, smiled, but then continued with their conversations.

It was quite confusing, considering Leila's confident, assured, and very forward way of moving towards her was all she had to go on.

She leaned back against a wall and felt the music thump its beat through it, and her, watching, taking it all in. Couples, who fit all kinds of stereotypes were being attentive towards each other. Groups of other people mingled, laughed, and talked animatedly.

Camille felt even more out of place.

She'd almost finished her drink, and was about to consider the rest of the evening a disaster and just go home, when she was finally approached by one of the women she'd made eye contact with earlier.

"Hi," she said, stepping in as close as she could to be heard. Her fingers brushed against Camille's torso and rested on her hip. "On your own?"

Camille continued to sip her drink before she replied, "Yes, for now."

The woman chuckled at that. Deep dimples popped on her cheeks. "Can I buy you another drink?"

Camille tilted her head to one side while she debated the offer. "If you like."

"I do like." She winked and said, "I'll be right back."

Camille observed her walking away.

She was shorter in height by an inch or two, but then Camille was wearing heels. The woman's long blonde hair trailed down her back, but there was something quite masculine about the way she moved through the crowd. Camille wasn't sure if that was a turn-on or not, but it definitely wasn't a turn-off. And she was nothing like Leila. That was the important part, wasn't it?

It didn't take long for her to return. Each hand held a drink as she carefully picked her way through the crowd.

"So, what's your name?" she asked, handing over a glass that didn't contain the same drink Camille had ordered earlier.

Camille said, "Jane," ss she accepted the drink with a half-smile. *If you could lie to yourself, then you could lie about anything,* Camille thought

"You're gorgeous, Jane. I'm Emma. Do you want to dance?"

Camille sighed. "No, not really."

"Oh, right, just chilling then?" Emma asked, sipping her drink and trying to appear nonchalant.

Instead, she looked a little nervous, and that was off-putting, Camille considered, but at least she'd had the balls to speak to her in the first place.

Unlike several of the others, who were still gawping in her direction, but didn't make a move.

Camille considered the question.

Honesty sounded like the best policy in a situation like this. She wasn't looking to be romanced.

"To be frank, I was hoping to meet someone who wanted to…hook up?"

Emma's eyes flashed between shock and excitement. She licked her lips as she envisioned the opportunity.

"Well, your luck might be in." Emma grinned, finally recovering her bravery and following it up with a large swig of her drink.

Camille contemplated the flirtatious offer.

Emma was attractive. That wasn't the reason for the hesitation. Something niggled at the back of her mind, but she pushed it away. This was what she wanted, wasn't it? No strings, no emotions, not impacting her actual life? Just fragments of enjoyment nobody else needed to know about.

"I have a hotel room." Camille smiled and then guzzled her drink, until the only thing remaining was the paper straw and the various fruit garnishes that bobbed at the bottom on a seabed of crushed ice.

"Sounds like we have a plan then." Emma moved in closer, moistening her lips once more, before she pressed them to Camille's.

A soft, warm, firm tongue then slid into Camille's mouth and reminded her why she was here, and what she was wanting from this exchange. She felt her clit clench, and despite the previous hesitation, Camille followed her body's urging and kissed Emma back.

THREE

The hotel room was basic.

A bed and a shower were all Camille needed for this little escapade. She didn't even plan on sleeping there, hadn't brought any luggage with her either.

Opening the door with the card, she walked in and shrugged off her raincoat, hanging it on the rail, while Emma followed and casually looked around, as though the room was of importance.

"So, this is—"

"Take your clothes off," Camille ordered, already frustrated Emma didn't seem to have the wits about her to read the situation, to read her. Leila would have had her cornered already, pressed up against the wall or a door with her underwear and clothing scattered.

Her brain would turn to mush as the accented voice spoke confidently against her ear and told her everything she was going to do to her.

"What will I find?" Leila whispered, once more, against Camille's ear.

"I uh—" Camille gasped when deft fingers parted her and slid effortlessly against her clit. "God, that's—"

"Wet." Leila chuckled, slowly circling the already engorged bundle of nerves. "I like that, Camille."

"Hm-hm."

"You like that, don't you?"

Camille nodded, biting her lip. "Yes," she finally got out, just before Leila's fingertip slid lower. "Oh, God."

"I will lead until you decide otherwise, Camille. You understand that, right?"

She pushed those thoughts aside.

Emma choked out a nervous chuckle. "Okay, eager. I like it."

It took Camille all of thirty seconds to kick off her heels and strip out of her clothes, tossing everything into a pile on the chair.

She needed this, to let loose with someone new, find out her longing had nothing to do with Leila, and had everything to do with finding who she was now. And getting that itch scratched, too.

She watched as Emma meticulously took each piece of her own clothing off, folded it neatly, and placed it on a pile.

In no hurry, or nervous? Camille couldn't quite decide, but Emma's slow pace irked her all the same.

Emma barely glanced at Camille, and when she did, her cheeks reddened. She looked away quickly, frustrating Camille in the process. She wanted to be looked at the way Leila had looked at her, to be explored visually, wondered about. She wanted her nakedness to be enticing and thought provoking.

"You can look at me," Camille said, intently watching Emma reveal small breasts and a small landing strip of pubic hair in shy glimpses.

Her mind flashed back to those inquisitive, searching, brown eyes that hadn't moved away from her from the moment they'd met, and held, with Camille's.

How much did it turn Camille on to be looked at that way?

Emma finally put her attention on Camille. Her eyes scanned Camille's naked form quickly, before settling back on her face.

"I make you nervous?" Camille asked.

The nervous laugh answered before the words did. "A little, yes. You're a bit more forthright than maybe I'm used to."

And right there and then, Camille understood what the nagging, niggling hesitation had been earlier. The warning in the back of her mind telling her this would not be the passionate engagement she'd hoped for.

She might as well have called a random date, like Roger, to come over for a quickie, but the thought made her stomach turn.

Sighing, Camille took Emma's hand and led her to the bed. At the very least, she would get an orgasm out of it – even if she had to do most of the work herself.

"Sit against the pillows," Camille instructed, and like a little eager puppy, Emma scrabbled into place and stared up at her expectantly.

Camille heard a voice in her head.

"You enjoy it, the way they scuttle around after you...but you don't respect them...because you think they are..." Leila paused. *"Weak..."*

Camille pushed the memory away and climbed onto the bed, moving to straddle Emma's thighs. Leaning back on her heels, she tilted her head until their mouths met again.

The one thing she could say was Emma did know how to kiss, hesitant for just a moment before she understood it was something she was allowed to enjoy. Her tongue pushed its way into Camille's mouth and dominated her tongue and for a split second, Camille thought this might be all that Emma had needed to push her into action, but no other movement followed.

In the end, Camille reached for Emma's hand and pushed it into the gap between her own thighs, into her wetness. "Fuck me," Camille pleaded.

The moment Emma penetrated her, Camille took charge, riding the digits to her own rhythm, and altering the way her hips moved in order to hit that ultimate spot, desperately pushing all thoughts of Leila from her mind.

Her hands pressed against the wall, bracing herself, as her breasts bounced and slapped against Emma's face. Frustrated, Camille nudged her nipple against Emma's lips until Emma finally got the hint and took it, but nothing she did had any real effect on Camille. Not until she finally succumbed and allowed Leila to intrude. Only when she dove into her memories, did she start to feel any sense of getting her needs met.

"Don't stop," Camille demanded. "Press your thumb against my clit." Her back arched the instant Emma did so. It didn't take long before she came, but when she did, she knew it wouldn't be enough.

It would never be the same. She'd never had to ask Leila.

"Explore," Leila said quietly. "Let your fingertips roam my body."

"I want to touch you," Camille admitted.

"You are touching me."

"No, I—not...I want to touch you." Her eyes opened, and she found Leila's eyes locked on her. "Your...I want to touch your..."

"Say it," Leila urged. "What do you want to touch, Camille?"

It was one thing using words in her head. Saying them aloud, however...

Leila leaned forward, her mouth against Camille's ear.

"You like that," Emma said, her words infiltrating the fantasy. "You feel so good."

Camille ignored it, focused only on those precious moments alone with Leila.

"Pussy?"

"Yes."

Leila took her hand once more and pulled it between her legs, until Camille could feel the heat against her fingertips, but not touch.

"Say it. Tell me." Their eyes locked once more.

"I want to touch…your pussy," Camille said in barely a whisper, still shocked at herself she would even think such language.

"Own it, Camille. Don't shy away when you are so close."

She was right. Camille knew that. In any other area of her life, she wouldn't be embarrassed or afraid to ask for what she needed. God, usually she just demanded it, so why was this different?

"Pussy." She spoke more confidently. "I want your pussy."

"So hot, baby," Emma continued, believing it was her that was causing this reaction. Camille wanted to scoff and laugh at her.

Why couldn't she just shut up?

Just shut up, Camille's mind screamed.

She just needed to come again.

Rising up, she looked down at Emma and pressed her hips forward. "Put your mouth to good use."

Emma looked confused until Camille slid her hand behind Emma's head and pushed forward. "For God's sake."

FOUR

Over the weeks that followed, Camille got better at picking women to share her bed, but none ever really got her. It was always the fantasy of Leila that tipped her over the edge; always her words, her voice, her touch relived, that gave Camille any sense of satisfaction.

She'd learned to appear demure and submissive, in order to attract the ones confident enough to take charge and be guaranteed to get her off, but it was always a trade-off.

She could never just be herself. She would always lead, somewhat, and it frustrated her no end.

Although, she could admit, she'd learned a lot about women and the different types available on the scene: those who would fuck her all night long and never let her touch them. Then, there were those who wanted to dominate just a little too much. Far too many had mummy issues, or not enough self-esteem, or were just simply inexperienced.

She never quite found anyone who fulfilled her the way Leila had, because it wasn't just sexual, and that was the problem. Camille had put her time with Leila into a box that didn't fit. Leila hadn't just stripped her naked and pleasured her body. Leila had stripped her bare mentally too, and then filled her with a sense of something she'd been missing, and longed for now.

Had she fallen in love?

Fallen for the exotic, younger woman who could calm her mind while sending her body into a frenzy? *Had she?* It was ridiculous to even think it. How could anyone fall in love with someone in such a short span of time?

And yet, Leila had been creeping into her thoughts more and more lately, hadn't she? Especially during moments like now, as she waited in the car for Rosie to come out of the airport.

Rosie, who'd flown off to Madeira, once again, to spend yet another weekend with her young lover – the same hotel where Camille had spent those wonderful nights with her own younger, gorgeous experiment.

Her phone beeped and pulled her from her thoughts.

Rosie: Coming out now. Where are you parked?

Camille: Wait at drop off. I'll drive around.

It took a few minutes to leave the garage where she'd parked to wait and drive back up and around the roundabout before turning into the airport and making her way to where people usually got dropped off.

She slowed the car and searched along the rows of people until she spotted Rosie, waving at her with an enormous grin on her face, red hair flying about in the wind.

Camille smiled and pulled in.

The back door opened in an instant, and Rosie pushed her case onto the seat before hopping into the front and collapsing as though she'd just flown halfway around the world.

"Welcome home," Camille said, indicating and pulling out again, before the security guard could tap on the window and tell her to move. "Good trip?"

Rosie's face lit up. "Very, thank you."

"Pedro is still around then?" The barest hint of a smile graced Camille's lips as she checked the rear mirror. She was sure one day she'd be doing this and dealing with a heartbroken Rosie, but she wouldn't ever tell her friend she felt that way. So far, Pedro had proved her wrong, so maybe he'd continue to be a decent guy. After all, Rosie was a catch, and had a lot to offer anyone.

"Of course, that's why I was there," Rosie said gleefully, then she bit her lip before saying, "Guess who else was there?"

"No idea, enlighten me," Camille said, but she felt the pull in her lower stomach. The knot tightened in her throat, her mouth drying as she prepared herself to hear the only word that made any sense in this situation.

"Leila," Rosie said softly, as though it wasn't a bomb being exploded in the pits of Camille's soul.

Camille felt the air being sucked out of her lungs., her heart rate rapidly increasing. She wouldn't rise to it. She couldn't.

"She asked after you," Rosie continued. "I said that you were well."

"Okay," Camille croaked out, before moistening her lips with her tongue, swallowing over and over to try and lubricate her mouth.

They drove in silence for a moment, with just the sound of the radio in the background and the tarmac under the wheels, as Camille joined the motorway and sped up, doing everything she could to push those thoughts and feelings and images away, but she just couldn't.

She needed to know.

"Was she—"

"By herself?" Rosie asked. "No, but I don't think it was a romantic situation."

Camille flashed her a glance before putting her eyes

back on the road again.

"What makes you think that?"

Rosie shrugged. "I don't know, just a vibe. They were laughing and talking a lot, but never doing anything touchy-feely." And then Rosie added, "More like how we are, not like she was with you, you know?"

Oh, she knew, alright. Leila's hands had been very touchy-feely. How she missed that touch, and the way Leila could play her body like a symphony.

"You should call her."

"What for?" Camille answered defensively. She stuck to the slow lane, not trusting herself to concentrate enough to be speeding and overtaking.

"Because you liked her."

"What does that matter? We have very different lives and I'm not gay. It was just an exploration."

Rosie sighed heavily, twisting a little in her seat to stare at Camille in that way that said she wasn't having it.

"Don't tell me that you haven't been out continuing to explore things with women. I know you, and I know when you're being sneaky."

Camille side-eyed her friend. "I am not sneaky."

"Really? So where were you last Friday when I asked?"

"I told you; I went out."

Rosie twisted in her seat some more. "Yes, and that's what I mean, no other details, just 'out.'" She used her fingers to emphasise speech marks when she said 'out.'

Camille huffed. "What do you want me to say?"

"I want you to be honest. At least with yourself," Rosie said. She reached into her bag and pulled out a vape.

Opening the window, she sucked on it and blew the smoke out. "The whole point of sleeping with Leila was to find out, and you *found out*, and now you're denying yourself anything substantial and dabbling in under-the-radar hook-ups."

Camille said nothing.

"Nobody else is going to care. None of your friends, work—"

"Oh, work would have a bloody field day," Camille spurted, unable to stay quiet. "I can't, okay, I just... I'm good with how things are. I get my needs met in other ways—"

"Bullshit." Rosie called her out. "This is me, remember? I know you, and you haven't been happy since the day we got back four months ago."

"My life is exactly what I need it to be."

"Your life is devoid of anything meaningful," Rosie accused.

"And because you have Pedro, you're the expert on meaningful relationships? A man half your age who you see once a month for sexual intercourse, and then leave to come home, to a dreary UK and the mundane life you've established?"

Rosie said nothing, but she twisted back around in her seat to face forward.

"I'm sorry, that was uncalled for and—"

"Yes. It was. My life is not mundane, it's complicated. I can't just up sticks and go, and if you must know, Pedro is visiting me next, and we plan to find out if there's any way he can stay. It's not so easy now, since Brexit."

Camille breathed deeply. "No, I imagine it isn't."

"All I am saying is think about it. Think about the life you could have, with someone who gets you."

"With someone who got me for less than a week. I can't base my entire life on a holiday fling, I can't, and I'm not ready to leave the closet. I'm just not."

FIVE

"I thought you'd want to know we've taken on some new analysts, Ms Franklyn," Vincent Hardy said, running a hand nervously over his tie.

Camille turned enough to look over her shoulder at him, and then glanced at the clock. It was 9:52 a.m. She'd been in the office since seven. "And why are you telling me?"

"I – I thought you'd want to know – they're starting today."

"Recruitment is your job, Vincent, not mine." She pulled her chair out from her desk and sat down, steepling her fingers as she now looked up at him. "My job is to make sure you're doing your job. I don't need to know the details. I'm sure you're quite capable of distributing them around to whichever department they need to be."

"Yes, that's…that's why I'm telling you. We have someone moving into your office. She'll be working alongside Pamela on the Connor deal."

"Again, why do I care?" Her stare was like ice and he felt it run down his spine. "Pamela is quite capable of organising the Connor report and dealing with any new staff on board. That's why we hired her. Will I be required to welcome the new staff? Maybe I should forget about all of this work." She waved her hand over the paperwork on her desk. "And do a guided tour. Is that what you'd like me to do?"

"Just keeping you in the loop." The nerves made it into his chuckle as he backed away, nearer to the safety of the door and an escape.

"Okay." She sighed and turned away. "Now, I have a meeting with Jacoby and Sons regarding their multimillion-pound cash injection into Wetherby's. Do I need to waste any more time on this?"

Vincent pressed his lips together and backtracked physically, towards the door. "No, I will organise everything and—"

"Correct. Close the door on the way out."

Camille Franklyn sat back and pinched the bridge of her nose.

Maybe a night out on the prowl would work. She needed something, someone.

Commitment-free, sapphic, sexual relations, with a hot and adventurous woman, willing to let her continue her exploration under the radar, even if it wasn't as satisfactory as she'd like.

She needed that today. At least she would, once she was done with these damn meetings.

Pulling on her jacket, she checked herself in the mirror. When she walked out of the office, all eyes would inevitably fall on her, and she wanted to make sure they never once got an opportunity to not see her put together.

Gathering her files and phone, she took a moment before she opened the door to her office and walked out.

Head high, shoulders back. The epitome of in charge.

She rolled her eyes when several underlings scurried and dipped out of sight. *Weak*, she thought to herself.

"Oh, Ms Franklyn…" Pamela called out from the opposite direction, but Camille didn't have time to deal with whatever that was. If it were important, Pamela would have to catch up with her and talk en route.

Otherwise, she knew to deal with it herself.

Outside the door to the conference room, she checked her watch, and at exactly ten a.m., she opened the door and marched in. Taking up her position at the head of the table, she glanced around at the predominantly white, middle-aged, balding men, and the one woman, who sat on the end, with her chair pulled as far away from the man she was sitting next to as she could get.

"Right, let's get this done, shall we?" she said, with all the authority of someone not to be messed with. "Tanner, fill me in."

Tanner, one of the few men in the room still under forty, smiled awkwardly as he stood up to deliver his part of the information. He worked on Wetherby's behalf and would put the case across as to why they needed a cash injection at all.

His monotonous voice almost sent Camille to sleep, but eventually, he got to the point and sat down again. In turn, she listened to the representative of Jacoby's rebut why it was they felt a cash injection right now would benefit nobody, least of all, Jacoby and Sons.

SIX

Leila looked up at the building. Her new office was on the 7th floor, and she smiled to herself as she pushed through the revolving doors and headed to the small reception desk where she knew her credentials would be waiting for her.

She signed in and waited while the security guard, whose nametag read Nick, went through to the back to find the envelope with her name on it. She checked her watch; 9.52 a.m. She still had enough time to get to where she needed to be and not be late.

The atrium was nice, all glass and shiny, and she caught her reflection in one of the windows. There was no way anyone couldn't appreciate her efforts to look professional.

Her hair was up and pulled into a neat ponytail. She'd considered plaiting but hadn't had time in the end. Makeup perfect, the exact tone of lipstick that said she had made an effort but wasn't trying to stand out.

Her suit was something she'd splurged on, wanting to make the right impression with anyone she met today. She'd ignored the traditional black and went with a soft shade of camel because it matched perfectly with her tanned skin and was the exact fit to accentuate her figure. The heels added to her height and lifted her from a reasonably tall 5'6" to a lofty 5'8". She'd topped it all off with a woollen brown coat that would keep out the late winter cold.

It had been so good to get away for a few days with Kristen before she'd moved her entire life halfway down the country for a job that seemed perfect for her.

Though, in hindsight, she probably shouldn't have gone back *there*. Everywhere she looked reminded her of Camille. The one woman who, no matter how hard she tried, she couldn't shake from her thoughts.

Common sense said she needed to get her head around it and move on. It was clear from the lack of contact that Camille had been true to her word and she'd seen it as nothing more than a fling. And wasn't the saying, 'no response is a response,' something she should accept?

But then the universe had stepped in, putting Rosie back in Maderia. Camille's best friend, Rosie, who recognised her and offered a friendly smile, and a discreet answer to her questions.

Synchronicity at play? Or just coincidence?

Leila didn't know, but potential for something more at some point, was playing with her mind and allowing far too many thoughts to play out her fantasies. It was easy to let herself believe the stars were aligned for her with Camille.

In much the same way, this job had felt divinely orchestrated. A message alert, on a job site where she was registered, had come through and she'd sent for more details immediately. She hadn't even looked where it was based, wanting to judge it purely on the job description and salary, because she'd already accepted she would move anywhere for the right step up.

It was a perfect fit.

Everything she'd have wanted in a job was being offered by Franklyn Financials. And like with most things in her life, she went off gut instinct, especially when she'd seen where the offices were based, and where she would need to move to if she accepted the offer.

Synchronicity again: Woodington.

The town where Camille said she lived, and Leila had no reason to think that was an untruth.

It had been a dilemma for all of a minute.

Leila would have the perfect job, and then, if the cards were dealing a favourable hand, she might bump into Camille, and then who knew what might happen.

"Here you go, Ms Ortez," Nick said, handing over a white envelope. "You should find your access card and lanyard inside. You'll find everything else you need when you get upstairs and speak to Pamela Naysmith."

"Thank you so much, Nick," she said, already peeling the envelope open. She peered in, pulled out the plastic rectangle with her face and name already printed on it, and placed the lanyard over her head to hang around her neck. "Do I just take the lift up?"

"Yes, turn to the left and walk straight through and you'll find them there. Use your card to activate them."

"You've been a big help." Leila smiled, already noticing his interest in her from the moment she spoke.

"French?" he asked as she was turning away.

Her accent did that to men for some reason. Of course, so did the way she looked, but at work she hadn't played on that. Her hair was up, and she wore the fake glasses that made her look more businesslike. Still, men like Nick would always be intrigued by her voice.

"Not really, no." She smiled and left him with the mystery. "Thank you again."

"Not at all. Have a good day."

She nodded and turned to her left, took a big breath in and blew it out slowly, and then proceeded to find where she needed to be.

Today was going to be a good day. She could feel it.

Travelling in the lift was super-fast, and when the doors opened, she was greeted by a thin woman with long auburn hair, looking pristine in a purple mohair jumper and beige slacks, smiling at her awkwardly.

"Hi. You must be Leila." She held out a hand and Leila shook it. "I'm Pamela. You'll be working alongside me, so I thought it prudent to meet you and show you around."

"That's so kind, thank you," Leila responded. "Have you worked here long?"

"About two years now," Pamela said, leading the way down the corridor to the left. "We have the entire floor to ourselves, unlike other companies in the building who share space. Franklyn Financials is one of the largest and Ms Franklyn likes us to spread out."

"Okay," Leila said, walking more quickly than she'd like, in order to keep up with Pamela.

"So, our office is at the end of this corridor. We're quite lucky in that we have a corner with lots of light," Pamela said enthusiastically. "HR is down here too, as is publicity, but they're a very small outfit of just one, and they have a right-side office, so no window." She pulled a face at that. "This is the staff room." Pamela opened the door to a room with four sofas around a large coffee table. At the back of the room was a long counter with a coffee machine, kettle, microwave and, surprisingly, an air fryer.

Beneath that were two small fridges and cupboards with stickers that said things like 'cups,' and 'plates,' and 'keep clean.'

"There's no policy on how many cups of coffee you have, or even how often you take a break," Pamela explained excitedly. "Ms Franklyn believes productivity is imperative, and if you need a quick break to refocus, then she's—" Pamela stopped talking when a harried-looking man entered the room.

Blustering and swearing, he threw down a clipboard and dropped down onto the couch nearest him before looking up at Pamela.

"I swear to God, *Elsa* is going to be the death of me. I'll either keel over from one of her death stares, or have a heart attack, if she bloody well smiles."

"Are you alright? I know she can be a tad prickly, but… she's not all bad, Vincent," Pamela said to him. Leila watched the interaction with interest.

"Not that bad? You heard what she did with Frost last week, right?"

"Yes, but…he did make quite a big mistake."

"Sacked him on the spot. She's a cold heart that one, I can tell you."

Pamela remained quiet for a moment before suddenly remembering why she was here. "Oh, Leila, sorry, this is Vincent. He's in charge of HR and recruitment."

Vincent stood up. "Ah, yes, Ms Ortez – wonderful CV. I know my colleagues were glowing about you following your interview." He held out his hand. "Sorry for my outburst, it wasn't very professional of me, but we do have a policy that what is said in here," he indicated the staff room, "remains in here, especially where upper management are concerned,"

"Of course," Leila responded. "I'm sure I'll find out soon enough the goings on and to avoid this, Elsa?"

"I don't think you'll have many dealings with Ms Franklyn," Pamela said, trying to be as diplomatic as she could, or trying to impose her importance, Leila wasn't sure, until she followed with, "I'm the lead on this so, it will be me that has that pleasure."

"Is she that much of a tyrant?" Leila asked Vincent.

"No, no, absolutely not," Pamela said quickly. "She's just...as I said—"

"Prickly?" Leila offered, thinking it was interesting how Pamela seemed in awe of someone others clearly had a different opinion of.

Pamela blushed, and murmured, "Yes."

They left the room and dropped Leila's things in their office. It was a nice room with big windows and a great view of the town, and she was pretty sure she could see her new flat from here.

She had her own desk and shelving for her files, and there was a nail already in the wall where she could hang something if she wanted to.

"Come on, I'll show you around. I need to drop this off with Ms Franklyn," Pamela was saying, as she scooped a small pile of manilla files into her arms.

Leila grabbed the door and held it.

"Thanks." Pamela smiled and led the way.

They were halfway down the corridor when Pamela became a little excited, and almost on tippy toes, she waved and said, "Oh, Ms Franklyn?"

All Leila saw was a flash of blonde hair as the person ignored Pamela and turned left, disappearing around the corner.

"She must be on her way to a meeting." Pamela tried to smile. "She's really not that bad. She's just...I think she's quite awesome, actually." Pamela blushed once again. "With work, she's very progressive, and we're given carte blanche to get things done."

"That's good to know." Leila smiled.

"She just...she makes people feel a little intimidated. She's so good at what she does, and we all just want to—"

Leila thought of Camille, and all of the people in her office running around and acting like Pamela.

"I guess we... I mean, I...I'd like to be like her one day," Pamela admitted.

SEVEN

It was gone seven when Leila opened the front door to her new flat and trudged inside.

Tossing her keys into a bowl, she kicked off her heels, shrugged off her coat and hung it with her bag, and then she remembered the lanyard. It joined her keys as she yawned and then stretched her neck muscles.

It hadn't been a difficult day, but any new experience always felt draining. There was a lot to remember, names and faces and the like.

"Wine," she said to herself, and headed to the kitchen. Most of her things were still in boxes, except for the kitchen. Kristen had helped her move in and insisted at least having the kitchen set up meant she wouldn't starve.

Opening the fridge, Leila smiled at the food lining the shelves; milk, orange juice, and a half-empty bottle of Chardonnay rested against each other in the door. She took the bottle from the fridge and a microwave meal of lasagne from the freezer.

Popping it into the microwave, she set it for eleven minutes as instructed and found a glass to pour a generous serving of wine into.

With the glass in hand, Leila wandered into the lounge and looked around at her things, all stacked neatly in boxes, in one corner next to the long cabinet. She didn't have a couch yet. It was on order and would take another couple of weeks. Instead, she had two garden chairs, even though she no longer had a garden.

The TV was up, and thanks to Kristen, it was all ready to go. Her satellite TV was plugged in; the same in the bedroom.

Her favourite part of the entire place wasn't a room, though, or a piece of furniture. It was the window, and she moved closer to it as she sipped her drink.

With the curtains still open, she stared out at the view of Woodington and further afield to Bath Street.

Way off in the distance, she could see the lights of the football stadium lit up. To the right, and much closer, she saw the tall structure that housed her new office, and down below, the park. It was dark and quiet right now, but she imagined in the summer, it would be a vibrant place to explore, and maybe just sit and enjoy.

She took a sip of her wine before placing it onto the side table between the chairs.

Walking towards the bathroom, disrobing as she went, she was naked by the time she entered the small room and felt the cool tiles on her feet.

A quick shower, then she'd eat and finish her wine while relaxing in front of the TV for an hour in bed, before she'd probably fall asleep.

She heard the microwave ping just as she finished drying herself off and pulling on her robe. She tied it tightly and then headed for the kitchen.

Her phone had one missed call, and she hit 'return,' putting it on speaker so she could attend to her dinner.

"Hey, how did it go?" Kristen's cheerful voice said loudly enough Leila could pretend she was in the room with her.

"Oh, you know. It's all information gathering on the first day. Trying to remember names and where to get paper clips from." Leila chuckled. She stuck a knife into the middle of the lasagne and then licked it to test the heat. It was cooked.

"But they're all nice, right? I know how offices can be."

"I guess so. They were nice to me, so that's all I can go on. Apparently, the owner of the company is a bit…" She recalled the word she'd offered Pamela. "Prickly? I don't know what this means as I've not met her, but—"

"I'm sure your charm will win her over," Kristen laughed.

"Yes, why not." Leila smiled and carried her dinner, and Kristen, into the living room. "My supervisor is nice, Pamela – though she's a little bit…I want to say timid."

"Then that's what you should say," Kristen said. "And how's the flat? Did you get anything else unpacked?"

Leila grimaced. "Uh, no, but I will spend some time over the weekend and—"

"It's your space. If you want to live like a pig in shit, you go for it," Kristen sniggered. "Want us to come down and give you a hand?"

By 'us,' she meant her boyfriend Paddy and his friend Elvis. Leila still hadn't gotten over that being his actual name and not a nickname they'd given him.

"No, I'm fine, honestly. But you're coming down the following week and I promise it will all be done, and the spare room will be tidy and ready for you."

"I'm looking forward to it. I miss you already."

"I know, me too, but this job, it's—"

"Perfect, yeah, I get it, and I know if it all pays off there's the opportunity for you to move up the ladder. I'm happy for you, Lei."

Leila smiled at the shortening of her name. Nobody else did that. It was their thing. Just like she'd gotten into the habit of calling Kristen 'Kris.'

"Right, I'd best get sorted for work tomorrow. I'm making Paddy's lunches while their canteen is under a re-do."

"Oh, lucky Paddy. Should I send him a gift card for Tesco?"

"Hey, my cooking isn't that bad, and anyway, even I can't cock up a couple of ham sandwiches and a packet of crisps."

"Poor Paddy," Leila laughed. "I'll speak to you soon."

"Night—"

Leila looked at the garden chairs and made a decision. She picked up her wine, her dinner, and her phone, and took it all to bed.

EIGHT

The lights were low, the music loud but not deafening, and Camille sat at the bar as she sipped a non-alcoholic cocktail and surveyed her options.

Her day had been stressful, and she'd barely stopped, with meeting after meeting and inept people to deal with. It was gone eight when she'd finally left the office.

She hadn't even had time to go home and change. Instead, grateful for the spare blouse she always kept at the office, she'd shrugged off her suit jacket, changed, and come straight to the bar.

Now she wondered if she should have just gone home and gone to bed with her vibrator. Mondays really weren't the night most women went out, but something had urged her to give it an hour. Blanca's wasn't her usual haunt, but she was getting frustrated with Art and the lack of anyone interesting there.

"Refresher?" the woman behind the bar asked, pointing to her almost empty drink.

"Sure, why not?" Camille said, turning fully on her stool.

"Don't see you in here often." The woman continued to make small talk. In any other situation, Camille would find it tiresome, but tonight, she welcomed the distraction.

"No, usually I—" Was it the done thing to say you preferred a different bar? "I don't get out much—work, you know how it is?"

"I do." She smiled and continued to pour various coloured shots into a shaker. Camille paid her more attention. Attractive. Somewhere near her own age. Confident – Camille glanced at her left hand – not married.

The woman clocked the subtle checking her out and laughed easily as she shook the shaker and poured the liquid over more ice.

"I don't have a ring but I'm not on the market."

Camille smiled. "Shame."

Pushing the glass towards Camille, she said, "Sadie."

"Camille."

Sadie took one step back and let her eyes scan Camille.

"Looking for fun, no commitments…probably hung up on someone else."

Camille smirked and then chuckled. Two drinks and this woman could read her like a book, too.

"Like I said – shame."

"Not many around like me," Sadie laughed. "I've spent a lifetime people-watching. Reading the room. It's not difficult if you just pay attention." She wiped the bar clean with a cloth from beneath it. "So, who are you hung up on?"

"I don't know that 'hung up' is the word I'd use," Camille said, twirling the glass between her fingers.

"Oh? What would you call it?" Sadie leaned on her elbows and gave Camille her full attention.

Camille sipped her drink as she thought about it. "Having my eyes opened to new possibilities, I suppose."

"As long as they're not permanent…" Sadie said slowly before adding, "or expect you to be open and out?"

Stiffening in her seat, Camille felt a sense of

apprehension settle on her. This woman was equally attractive, thrilling, and terrifying, much like she'd felt around Leila.

"My life is— I'm content with it – with how things are."

"I get that. So, who opened your eyes to something different?"

Camille couldn't help but smile. The disarming question had provoked an instant thought and an image. Dark eyes, sultry smile, and a body that most would kill for.

"It was a holiday fling, you know. Eyes meet across the pool, and before you know it, you're doing things you never imagined you wanted to."

"Yeah, had a few of those in my time," Sadie admitted. She glanced along the bar and saw someone waiting. "Be right back."

For a moment, Camille considered just getting up and leaving. Did she really want a complete stranger to know her innermost thoughts? Did she want to discuss Leila? Wouldn't that be dangerous?

"So, where were we?" Sadie said, settling back onto her elbows. "Does she have a name?"

"Of course she does." Camille smiled.

Sadie mirrored her. "But you don't want to say because saying it out loud is too much and you might not be able to push it all the way back down there again if you give it airtime?"

"You're quite perceptive." Camille laughed nervously. "I can admit that she lives rent-free in my head."

"And you've no way of contacting her?"

Camille looked at her drink and stirred it slowly.

"Oh, you can but you're choosing not to? Why?" Sadie asked, before working it out. "Ah, because she won't let you hide in the closet."

NINE

The office was quiet when Pamela stepped off the elevator and strode down the corridor with purpose. It was seven minutes past seven and she could have kicked herself for the extra ten minutes she'd allowed herself to sleep.

One red traffic light too many and the bus had gotten her here later than planned.

Still, she'd made the effort, and that must count for something. She was sure of it. The coffee machine kicked into life and by a quarter past the hour, she had two steaming cups in her hand.

Knocking lightly, she opened the door the moment she heard the permissive, "Enter."

"Good morning, Ms Franklyn. I was making coffee and thought you'd probably—" She noticed the cardboard cup from the local café on the desk and felt her shoulders sag.

"I'd love one actually," Camille said, surprising her. She spun around in her chair and looked up at Pamela. "I don't know how that café stays in business with the muck they're serving. Can you get rid of that for me?" She pushed the cardboard cup towards Pamela.

"Oh, yes, absolutely," Pamela answered, swapping the cold cup for the hot mug. "I will be in my office all day with the new—"

Camille held up a finger and then started talking. "Yes, I am aware I said that." As she turned her head, Pamela noticed the earpiece. "Well, that's all well and good but...hold on a moment—" She turned to Pamela. "Was there anything else?"

"No, all good. I'll be…" She pointed over her shoulder. "In my office."

"Great. Thank you for the coffee."

Pamela backed out of the room and closed the door. She gave herself a small grin. "That went pretty well," she said to herself as she walked back towards her own office. As she passed the lift, it dinged and out stepped Leila.

"Good morning. Are you planning to greet me every day?" Leila smiled at her.

Pamela looked perplexed. "What? Oh, no." She laughed nervously. "I was just…I mean, I got in early and made coffee so I took a mug in to Ms Franklyn. She's very busy."

"Okay," Leila said, clearly amused. "So, you mentioned coffee?"

Camille pulled the mug towards herself while Rosie continued to yap in her ear. She took a swig and savoured it. Being able to enjoy an excellent brew was much more pleasing to her day.

"So, I am thinking, we should plan our next break away," Rosie continued, "Because you said we should make it a regular thing and—"

"Yes, I am aware of that too."

"Right, so I'll be round tonight, and we can order in and pick the perfect spot. Unless you just wanted to go back—"

"No, I think somewhere new would be best." *Somewhere I'm not likely to bump into Leila,* she thought to herself.

"I know you say that, but…and hear me out, what if we

went back and she was there and—"

"Rosie!" Camille warned.

Rosie ignored the tone and carried on making her point. "It would be fate, wouldn't it? Kismet. You couldn't ignore it then. And if she's not there, well then, we'd just enjoy the week and get drunk a lot."

"Firstly, going back there wouldn't be the same. For a start, you'd be with Pedro, and I'm all for that, but I'd be a spare wheel, which isn't the point of our girl's week away. And secondly, it's not kismet if you're orchestrating it."

"Tsk, don't be such a Debbie Downer."

Camille rolled her eyes and blew against the hot coffee before taking another sip.

"Anyway," Rosie said, "I'll be at yours for seven. Do not stay late at work."

"You're very bossy this morning," Camille chuckled.

"I know, I think I'm having Pedro withdrawal. Anyway, I'll bring the wine. You find a take-away you fancy."

"Fine, but I'm not making any promises. I can't just swan off right now."

"Well, I won't keep you from your empire. See you tonight."

The call was disconnected before she could say another word, and she sat back with her coffee warming both hands. She let her mind drift just for a moment, to sunny days, a pool, and dark eyes staring at her.

TEN

By eleven, Leila was more than grateful to be able to just get up and wander down the corridor to make another coffee for herself and Pamela.

They'd been working hard, focused and strategic. Pamela was a breeze to work with. Leila was pretty sure they'd have this report wrapped up early.

There were two people sitting quietly at a table in the staff room when she entered, and she smiled and offered a cheery, "Good morning."

The man looked up instantly and grinned. "Ah, the newbie." He pushed his chair back and sauntered over with his hand out. "Sullivan Price, I'm in accounts. This is Elliot Schreiber," he said, pointing to the other guy, who then got up too and came closer, peering over round spectacles. "How are you finding things?"

"Oh, pretty good so far," Leila answered. She quickly rinsed the mugs she was carrying and then reached up for the canister that held the coffee grounds.

Sullivan reached for it at the same time and chuckled in a way that he probably believed sounded charming. "Sorry, just thought—"

"No problem. I'm taller than people think," Leila said, giving him a pass this one time. She waited for him to step back before she continued on.

"So, where's that accent from?" he continued.

"Sounds French," Elliot said, pulling a 'don't ask stupid questions face' at his colleague.

Leila smiled at him. "Yes, it's French, but I'm not French."

Sullivan leaned against the counter and reached for an apple, tossing it and catching it. "Sounds intriguing."

"Does it?" Leila continued to smile as she put the coffee machine to work.

"I think so. You know what? You should tell me about it over lunch," Sullivan persisted. Elliot rolled his eyes and sighed.

"Are you asking me on a date, Sullivan?" Leila turned to him and gave him her full attention.

He straightened up and put the apple down. "I mean, I—sure, if you like."

She patted him on the shoulder and leaned closer. His aftershave was somewhat overwhelming. "I'm not into men."

"Oh, that's cool. I mean, just being friendly and all that." He took the rejection quite well, Leila thought. "So, right, well, we should get back to it…don't want old icy drawers catching us and thinking we're skiving off."

"Were you skiving off?" Leila asked, acting a little shocked by the statement. "I've heard Ms Franklyn is a fair woman."

Sullivan scoffed. "Is she? I mean…shit." He looked flustered and as though a new thought had just entered his mind. "You're not…going to tell her, right?"

Leila laughed. "I haven't met her yet. I just came in here to make coffee."

"Right." He laughed nervously.

"Oh, for goodness' sake, Sully," Elliot intervened, "She's not a spy been sent in to find out what we all think of Ms Franklyn. Get a grip man." He started to nudge Sullivan out of the room. "Sorry about that. Everyone's a bit jittery since she fired Foster last week."

"I heard about that. What did Foster do?"

"Missed an important deadline that cost a two-week setback and a huge sum of money."

"Oh, that's—"

"Ms Franklyn doesn't do incompetence," Elliot added. "Anyway, best get going."

Leila waved them off and returned to her coffee making. With two mugs filled, she glanced at the clock. 11:11. She liked that time. It had a spiritual meaning and for her it meant she was on the right path.

ELEVEN

Camille slammed down the phone.

"Honestly, it's not that difficult," she said to herself, as she pushed her chair back in frustration and stood up. Breathing deeply, she let the exasperation leave her body and noticed the empty coffee cup.

For a moment, she contemplated buzzing through to her assistant for a refill, and then changed her mind, deciding it wouldn't hurt her to get it herself. After all, she didn't want to give the staff the impression she was above doing anything, or too lazy to get her own drinks. 'Lead by example,' that was her motto.

She checked herself in the mirror and then strode into the outer office.

"Ms Franklyn," Fatima said quickly, as though she were at school and had been caught doing something she shouldn't. "Is everything alright? Do you need something?"

"Thank you, Fatima, but I'll be fine." She held up the cup. "Just getting a coffee."

Fatima smiled and continued with her work. She was one of the few staff members Camille actually liked; rarely fazed by anything, not afraid to give an opinion when warranted, always on time, and always impeccable.

"Would you like one too?" Camille asked.

"You know I'd love one, but apparently I need to cut down on my caffeine intake, so I'm on this…" She pulled a face and held up a bottle of water.

"Make sure to order in some caffeine-free supplies."

"Will do. And don't forget you have a meeting at twelve."

Camille rolled her eyes. "Yes, not that I'm looking forward to listening to Tanner bore on for another two hours. What time is it now?"

"Ten past eleven."

"Right, coffee, and then I'll be ready for Tanner."

She opened the door to the corridor and walked towards the staff room. Really, she should just put a coffee machine in her office and save the hassle, but she'd always believed that management shouldn't split themselves off from everyone else. Even if everyone else annoyed the hell out of her most of the time.

As she looked up, she caught sight of a dark-haired ponytail, the owner of which had already turned the corner, and it brought an image of Leila once more.

Her heart raced, her innards liquified, and then she laughed at herself.

"Now you're imagining out of your head. Ridiculous," she said to herself, entering the staff room, only to be overwhelmed by the scent of something she hadn't even considered she knew, until that very moment when it hit all of her senses. Perfume…a very familiar scent.

She felt her knees weaken and gripped the countertop, thankful the room was empty.

"Get a grip," she scolded herself as she set the cup down to work the machine. With the machine getting itself ready, she quickly washed her mug and was just about to set it under the coffee drip when the door opened behind her.

She turned slowly to see who it was and was so startled, she dropped the mug, smashing it to smithereens.

"Leila?"

TWELVE

"Camille?"

Leila stared back at Camille with a look of incredulity that matched Camille's panic.

She'd forgotten sugar in Pamela's coffee and had quickly returned to pick up a couple of sachets. The last thing she had expected was to open the door and be confronted by the woman she'd been unable to forget, standing there with a mug in hand as though she had every right to be there.

"What are you doing here?" Camille asked, her eyes darting behind Leila to the still half-opened door and the gawping faces who'd appeared at the sound of something breaking.

"I work here," Leila answered, finally stepping forward to let the door close. She held up her pass and lanyard as proof, because the look on Camille's face was sceptical.

Camille took a step back.

"What do you mean, you work here?" Camille continued to question. The lines between her brows creased further.

"It's not a difficult scenario, Camille. I applied for a job, I got the job and here I am." Leila smiled and took another step forward. "It's good to see you."

Camille just stared at her with an icy glare.

As Leila held the stare, she began to fit the pieces together, all the clues racing around her head and dropping into place. She remembered back to their time together and the conversation they'd had.

"*You work somewhere where you're in charge. You're the boss in some capacity or another. Total control. You're a perfectionist. You expect, no, you demand respect. Everyone tiptoes around you. Nobody wants to poke the bear and have her lash out at them, punish them. You enjoy it, the way they scuttle around after you...but you don't respect them...because you think they are...*" She paused. "*Weak. And yet, it makes you feel powerful.*"

Camille stiffened, yet said nothing, but she took a sip of her drink and didn't take her eyes from Leila's.

"*It must be exhausting always having to be so...limited.*" *Leila finished her analysis.*

"So, what is it that I desire?" Camille asked, putting her glass down. "If I'm such a control freak..."

"Oh my God, you're Ms Franklyn."

Now Camille frowned. "What does that mean?"

Leila chuckled. "Nothing, I just... I'd heard about you, but nobody mentioned your first name, but now...yes, I see it. God, can you believe it?"

Camille ignored the question. "What do you mean, 'Yes, you can see it?'"

"Sorry, can we start again?" Leila said. "I can't believe you're here."

"Where else would I be? This is my company," Camille grumbled. "I thought we agreed we wouldn't see each other."

Leila felt the gut punch of that comment, and was about to respond, when the door opened, and Pamela stepped inside.

"Everything alright? Someone said they'd heard a crash."

Camille came to her senses quickly. "Yes, just a dropped

mug." She turned to look at the coffee machine. "Clean that up and then get back to work."

"Yes, of course," Pamela said, as the door closed behind Camille and Pamela shrank, shoulders sagging. "So, now you've met Ms Franklyn."

"Yes," Leila said, watching the door. "Now I have."

THIRTEEN

This was not happening, Camille told herself, over and over, as she stormed back to her office.

"Forgot your coffee?" Fatima asked, grinning at her.

"What?" Camille said, stopping in her tracks. "Sorry, what?" Her mind was awash with more than she could deal with right now.

Just one look at her and everything flooded in. All the words, the images, the feelings Camille had pushed down and ignored all these months, now had free rein in her head.

"You went to get coffee?" Fatima said. "Is everything alright? You don't look well."

"No, I—" Camille rubbed her eyes between finger and thumb. "I need you to cancel my meeting. Rearrange it for Friday."

"Absolutely," Fatima said, already lifting the phone from its cradle. "What shall I tell them?"

"Tell them I've had a sudden emergency, and then cancel everything in the diary. Rearrange anything important for Friday. Anything else can hold over till next week."

"Are you sure you're alright?" Fatima asked once more. A look of real concern flashed across her face.

"No, no, I don't think I am," Camille answered, unable to pretend otherwise. "I'll be out of the office till Friday. Emergency calls only. Understood?"

"Of course."

Camille nodded, and then turned and entered her office. Closing the door, she slumped against it. She couldn't breathe. Every expansion of her lungs just felt more suffocating.

"What. The. Fuck." She rubbed her eyes again. They were dry and scratchy. The urge to cry came over her as she considered what to do. "This isn't happening…you're just stressed and—" She pushed off from the door and found her bag, throwing her things into it without even thinking.

When she was done, she pulled her jacket from the back of the chair and slid it on. Stopping at the mirror to check her appearance, she reached for the door handle and then stopped. Rummaging in her bag, she found her sunglasses and put them on.

And then, for the first time in Franklyn Financial's existence, Camille Franklyn left early.

Not one person dared to speak to her.

They all just stared and watched as she left. When she got to the elevator bank and pushed the button twice, she thought for one minute Vincent would have the balls to say something, but after one step towards her, he changed his mind and backed away, for which she was grateful.

She jabbed the button. In frustration, she pressed the button again and again, before she remembered where she was and got control of herself.

She just needed to get out of there.

The elevator finally dinged, the doors opened, and she stepped inside, spinning instantly to jab at the buttons again. When she turned to watch the doors close, the last face she saw was Leila, looking sad and confused.

Camille closed her eyes to it.

The moment the doors shut, and the lift juddered into life, she fell back against the wall and thumped it with her fist.

"Fuck." She stamped her foot. She wanted to cry. That hadn't happened since Tom had left and she'd fallen apart.

It took several deep breaths before Camille calmed enough to pull her phone from her bag and type out a quick text.

Camille: Emergency Code Red.

The elevator had barely hit the ground floor before the message was returned with no sound, just a vibration in her hand.

She smiled wryly when she read it.

Ever dependable Rosie. Her best friend for over thirty-five years.

Rosie: On my way.

FOURTEEN

Pamela eyed her from her desk, but Leila paid no mind to the visual interrogation. Her own thoughts were going haywire just now, with images of Camille moving around her memory banks – flashes of nakedness and then, as she was now, glowering at her as though she were the devil incarnate.

Obviously, in her logical brain, she could understand the reaction. Camille was so far in the closet, Narnia beckoned, but still, not a flicker of delight at seeing her had stung Leila's ego a little.

After all, she'd spent months daydreaming about this woman, but maybe a summer fling was all it would ever be, and any ridiculous notion otherwise was simply leading her to more disappointment.

"I've never known Ms Franklyn to leave early," Pamela said, still musing over the situation she had inadvertently stumbled into. "Not once, in all the time I've been here."

Leila pretended to be reading something on her screen. "Is that so?" she said, wanting to sound disinterested, but who was she kidding? She wanted to know everything about Camille Franklyn.

Then the idea hit her, and she flicked the program off and pulled up Google, typing into the search bar: 'Camille Franklyn, Franklyn Financials.'

A whole list of options flurried onto the screen, and she scanned down them for anything that stood out.

Woodington hotshot lands the big one

She clicked on it and an image of Camille filled the screen, smiling into a camera and holding a large glass trophy.

Leila studied the image.

She was gorgeous; a little younger maybe. She checked the date. The event was ten years prior, and a tall man with a moustache stood beside her, clutching gently at her elbow, and looking very awkward and out of place, as she enjoyed the limelight and the appreciation.

The line beneath it listed those pictured: Gareth Tudor, Fred Kilburn, Camille Franklyn, and her husband, Tom.

Leila read the article.

Businesswoman of the Year was bestowed on Camille Franklyn today at the Woodington Business Innovation Awards. An annual event that highlights the work of those, within the town and surrounding areas, who are lighting the way with progressive, modern, and successful working practices and ideas.

Camille started Franklyn Financials almost fifteen years ago when she was unexpectedly made redundant from her job in the city. She told our reporter:

"When you have two young children at home, you need to find a way, and I did that. Utilising the knowledge I'd collected from education and previous working partnerships, I knew I had a strong foothold with which to build a competitive business, and I'm very proud of what we have achieved as a company."

Leila clicked out of it and scanned further. It was all business-related and nothing much to tell her anything more about Camille than she already knew, or had deduced.

"I wonder if she's okay?" Pamela said, still ruminating about it all. She suddenly got very serious. "Maybe she's unwell. Oh, I do hope there isn't a bug going around, I really can't afford to be off."

Leila peered over her screen at her. "I'm sure it's just

something and nothing."

Oh, it was something alright, but nothing Pamela needed to worry about. She turned her attention back to the screen and noted a social media post for Tobias Franklyn.

She let the mouse hover over it and contemplated whether it was right to invade Camille's privacy, arguing in her head that it was a public search engine, and available to anyone to open and look at, but her own morals meant she moved away and clicked Google off completely.

"It's just so odd. Did she say anything to you?" Pamela continued.

The question threw Leila for a moment, but then she gathered her wits and said, "What would she say to me?"

"I don't know, you were talking to her, so I assumed —She's not rude enough to completely ignore you if you happened upon her in the staff room."

Leila nodded. "Well, I just said hello. I guess I made her jump because she dropped the mug…" *Made her jump? She looked like you'd threatened her with an excruciating death.*

"It's just not like her at all. I've seen her in her office with the worst flu and colds. Unless she has annual leave and leaves the country like she did last year, then she's in the office."

The mention of the holiday had heat rising up Leila's neck. Wishing she'd worn her hair down to hide her face behind, she ducked lower and hid the blush behind her screen.

"She probably needs another holiday. Honestly, if you'd seen her when she got back, she was like a different person for a couple of weeks, and then—"

"And then?" Leila perked up.

"Oh, I don't know, she just seemed…what's the word?" Pamela thought for a moment and Leila wanted to shake the word out of her.

"Melancholy? She was sad?"

"Yes, I think so, and then she was back to being the Ms Franklyn we all love and adore," she gushed, and Leila looked away again.

Happy and then sad? That made sense, didn't it? It was exactly how Leila herself had felt. Elated, and then desolate.

"Maybe I should send some flowers," Pamela was saying. Rhetorically, Leila assumed.

Bringing the conversation back to work, Leila asked, "Do you need me to email these over to the Connors' representatives?"

"Oh, no, send them to me and I'll pass them on once I've added my sheets to it. Might as well have everything in one place."

"Good idea." Leila smiled.

She'd found Camille, and yet, she felt further away than ever.

She needed a plan.

FIFTEEN

Camille climbed out of her car and locked it with the fob, over her shoulder, as she strode with purpose to the front door. Fighting with the key to get it into the hole, her hands were still shaking as she turned it and opened the door. Whereupon her legs almost gave in, and she stumbled across the threshold and into her house.

Safe.

Dumping her bag down, she pulled off her scarf as though it were a boa constrictor suffocating her. She dropped it to the floor without a care and the coat followed, as did the heels.

And then she was in the kitchen and trying to decide whether coffee, or the unopened bottle of chardonnay in the fridge, was the answer.

Glancing at her watch, she flicked the kettle on. It was too early for wine, wasn't it? As the kettle steamed and hissed to life, she leaned back on her hands, against the countertop, and replayed this morning over in her head.

Leila had been in the staff room. Her staff room!

Leila, with her tanned skin, her hair pulled back and wearing those cute, sexy glasses. Just standing there, looking every bit as though she belonged, smiling at her. And then, the audacity to simply ask how she was had completely thrown Camille for a loop.

Beautiful, stunning, confident, Leila.

Camille rubbed her hands over her face and growled.

This couldn't be happening. This was not how things were meant to be.

The kettle clicked, and she spun around to pull a mug from the cupboard just as the doorbell rang, quickly followed by the front door opening and closing.

Rosie, with her own key.

"Cami?" Rosie shouted out. "Where are you?"

"Kitchen," Camille called back, and took another mug from the cupboard, as Rosie rushed into the room looking harried and flushed. A 'code red' message had only ever been used once before— when Tom had left.

"What's wrong? Are the boys alright? You're not ill, are you?" Rosie asked quickly.

"Yes, they're fine. I'm not ill. Coffee?" Camille said, feeling a sense of calm come over her now that her friend was here.

"You called a 'code red.' I expected to find you in a heap on the floor like last time."

The reminder of Tom, and his subsequent leaving, didn't have the same effect now as it had back then, when her world had collapsed. And in truth, Leila's appearance hadn't created that same sense of foreboding, but it had rattled her in other ways.

"I saw her," Camille said, spooning coffee into cups.

Rosie closed her eyes. "Okay, are we going to elaborate or continue to be cryptic for the entire conversation, because —"

"Leila. I saw Leila."

Rosie's eyes widened. "Where?"

"In my office," Camille spewed out, the teaspoon clanging in a cup as she dropped it.

"What? How? Is she stalking you?"

Camille turned to face her. "Worse. She's working for me."

"Holy fuckaroni!" Rosie's mouth gaped. "How?"

"Yes, holy fuckaroni indeed. I went to get a coffee from the staff room, and she walked right in, bold as you like," Camille said, but didn't add, *and sexy as fuck* with it. "We were hiring recently. I guess she applied and got it, which means she's going to be bloody good at whatever— " she stopped to think, "the Connor report, she's on the Connor report, and that means…"

"And it was definitely her?" Rosie asked.

Camille stared at her silently.

"I mean, you didn't get someone else confused—"

"Do I look like someone who gets people I've slept with confused with random strangers, Rosie? I know it was her. We spoke. She asked how I was." *In that same sexy accent.* Camille turned back to the coffee and stirred each cup vigorously as she added hot water.

"And you said?"

The teaspoon clanged again.

"I left. Pamela walked in. I'd dropped the mug I was holding. Leila was looking at me all…all…" *Those eyes; all they'd done was look at her, and it was enough to send Camille into meltdown.* "I told Fatima I wasn't feeling well and to book me out of the office till Friday."

"You did a runner?" Rosie said, almost laughing at the idea.

"I did not do a runner. I left— there's a difference," she replied indignantly.

Now Rosie did smile. "You legged it. Admit it."

Camille picked up both mugs and brought them to the table, pulled out a chair, and slumped into it.

"Fine. I legged it."

Rosie touched her shoulder and pulled out the chair next to her. "I don't blame you. It must have been quite the shock."

"You can say that again." Camille sighed and glared at Rosie when she was, indeed, about to say that again. "I guess it hasn't helped that she's been on my mind a lot lately, too."

"Oh, why's that?"

"You know why." Camille reached for her cup and took a sip.

"Yes, but it's always more fun making you actually say things out loud and acknowledge them."

Camille slouched, huffed, and then picked at imaginary fluff on her skirt. "I think I'm in love with her, or at least, a version of her, but no matter how I look at it, I can't imagine it working out, and I'm not prepared to put myself through the whole coming out saga just for it all to end anyway." She finished speaking, and finally looked at Rosie, before she added a further admission. "She's younger than me, she's gorgeous—"

"You're no slouch in the looks department, Cami," Rosie offered sincerely. "And so what if she's younger? She's not a child. This isn't some kid in their twenties with a M.I.L.F. fascination. She's almost forty for goodness' sake."

"Imagine it, the office gossip about the old crone and the sexy trophy wi—"

"Go on, say it." Rosie grinned. "Trophy what?"

Camille ignored her. "I'm 52. I'm old enough to have been her babysitter."

Rosie stared with pursed lips and then a look of disdain. She wasn't taking any of this personally, despite Pedro only being 31, but she was getting seriously fed up with her friend's excuses. "You're being an idiot; you know that right? I mean, you are at least aware of how ridiculous you are being?"

"Well, thank you so much for your support," Camille snarked, and got up, taking her mug to the sink. She poured the still-steaming coffee down the sink and dropped the cup into the dishwasher under the counter.

And then she reached for a glass and opened the fridge, no longer caring what the time was. She needed a drink.

"I'm aware that my choices don't make sense to you, but they are very clear to me. And my getting involved with Leila isn't going to happen."

"Alright, so what are you going to do?"

"I've no idea." Camille poured a small glass. She wasn't an alcoholic, after all.

"You could fire her," Rosie offered as a solution.

"I'm not adverse to firing anyone who deserves it, but no. How would that look?" She shook her head. "No, I'll just have to avoid her."

Rosie laughed, "Oh Cami, you really think that's going to be possible?"

"I have no idea," she repeated.

SIXTEEN

"Are you kidding me?" Kristen shouted down the phone. Her gleeful tone meant she didn't quite grasp the seriousness of everything. "So, let me get this straight. You met the woman of your dreams on a holiday you weren't planning to go on, and then you get the job of your dreams in a place you weren't planning to visit, let alone live, and now you've discovered the very woman you've been fantasising about is your boss?"

"That's about it." Leila sighed and slumped back into the garden chair.

"So, what happened? Because you don't sound like she fell into your arms."

"No, she didn't. In fact, I think I might be getting fired tomorrow."

"What? Why?"

"Because she's not just my boss, she's the owner of the company, and I am clearly not someone she expected to ever see again." She slapped her forehead. "God, Kris, if you'd seen her face and the way she looked at me, like I was the most terrifying person on the planet."

Kristen laughed. "Because you are."

"I know, logically, I know, that for her, my turning up like this will be hugely shaking her world. We are not in Madeira now. This Camille is a very different animal and needs to be gently prodded."

"So, you're going to prod?"

Leila laughed. "Yes. Of course. When have you ever known me not to go after what I want?"

"That is true," Kristen giggled. "Unless she sacks you."

"I was being dramatic earlier. She won't fire me. How does she explain that? It would create more questions than she's prepared to deal with, so no, she will avoid me."

Kristen sighed. "She sounds like a nightmare. Are you sure she's worth all of this? You could just get your head down, work hard, and find that promotion elsewhere."

"You're right, I could. But the thing is this: my instincts are rarely wrong. I was blessed with the ability to see through people and their bullshit, and I see her, and I like what I see."

"Well, you know where we are if it all goes to shit, but I have to agree, you do seem to know people."

"Grow up with a narcissistic mother and an emotionally unavailable father and you soon learn to read every situation you're in." Leila laughed it off, but the truth of it hurt still, despite walking away from them. Reading a multitude of self-help books, she knew more about people and the way they behaved, and yet, it still burned to think about the child she'd been, who had lived through that.

And survived, she reminded herself.

"I'm proud of you," Kristen said. "Whatever life throws at you, you deal with it, and I don't think I've met a more secure person in my life."

"Thank you, bestie, and I am proud of you too. We're good people."

"Damn right we are," Kristen whooped. "Hold on a sec." The phone went muffled, but Leila smiled when she heard, "I'm on the bloody phone. Just look in the dryer, Paddy." And then she was back. "Sorry, Paddy's lost his lucky pants and it's football tonight, so…"

"Well, you had best go and find his pants. I'm going to get a bath and relax, have a little think, and then get to bed."

"Alright, you take care and keep me updated!"

"I will."

SEVENTEEN

Friday came around way too fast for Camille's liking, and if it hadn't been for this meeting being so important now, she'd have blown it all off and not been back until Monday.

But, leading by example meant she had no other choice than to get up, and get it over with.

She'd gotten in early, before anyone else had arrived, and brought coffee from that horrendous coffee shop downstairs, rather than venturing to the staff room again and risking an impromptu meeting with Leila.

She did, however, browse back through her emails, to Vincent's hiring update. Shaking her head, Camille rebuked herself for ignoring it. It was unlike her to let things slide quite so easily, but then, she hadn't had a lesbian awakening taking up her every thought before.

Leila Ortez. CV for perusal.

She did, indeed, peruse it. Impressed, she couldn't complain HR hadn't done its job and found a suitable—more than suitable, she considered— candidate for the job.

Leila came with glowing references. 'A superb acquisition to any company roll call,' her previous employer had gushed.

She closed the email.

By eight-thirty, she had completed all of her outstanding reports and gotten a head start on some planning for the following week. With the meeting scheduled for ten, all she had to do was hunker down, get through lunch, and she would avoid Leila for most of the day.

A moment later, there was a gentle knocking on her door. Camille reached for her mug, assuming Fatima had arrived and would be willingly offering to get her a refill.

"Come in," she said, not bothering to look up. "I'd love a coffee if you have a spare minute."

"Of course, Camille."

The words filtered through and shook her to her core; soft, accented, sexy.

It wasn't Fatima.

Camille slowly raised her head and almost gasped when the vision of Leila came into her eyeline. The woman would be the death of her, she was sure of it now.

Standing there, in a white pantsuit with a black shirt underneath, opened just enough to reveal a hint of her cleavage, with the locket Camille had bought her on full display.

Leila wore her hair down, framing her face in soft curls. She looked breathtaking. Camille couldn't deny that; everything about Leila screamed confidence and sensuality, and Camille felt it hit every nerve ending in her body, but she held it together, and even managed to keep her face passive when Leila slowly pulled the glasses away from her face and smiled.

"Leila," Camille said.

The smile spread more widely across Leila's face, and almost broke Camille's resolve.

"I wanted to have a quick conversation about this… situation." Leila stepped forward, her hand landing on the chair. "May I?"

Afraid to open her mouth, unable to create words, Camille just nodded.

When Leila was comfortable, she sat back, one leg elegantly crossed over the other, and observed Camille, mirroring her perfectly.

The silence, though awkward, had given Camille enough time to reset herself.

"So, what did you want to say?"

Leila's smile lazily spread once more, and Camille was stuck between enjoying it and wanting to wipe it off her face. *Stop tempting me.*

"This situation," Leila said slowly, breaking into Camille's thoughts. "I want you to know that it wasn't planned. I had no idea this was your company." The corner of her mouth lifted as she continued, "I admit, that when I discovered the job would be in Woodington, I was hopeful that maybe we might bump into one another, but this…" She glanced around the office. "I'm sorry that it was such a shock for you. For me, too."

Camille listened, hoping there would be some solution offered. "Go on."

Leila chuckled, and then bit her lower lip, as she settled her gaze on Camille's face. She breathed in, and then out, slowly and controlled. "I'm not going to sit here and say I'm unhappy to be here, to work here, or to see you again."

"I could just fire you," Camille said coldly.

Leila stared at her unmoved. "You could, but…" She shrugged a little.

"But?"

"You won't." Tilting her head a little, Leila said, "You're scared again."

Camille said nothing and stared at the pen on her desk.

"You're worried, not that I'll tell anyone, but that you won't be able to hide it. I can see it; the way you're avoiding looking at me now. It's still there. The desire for me." She paused and waited for Camille to look up, before adding, "For us."

Camille stiffened in her seat and breathed deeply, squeezing her clenched fists under the desk until she felt her nails dig into her flesh.

She would not bite; would not be drawn into this flirtation. Because Leila was an expert at it, and Camille would not stand a chance if she engaged with her.

"Do you still see my desire for you?" Leila tilted her head the other way. "Those nights together were—"

"Enough," Camille said, more loudly than she'd have liked. "If you are to continue working here, then it would be advisable to stop this game right now."

Leila leaned forward. "I'm not playing a game, Camille. But now I know you're here, I'm playing for keeps." She stood up abruptly and smoothed out her jacket. "I am aware you will go out of your way to avoid me at all costs. I'm prepared for that." She leaned on the desk with her palms and waited until Camille finally locked eyes with her. "We're going to work this out."

"I told you before, this isn't *Pretty Woman*, and I am not going to charge in and save the girl," Camille said.

Leila laughed. "*I'm* not the girl who needs saving, Camille." Leila held Camille's stare for a beat, before pushing up off the table and stepping back. "Like I said, we're going to work this out. In the meantime, I am going to head to my office and continue with my job. I suggest you think about things."

"I can't do this, Leila, I'm sorry. I like you, I do, but what you want from me is just impossible."

Leila glanced down at the empty cup and picked it up. "Coffee?"

She continued to stare at Camille until Camille finally nodded.

And with that she turned, hips swivelling as she walked away. Reaching the door, she glanced back, and had the temerity to wink, before she opened it and disappeared. Camille sank into her chair just a little further than she'd ever done before.

EIGHTEEN

It wasn't unusual for Leila to enjoy the attention of admiring glances as she passed by. In fact, she encouraged it by always making sure that she looked her best. It helped build her self-esteem back in the days when she had none, and now, it was like a cosy safety blanket she didn't need, but knew was always there.

Sully and Elliot both leaned against the wall by the lifts, talking quietly, until Sully caught sight of her and nudged Elliot. Two sets of eyes scanned top-to-bottom, and back up again, mouths gaping as she gave them a friendly nod of 'hello.'

"Tanner. My office, now." The icy voice had them all turn and glance back towards Camille's office. She was standing there, hand on hip, pointing with the other at the open door, as Tanner moved swiftly along the corridor.

Leila made eye contact with her and shook her head slowly. She felt a little bad for Tanner. He was copping the brunt of Camille's frustration with herself, after all.

"Wonder what he's done?" Sully asked, but nobody answered. Leila had already turned and was walking away when she heard. "I'm not paying you all to stand around and gawk."

Swishing into the staff room, Leila washed Camille's cup and then reached for two clean ones. Members of staff wandered in and out, mostly talking about Tanner and the impending doom he was facing. Leila set up the coffee machine to make coffee for herself, Pamela, and Camille.

"Ah, there you are," Pamela said, squeezing in through the door as someone else left. "I've set up a meeting for quarter past. I'd like you to sit in on it. That way, you should be able to get a real understanding of what we're up against with Mr Connor." She frowned and then her eyes lit up. "Oh, is one of those for me?"

No mention of the scene outside.

Leila said, "It is indeed, and also, one for Ms Franklyn. I figured you could maybe take it to her while I finish off?"

Pamela considered the opportunity, her mouth moving from side to side as she contemplated whether she had enough time. Deciding she did, she smiled as she said, "Of course." And then something else entered her mind. "So, you've seen Ms Franklyn?"

"Yes. This is her mug, no?" Leila said, pointing to the plain white ceramic mug, slightly bigger than all the other mugs in the cupboard. "We spoke briefly this morning when I arrived. I said I'd get her a coffee, but I assume you..." She turned with the mug in hand, steaming, as she passed it to Pamela. "...would want to speak with her."

"I uh... Yes, I guess I can fill her in on where we're at."

"Okay, you do that, and I will take these back to the office, yes? And get myself ready for the meeting. I'm looking forward to it."

"Me too," Pamela said quickly, before taking the mug and heading to Camille's office. Leila smiled to herself, imagining Camille riled up over Tanner and on tenterhooks as she waited, expecting Leila herself to return.

"That should keep her on her toes," Leila said to herself, finishing off making the other two coffees.

Camille thought back to when Leila had left her office. She hadn't moved. An entire minute had passed, and she hadn't moved a muscle, except to squirm in her seat, once.

Her mind had been awash with thoughts and questions, all rushing at once, and never staying long enough to find an answer to any of them.

Except for the one that ended with Leila on her knees.

She'd needed to inhale deeply and slowly release the breath, feeling her heart beat faster than was humanly safe, she was sure. Inhaling once more, her eyes closed as she exhaled, repeating the pattern until finally, a sense of her own being began to re-emerge from whatever this Leila-infused habitat was.

"Fire her," her brain screamed, *"It's the only solution."*

"But you won't," she heard Leila's voice reply, with the lazy, oh-so-sexy smile. Curling her lips until those dimples popped, and her eyes shone with knowing and longing. And just an air of mocking, perfectly placed to push Camille out of her comfort zone, even more than Leila's presence here was already doing.

Then she had opened the email from Tanner and felt her blood boil. How unlucky for him he was passing just as she opened the door to her outer office.

By the time he'd stepped inside, however, she'd realised it wasn't him she was mad at. So she'd kicked him out with a clear instruction to get things in order before the meeting.

She didn't hear the gentle tap on the door the first time. But the louder knock brought her from her thoughts with another shot of raised heartbeats. Her back stiffened, her thighs clenched, and a bead of sweat dripped slowly down her back.

Forcing the air from her lungs, she quickly said, "Enter."

And then she waited.

Lips pursed, determined not to bite when Leila waltzed in with a mug of coffee and more flirtations that were not wanted.

But it wasn't Leila.

She breathed a sigh of relief as Pamela pushed the door open enough to smile at her and hold up the mug.

"Leila said you wanted a coffee?"

Camille stared at her. Words, Camille, words, she reminded herself. "Yes, thank you, yes, coffee. That's…yes, thank you."

Pamela stopped in her tracks and looked at her. "Are you…" She frowned. "Everything alright?"

"Yes, absolutely fine. Why?" Camille said, holding out her hand for the coffee mug.

"No reason…you just seem…a little out of sorts?" Pamela risked handing over the hot drink. "I saw Tanner leaving and—"

The glare was enough to end that line of conversation.

Taking the mug with one hand, Camille rubbed her temple with the other. "Headache, I'll be fine. Thank you for the coffee."

"Of course. You're welcome."

Camille tried a smile, but judging by Pamela's face it wasn't doing what she expected it would. "You can go. I have work to get on with."

Pamela nodded. "Yes, me too. I have a meeting

organised with—"

Camille's eyes bugged and she stood quickly— too quickly. The blood rushed to her head, and she needed to steady herself.

"Ms Franklyn?"

Heat travelled up Camille's face until the tips of her ears felt like they were on fire. She could have kicked herself, allowing Leila to get to her like this.

"I'm fine, Pamela," she said sternly, glancing at the clock. It was three minutes past nine.

She was late for her own meeting.

And Camille Franklyn was never late.

NINETEEN

Camille dropped her bag down onto the kitchen island, like she always did, and let her keys dangle from her finger as she considered the shitshow of a day.

Tossing the keys into her bag, she turned on her heel and opened the fridge, pulling a cold bottle of lager from the shelf. She twisted again and slid the cap under the wall-mounted opener, popped it off, and then swigged straight from the bottle.

"Bad day?" the deep male voice said from behind her.

"You could say that, yes." She kicked her shoes off, just as her eldest son, Tobias, came into view, reaching past her to get his own bottle. "How are you doing?" she asked, softening when she noticed his red-rimmed eyes, unbrushed hair, and the same wrinkled clothes he'd been in these last couple of days, by the look of him.

His handsome face scrunched in a lopsided grin that soon disappeared with the bottle between his lips. "You know, about the same as you." He shrugged. "Thanks for letting me stay."

Camille patted his arm. "I'm sure things will work out. All couples argue. It's what creates the passion."

"I guess. It's just a lot more arguing than usual, and honestly, I don't think she wants to fix things." He took another swig. "What was wrong with your day?"

She sighed, sagged, and her head fell back all at once, as the bottle landed gently on the countertop. "If it could go wrong, it did." She smiled at him. "Just one of those days," she said, leaving it there. There was no way she was going to explain Leila, and the entire day spent thinking about her, and the things they did together in Madeira. Instead, she decided Tobias would be her distraction. "Have you eaten?"

Tobias shook his head. "Not sure I'm hungry."

"I remember feeling that way when your father left, but I also remember how much better I felt when Rosie kicked my backside and made me rejoin the world. So, tonight, I'm going to be Rosie. Upstairs. Shower and shave." She wrinkled her nose at him. "And for God's sake, put on some clean clothes, and then we are going out to dinner."

He smiled. "Yes, Mother." And then he downed the rest of the bottle, tossing it into the recycle bin before he left the room, and Camille heard the pounding of feet going up the stairs.

She picked up her lager and took another swig.

Leila sat by herself at the table and sipped a large gin and tonic from a gin bowl filled with sprigs of rosemary and ice. Floating on top were some little orange balls of fruit that she thought were called physalis, but she wasn't sure. It didn't matter; they looked pretty, and the drink tasted fantastic.

She'd googled the bar. One of three gay bars that were reasonably local if she grabbed an Uber to get herself home. Not that it would be a late night; she had an early start in the morning once more.

Sitting back in her seat, she watched a group of women laughing and dancing. *Equal numbers. Probably all couples*, she thought. She missed that; having someone to enjoy life with, someone to share everything with. Despite the bravado and confidence she pushed out into the world, she wasn't promiscuous. Rarely did she meet anyone who matched her energy or sparked that part of her that wanted anything serious.

Except Camille had.

She smiled when one of the women made eye contact, but looked away before it became an invitation. Coming out tonight hadn't been with the intention of making new friends. She'd just needed to unwind from a hectic day.

Other than her impromptu meeting with Camille that morning, she hadn't had any further contact with her, which was fine and expected.

Swallowing down the last mouthful, Leila smiled; Camille Franklyn was an enigma. And that was a code she planned to crack, but it would take patience, she knew that much.

Glancing at the time, she emptied her glass, stood up, and walked to the bar. One more wouldn't hurt, would it?

TWENTY

"So, what are you and Tina arguing about?" Camille asked when they'd made their order and the waiter had walked away, leaving them to talk and sip the glass of wine they each had.

The restaurant she'd chosen was based more on whether there would be a table free at such short notice than anything else. It was situated in a more residential part of town she didn't visit often.

Tobias leaned an elbow on the table, resting his cheek in the palm of his hand, lips pressed tightly together. It took him a moment, but eventually he said, "When we got married, we were on the same page about everything really. But now..." He shrugged. "It's like everything I thought we were working towards, she doesn't want now."

"Like?" Camille asked, sitting back in her seat, more relaxed now she could focus on Tobias.

"Kids?" he said, sitting up and bringing his hands to his lap. "We both said we wanted them, and that once we were in a good place financially, and settled, we'd talk about it." He picked up his glass. "But now she says she's not sure it's what she wants."

"Ah, that's quite a big turnaround."

"Yeah, I mean it's just—" He leaned forward and exhaled. "I want kids, Mum." His eyes went glassy, and he blinked rapidly.

"Tobi," Camille said gently, reaching for his hand.

"There's still lots of time for her to change her mind."

"I'm twenty-nine. She's thirty-two. How much longer do we wait? And what if the answer is still no and then I'm thirty-five and looking for a new relationship and don't get the chance to be a dad until I'm nearing forty and—"

"Tobias, take a breath." Camille smiled. "You've already decided this is where you're heading. How are you supposed to talk things through with the attitude that it's all over anyway?"

"I know, I know, I just… I didn't think we'd be having this conversation at all, and she's so adamant that… I guess I'm panicking."

"I didn't bring you boys up to panic when shit hits the fan." She frowned. "So, what's the deeper problem here?"

Tobias stared at her, glassy eyes now ready to spill.

"I don't want to lose her. And I'm afraid it will be me that has to make a choice, and I'll pick her, but I'll always resent it." He wiped his eyes. "I'll resent…her."

"Has she said why she doesn't want children?"

"That's the thing— she won't talk about it. She just says she's changed her mind, and I need to deal with it and get over it…in nicer words than that. But that's the crux of it."

"Tobias, you're a little bit like your father at times." She smiled at him. "Burying your head, when you should face the issue head-on. You need to find a way to get Tina to open up. What was her reaction when you left?"

"Cold. Standoffish, like it didn't matter."

Camille stiffened just a little. Not just because her child was hurting, but also, because she recognised that reaction in herself. It was always easier to go cold when one was hurting or unable to process something in the moment.

The waiter appeared and placed their food down in front of them, not lingering to see if they needed anything else. Camille raised a brow, but said nothing as she focused back on Tobi.

"She does care. She cares very much, despite the wall and the bravado otherwise," she said, speaking from experience.

"How can you know that? You didn't see her." Tobias shook his head.

"Because, my darling, whether you realise it or not, you married a woman very much like your mother."

His eyes bulged. "Oh, that just sounds creepy."

Camille laughed. "It's a known fact many men do. I mean just look at your father and granny—" She stopped speaking when she was distracted by a car door opening. Someone very familiar stepping out from the back seat, with a phone pressed to her ear.

Camille's fork clanged on the plate.

Leila.

"What's wrong?" Tobias looked in the direction she now stared. "Who is that?" he asked, as Leila smiled at something the person on her phone must have said. "Mother?"

"What? Oh, sorry, I—" What could she say? *That, darling, is my young lesbian lover?*' "Nobody. I thought... Probably someone from work."

Tobias continued to stare at Leila as she waved off the cab and stood on the roadside continuing her conversation.

"I didn't realise you had models working for you now," he said, still gawping at her.

"Don't be ridiculous," Camille scolded him, picking up her fork. "Your food will get cold."

Finally, he glanced back at his plate. "I'm really not hungry."

From her periphery, Camille felt it. She closed her eyes and tried to ignore the emotional and physical pull she felt towards Leila, but it was impossible. She knew, intimately, what it felt like to have those eyes on her, like they were now.

She pressed her lips together and forced herself to put her attention back on her son.

"You need to eat something. Try. For me."

When she looked up again, Leila was gone.

"Are you…alright?" Tobi asked, when Camille stared blankly out of the window again.

Was she? Was she alright? That was the question, wasn't it? One she didn't have the answer to.

TWENTY-ONE

Apparently, Camille's office was now the meet-and-greet area of the building. At least, she assumed that must be the reason why Leila was, once again, in here, waiting for her, first thing on a Monday morning. Her arms rested easily on one leg that was crossed over the other, making her skirt rise just enough up her thigh that it bordered on indecent.

She looked stunning, which Camille assumed had been the point. To entice her.

A captivating temptress lying in wait in Camille's own lair.

"That's my chair," Camille said firmly, dropping her bag on her desk and refusing to show any emotion around Leila's proximity. She couldn't deny that her heart raced, and her mind was awash with possibilities, so many…possibilities.

"It's a very comfortable chair." Leila smiled up at her. "I can see why you like it. Lots of…potential."

The way she said those words sent a shiver through Camille that hit exactly where she knew Leila had intended. Because she understood all too well what those possibilities were too, and as usual, had read Camille like a book.

And every opportunity to bring any potential to life, revolved around one of them being on their knees. *Why was that always her go-to image?*

Camille pinched the bridge of her nose and sighed. "Leila, what are you doing here?"

"I brought you coffee, and a little something for breakfast." Leila looked towards the white paper bag with cardboard handles next to two take-out coffee cups from the awful café.

"Right, well, thank you. Now you can leave."

Her hope was that Leila would get up and scurry off. Of course it wouldn't be that simple, would it? Leila wouldn't scurry. Leila could read her like a book.

"I have another ten minutes before I'm needed in my office." Leila leaned forward and rested one elbow on the desk, twisting a little to stare at Camille. "We can do so much in ten minutes."

"You're in my chair," Camille repeated. *Do not bite*, she told herself.

"Oh." Leila let out a chuckle. "You'd prefer it were me on my knees. I can—"

"Enough." Camille glared at her, but remained silent.

Leila sighed.

"Maybe we could have dinner?" She posed the question as she stood up and perched herself on the corner of Camille's desk. "At that nice little restaurant you were in on Friday?"

The look of mirth on Leila's face when Camille rolled her eyes did nothing to stop the attraction Camille felt.

Take control of this, Camille thought.

She pulled her chair away and sat herself down, rolling it forward and into position at her desk, despite Leila's proximity.

Dangerous – so fucking dangerous – and yet, Camille couldn't stop herself from wanting to be near her. Leila's heady scent filled her senses.

She was so close that when Camille reached up to open her laptop, her forearm grazed against Leila's thigh. The softness of her skin felt so appealing and warm and natural. She had to force herself not to reach out and run her hand along the flesh.

"We are not having dinner," Camille spat out, managing to sound convincing as she said it, all the while internally screaming at herself to accept the invitation.

"You know, I live just next to where you were dining…" Her head tilted. "In that block next door, number 405."

Camille sat back in her chair and didn't respond.

"You should also know," Leila continued, speaking slowly, edging along the desk, sliding one leg over Camille's knees until she was sitting directly in front of Camille. "I'm going to dine there every night this week, if you want to join me." Leila leaned herself forward and found purchase on the arms of Camille's chair, with her palms, to steady herself, and bring their faces as close as they'd been since Madeira.

When Camille looked away, Leila raised one hand, and with one finger, she gently lifted Camille's chin. Camille had no choice but to look at Leila when she said, "I think you want to come, no?" She smiled lazily. "For dinner, I mean."

Camille held her breath.

She remembered a time when Leila had used that trick before: leaning in, as though she was going to kiss her, and then at the last minute, saying something to throw her off guard.

She pushed her chair back and away from the temptress and Leila almost fell off the desk. She righted herself at the last moment, to remain perched there, staring at her with that sexy grin.

"If I do, it won't be with you," Camille said, feeling

pleased with herself for withstanding the way Leila could weave a magic spell over her. "Now, it's been ten minutes, and you're late. That would give me a reason to give you a warning. Three of those and I could fire you."

"Hm, you could…" Leila laughed, and slid off the desk, walking around to the opposite side, where she placed both palms on it and leaned forward. "But you won't…because deep down you know you want this."

"I don't."

"Okay, Camille." Leila winked. "I'll see you at lunch?"

"You won't," she said loudly, as Leila exited the room with a little wave over her shoulder. "Because I won't be here," she muttered to the closed door.

Of course, Camille hadn't taken into account meetings would now include Leila, along with Pamela's presence.

From her place at the end of the boardroom-style table, Camille sat back and listened intently as each member of staff that was required to spoke up and informed her of anything she needed to know, all the while feeling the intense stare in her direction.

Allowing her attention to be drawn away from the current speaker, Camille glanced at Leila.

Dark eyes, smouldering in her direction, burned her with intensity. Just like when children used a magnifying glass to burn paper.

Mischievous eyes smiled playfully at her, as those plump, kissable lips sucked on the end of a pen.

Leila's tongue flicked out around the tip of the pen,

while she coyly tilted her head and bobbed her foot up and down, heeled shoe dangling from it, visible from under the table.

Camille looked away, focusing back on Sullivan and his report, but she couldn't deny that she felt it: the desire, the chemistry. It was all off the chart, and all so out of bounds.

This wasn't Madeira.

TWENTY-TWO

Walking into her home, after a long day with more meetings and avoiding any more interactions with Leila, the last thing Camille expected to find was the kind of disarray she'd dealt with, over a decade ago, with two teenagers and their friends in the house.

Camille surveyed the kitchen from the doorway and for a moment, wondered if someone had broken in and raided the contents of her fridge and cupboards.

Empty, used, still dirty bowls and plates littered the worktop....ironically, on the countertop above the dishwasher and next to the sink.

"For God's sake," she fumed and turned on the tap. Piling the dishes into the sink and under the water, she drenched them with a quick squeeze of washing up liquid.

The island was covered in peelings from potatoes, and one of the drawers to the air fryer, as well as various half-eaten packets of crisps and breakfast cereals, including her favourite granola, and a sticky red knife that lay in an equally red splodge of what she could only assume was jam.

She pursed her lips, turned off the tap, and closed her eyes as she breathed deeply and let the annoyance out with a loud sigh. Opening her eyes, she turned and walked back out into the hall, listening for any sound that might suggest her son was around, because he was in a whole heap of trouble.

The faint sound of music playing drew her closer to the stairs.

"Tobias?" she called out. When there was no response, shouted up again, more firmly this time, "Tobias!"

"Oh, hey Mum," he said, grinning at her over the banister, headphones on, one side sitting properly, the other pulled lower to hear Camille.

"Can you come down here a moment, please?" she said calmly, walking away before he had any option, or the audacity to say no.

She went back into the kitchen and leaned against the island and waited, seething when she watched Tobias saunter into the room without a care. He finally looked at her, his eyes then flicking towards the mess, then away to the floor, where they stayed until she spoke.

"I'm not sure what it was I said last week that gave you the impression you can revert back to a fifteen-year-old boy while you're staying here, but you were very much mistaken," Camille said, sweeping her arm around at the room. "You have never had a maid at your beck and call, and I am not about to become one."

"No, I was going to—"

She held her hand up.

"Is this how you behave at home?" she asked. "Leaving your mess everywhere?"

"No, I mean, I'm usually at work, or Tina cleans—"

She smiled at him. The smile that said she'd got the information she needed.

"Tobias, you are a grown man. A married man. And quite frankly, I can understand perfectly well why Tina doesn't want to have children, when she's already got one." Her voice was louder than she'd planned, but still, it needed to be said. "How on earth do you expect to be a father, when you can't even clean up after yourself? Do you think babies self-clean?

Or have I somehow produced a child who believes a woman's place is in the kitchen, because I'll tell you something for nothing, young man, I certainly did not."

Heat rose and coloured the tips of his ears and cheeks as he swallowed down the embarrassment.

"This…" She swept the arm again. "Is not on."

"No, of course. You're right, I just—"

Camille stepped away. "I don't want to hear it. Get this cleaned up. How is anyone supposed to cook dinner in this?"

He started to pick things up and shove rubbish into the bin. "Maybe I could take you out to dinner? Repay the other night?"

It was an option. But so was meeting Leila, and she'd turned that down.

"I just wanted a quiet night in." She glanced at her watch. It was gone seven already. The last thing she actually wanted to do was cook. "I'm going out. And I want this place spick and span by the time I get back."

TWENTY-THREE

She would be a liar if she said she hadn't, just for a brief second, considered she knew where Leila would be. It would be just as easy to turn left at the bottom of the road and head for the part of town she now knew Leila lived, and the restaurant she also knew she'd be eating in.

But she turned right and headed for the bridge that would take her out of Woodington and into Amberfield and to Blanca's, the bar she'd been preferring more recently.

The lights were red, and she slumped back in her seat and blew her cheeks out, closing her eyes as, once more, images of Leila hovering above her flooded her mind, creating that frustration within her again.

The beeping horn from behind made her jump. She put the car into gear and pulled away, raising a sorrowful hand to acknowledge to the driver behind – she understood their frustration with her, too.

Just to worsen the dismal evening a little bit more, it had started to rain; that incessant drizzle that soaked in deep to the core and froze everything. "Just like divorce," she chuckled to herself as the wipers swept across the screen and cleared it just long enough before the rain covered it again, and the process began its next cycle.

Camille turned the heating up a notch and pressed the accelerator just a tad more. The roads were quiet as she continued on.

She switched lanes and turned left to take her along the

other side of the river, until she reached the smaller bridge she would walk across to get to Blanca's.

She found a space and parked the car.

Leila placed her knife and fork down and delicately wiped her mouth with the linen napkin. An enjoyable meal, and a nice glass of wine to go with it. The only downside was the lack of company. And by company, she meant Camille, of course.

Not that she expected Camille's stubbornness would give in quite so quickly, but there was always hope, wasn't there?

She smiled to herself. The game plan was in play.

"Can I get you the dessert menu?" the waitress asked with a bright smile.

Leila returned the friendly manner. "You know, I wasn't going to, but...why not?" She let her eyes linger on the waitress's face just that moment longer than was needed, enjoying the gentle heat that rose to her cheeks. "What would you suggest?"

"Oh, well, I guess my favourite is the salted caramel toffee pudding, with a scoop of vanilla ice cream."

Leila held her gaze. "That sounds delicious."

The waitress leaned in and lifted the empty plate. A gentle and feminine scent floated with her. Another time, another place, and maybe Leila would have made a move.

"I'll get that for you."

"Thank you, so much." Leila continued to smile, watching her walk away. *Not that it would be so terrible to have some fun, would it?*

"Back again," Sadie said, already reaching for a glass as Camille smiled wearily and took a seat at the bar.

It wasn't that busy, not that she expected it to be, and was another reason why she'd picked this over Art.

She sighed. "Must be the company."

Sadie nodded. "You know, I get that a lot."

"I can imagine," Camille said, before nodding when Sadie held up the bottle of white wine she'd had the last couple of times she'd been in. "Quiet tonight?"

"Hm, Mondays usually are, that's why I like working them."

"I think it would drive me crazy," Camille admitted, accepting the glass and handing over her card for the tab.

Sadie leaned on her elbows, dark blonde hair tied back, a light dusting of makeup on her face. They could be sisters, Camille thought, as she looked at her.

"Too much thinking time?"

Camille laughed. "Lately, yes. My brain needs to keep busy, otherwise..." She shrugged and took a sip of her drink.

"Ah, still the one that got away." Sadie winked.

"No. The one I chose not to pursue," Camille clarified. She pressed her lips together before saying, "But apparently, that doesn't matter."

Sadie's eyes narrowed. "What do you mean?"

Camille closed her eyes and breathed deeply. "I'm employing her."

"What?" Sadie's laugh burst out. "How?"

"Obviously, *I* didn't employ her." Camille shook her head. "My company were recruiting and she…"

"Got the job?" Sadie bit her lip, wide-eyed. "Wow, that's… So, she's searched you out?"

Camille shook her head. "No, I never gave her any details other than my first name and the town I lived. She claims she applied for the job based on the position. She said once she realised it was in Woodington, she hoped we might bump into one another, but she had no clue I owned the company."

A grin slid across Sadie's face. "So, she's here and you're horny as fuck…"

Camille slapped her hand against her forehead, letting her palm slide down to her cheek to cup it as she too leaned an elbow on the bar.

"I know." She sighed.

TWENTY-FOUR

Leila yawned.

But she couldn't complain. Being tired was her own doing, after all.

The waitress, Chloe, had turned out to be a lot of fun to stay up with, drinking tequila far too late. Leila was right; another time and place, and who knew, but it had been nice to talk to someone else about Camille.

And she could have had an extra hour in bed had she not been on her mission to melt Camille Franklyn's cold heart, once and for all.

"Late night?" Sully asked, entering the staff room and catching the end of the yawn. He thumped his insulated coffee cup down into the sink.

"You could say that." Leila smiled but said no more.

"Lucky man."

"Sorry?" Leila understood the implication, and she wasn't going to let it go. Potential office gossip needed to be nipped in the bud. In her experience, the best way to do that was to hit it head on.

His ears went red, along with his cheeks. "I just meant, you know…if someone got to spend time with you last night, you know then, he'd be—"

"She," she said, glaring at him just enough to keep him on the back foot. "If I'd spent the night with anyone, it would be 'she.' Not that it's any business of anyone here at work."

"No, of course, I was just—"

"You were just implying that my being tired must be down to the workout a man gave me?"

"No, no, absolutely—" His face was now beet red, and he looked as though he wanted to shrivel up and fall through the floor. "I—sorry, I shouldn't have made any comment."

She shot a finger gun at him. "Correct." She picked up her mug and the one she'd made for Camille. "And it won't happen again, right?"

"Right, yep, never again."

"Good." She stared at him and then the door. "Can you?"

"Oh, yes…" He grabbed the handle and opened the door for her. "Again, sorry, I didn't mean anything by it."

Leila smiled. "Okay, you are forgiven."

Camille looked up at the quiet knock on the door and held her breath.

"Come in," she said with authority; as much authority as she had for someone who'd already accepted defeat. Because in her heart, she already knew it wasn't Fatima or anyone else. She could almost sense it in her core.

It would be Leila.

The door remained closed, but another gentle knock came.

"Yes, come in," Camille said a little louder, irritation seeping in. When the door still didn't open, she huffed and pushed her chair back, stalking across the office to yank the door open. "I said, come—"

She was greeted by Leila, of course, smiling and holding two mugs of steaming coffee in her hands.

"Sorry, my love, I couldn't...with the door, you know, only one pair of hands." She pushed past and into the office, leaving Camille to glare after her.

"I don't recall asking for coffee."

Leila set both mugs down onto the desk and turned brightly. "No, of course not. Because you don't ask for your needs to actually be met. You expect everyone to work it out and supply you, so here." She waved at the coffee. "Supplied."

She sat down before Camille could say another word.

"Pamela told me you don't like the coffee from the café, so I figured I'd get in a few minutes earlier and make it myself."

This was one of those moments when Camille fought the urge to vent her spleen, because what could she say? *How dare you be so presumptuous to make me a delicious cup of coffee? How dare you care so much? Be so wonderful?*

Camille walked slowly and silently back to her chair.

She stopped and glanced quickly at Leila. She'd never understood the saying, 'can't take my eyes off of you,' until now. Because it took everything she had to pull her gaze away from the elegant woman, looking quite at home with her leg crossed over the other, her mug in hand, sipping and blowing on the hot liquid. Plump, kissable lips pouted with every breath.

"As grateful as I am, I would prefer you didn't bring me coffee every morning moving forward."

"Because you don't want coffee, or because you're worried what it might say to other members of staff?" Leila said, clearly amused, judging by the smile on her face. "Or is it that seeing me is just a little too much, and you're struggling to avoid looking at me in that way that I know you enjoy?"

"Stop it, Leila, please, just stop this before it goes too far." Camille pulled the chair out and sat down. "I can't give you what you want, alright? So, find a way to deal with that, or find somewhere else to work, but this..." She pointed to the coffee. "This all stops, right now. If you have any feelings for me, then you'll stop this and let me go."

She finally held Leila's gaze, refusing to look away. It didn't matter how attracted Camille was to Leila; this wouldn't work.

Leila smiled sadly, nodded once, and made a little 'humph' noise, before she stood up and turned away. At the door, she stopped and looked back at Camille.

"I will look for employment elsewhere. Your secret is safe with me. In the meantime, I will work quietly, and you will not be bothered by me anymore."

The door opened and closed, and Camille fell against her arms, onto the desk. *What have you done?*

TWENTY-FIVE

Leila took off the moment she was able to, heading home before Camille would even think to leave her office. She'd gotten through the day with a mixture of annoyance, frustration, anger, and despondency.

But she'd managed it.

And now, as she pushed the key into the door and shuffled through it and into the flat she was finally beginning to call home, she felt the emotion of it all erupt, and she burst into tears.

Dropping her bag, she moved quickly to her room and collapsed onto the bed.

Nobody said this would be easy, she reminded herself. This was not going to be a walk in the park. True love never ran smoothly, did it?

Maybe it was foolish to have thought otherwise, and yet, she couldn't quite believe Camille didn't want them to be together.

"It's just bullshit," she reminded herself but thumped the pillow for good measure. "You've seen the way she looks at you."

Several deep breaths later, she felt the release of all that pent-up frustration leave her body and finally relaxed.

Sitting up, she wiped her face. Emotional outburst over, she got up and undressed out of her work clothes.

"Let's see just how serious Camille is about losing me."

She nodded to herself.

A quick shower later, she pulled on freshly cleaned jeans and a jumper, and went down for dinner, as planned. And then, who knew, maybe some drinks at Art.

She was just about to walk out of the door when her phone rang. She smiled as she flicked the answer button.

"Hello, bestie," she said, placing the phone in the crook of her neck as she pulled her jacket on. "I'm just heading down to dinner."

"Oh, well I won't keep you long. I was just checking in, seeing how it's all going down south with the enigmatic Camille."

Leila sighed.

"What's up?"

"As with every plan, there are always bumps in the road, no?" Leila said. "She's pushed back as much as I think she will. And so now, I have to give her what she's asked for."

"Which is?"

"Stop chasing her."

"Okay, and that will mean what?" Kristen asked slowly as she thought about it.

"As of tomorrow, I will back off," Leila said, closing the door behind her and walking towards the stairs. "No more coffee. No more being around to remind her. I'll give her what she thinks she wants."

"And you think that will work?"

Leila thought back to their time at the hotel, when a woman had stopped her to ask an innocent question, and Camille had become instantly jealous, though she'd never admit it.

"Yes, I think so..." She took the stairs down. "She came home and convinced herself she'd never see me again. That's not the case now. I'm right here, she can't avoid me."

"I hope you're right. I don't want to see you get hurt."

"You never have to worry about me, Kristen."

"And yet I do," Kristen said, a smile in her voice. "So, I'm going to be arriving Friday night. Let's go out and get drunk."

Leila laughed. "Really? Is that all you want to do?"

"Well, I mean, we need to let our hair down, duck."

Smiling at the familiar term, Leila said, "Alright, I'll take you to my local gay bar. How does that sound?"

"Does it have fancy cocktails?"

"Of course." She stepped out of the lift and exited the building, turning right and walking until she was looking through the window of the restaurant. "Okay, I need to eat before I waste away."

"Okay, Lei, see you Friday?"

"Will do."

TWENTY-SIX

For the rest of the week, Leila was good to her word. Camille made her own coffee, or had Fatima do it. She walked the corridors and went to meetings, and if Leila attended, she kept her head down and sat as far away from Camille as she could.

And Camille hated every minute of it.

The feeling surprised her, not least because it was different now. When they'd parted ways after Madeira, it was fine, because Camille could wake up every morning and pretend Leila didn't exist. She could put it all down to a dream, to a memory, and leave it there.

But now, Leila was just down the corridor. Her name was on emails, her signature on paperwork. Leila Ortez was no longer someone Camille could pretend didn't exist.

And what was most annoying, was it was no longer on her terms. Now, it was Leila who was avoiding her.

She checked her watch.

It was almost three in the afternoon. Everyone would be congregating in the meeting room, waiting on her arrival. Everyone, including Leila.

For the last thirty minutes, Camille had been preparing herself. Now though, she didn't have any more wriggle room on time.

She slid on her suit jacket, picked up her things, and left the office.

Leila made sure to arrive for the meeting early. She wanted to pick the best seat, have her coffee steaming, and be ready for everyone's arrival, and by everyone, she meant Camille.

There were fifteen chairs around the long table; seven either side and one at the end. Usually, she'd sat further away, but still giving Camille the long view of her. She'd noticed the surreptitious glances from Camille anytime she'd worn a skirt.

Camille was very good. Leila had to admire that.

Barely anyone would notice the covert glances, unless they knew to look for them, which of course, Leila did, and she'd played on them.

Anytime Camille had looked her way, she'd been looking right back at her. It amused her to watch Camille struggle to fight the inclination to gawp.

Let's see how you deal with not seeing me, Leila thought to herself, pulling out the seat furthest away. She laid out her planner, pen, and went to the machine to get a coffee.

Sully and Elliot arrived next, talking to one another loudly and laughing about something of no interest to Leila. She turned to acknowledge them both and smiled when Sully sat exactly where she assumed he would.

Right next to her.

Sully was a big guy, over six feet tall and built like a rugby player. All Leila needed to do was lean back in her chair and she would be completely obscured from Camille's view.

Half a dozen more people entered the room, including Pamela, who looked quite confused to see Leila sitting so far away from the optimal position she wanted them to sit in. As close to Camille's right hand as Pamela could get herself. It amused Leila to watch the indecision play out across her face, as Pamela considered whether she should abandon her own hope of being centre stage; eager and willing should Camille pay her any attention, or would it be rude to abandon her working partner and sit apart from Leila?

Pamela then looked at Sully, and the unavailability of a chair for her to sit on, and made her decision, placing her things down at the space she usually took.

She mouthed a silent, "Why are you over there?" at Leila. Her response was a silent shrug and smile, to which Pamela pulled a face and looked around, as the door opened and Camille swept in.

Their eyes met and held as Camille glided around the room to take her seat. Leila looked away, leaned back, and disappeared from view.

The other vantage point Leila had with this seat was the windows. With the blinds open, and the lighting the way it was, she had a perfect reflection of the room, and of Camille.

She could watch as Camille took her place at the head of the table, and as casually as she could, looked around at those seated, lingering on the end where Leila was now out of sight.

"Who's missing?" she said abruptly.

It was Pamela, of course, who answered, "Just Tanner, I think."

Camille glanced around once more.

Leila reached for her mug, revealing her tanned hand, and the tattoos covering her arm peeking out from her sleeve as she pulled the hot drink towards herself. In the reflection, she noticed Camille pull her seat forward.

Looking at her watch, Camille said, "Right," in a tone that said Tanner had about thirty seconds to get his backside in the room, and just on cue, the door opened and an out-of-breath executive walked in.

"So sorry. Got held up on a call with New York," he said, taking the only seat available and nodding apologetically to anyone who looked his way.

"Seeing as we've all been waiting for you, Tanner, you might as well start," Camille said, and Leila allowed herself to enjoy a little thrill at the way Camille commanded the room. It was intoxicating, and she could perfectly understand why it was Pamela found herself so drawn to the woman.

She watched Pamela.

It wasn't sexual. Her interest in Camille was all about validation. If she had to lay money on it, Leila would guess Pamela's mother was just like Camille.

Tanner stood up, cleared his throat, and began to speak in that monotone voice he had. Leila drowned him out by focusing on the reflection of Camille in the window.

For the most part, Camille kept her head down, reading along with reports, occasionally interrupting with a pertinent question, jotting something down. But each time she did so, she'd glance towards the corner, to where Leila was sitting, out of view.

At one point, Camille even sat forward, fidgeting and adjusting herself in her seat. It was no use. Leila just pushed her feet against the floor and let the chair slide back another inch.

And when it was all over, Leila was the first to pile up her things, pick up her cup, and exit the room without a backward glance.

If Camille Franklyn wanted to see her, *she'll have to work a lot harder*' she told herself and headed for her office to pack up for the day.

TWENTY-SEVEN

Kristen arrived at the flat a little after seven. Trouble with trains and connections had meant she'd arrived later than Leila was expecting, but none of that mattered once her friend was through the door and they hugged.

"It's so good to see you," Leila said, pulling back and looking at her friend. Her blonde hair poked out at the bottom of the woolly hat Leila had gotten her for Christmas. "How tired are you?"

Kristen laughed. "I had a nap on the train. Why? What's the plan?"

"Well, there's this bar I wanted to check out but it's a cab ride away, and I just thought we could get something to eat and then go out, but I realise we're not as young as we used to be."

"Hey, speak for yourself." Kristen pushed her playfully. "Let me get sorted with my bags and then I'm all yours."

"Great. I booked a table at my regular spot downstairs. It's really nice. And I'll book a taxi for 8:30?"

"Sounds good to me." She bustled past Leila with her rucksack towards the spare room and opened the door. "Not gonna lie— I didn't think you'd have got this done."

"Cheek. I said I would, and you know I always do what I say I will."

"True. Shame on me for being so negative."

"I'll be in the lounge. Take your time. Table's booked for 7:30."

Kristen poked her head back around the door, "Okay... Casual or dressing up?"

"I'm going for casual."

Narrowed eyes smiled back at her. "I know what your 'casual' means, and it's sexy, hot, and not jeans and a shirt. Right, full on for me then."

Leila laughed. "You know me better than I know me."

Camille stared into the mirror. Her blonde hair was darker now, without the sun's kisses that had lightened it after her holiday. Twirling it into ringlets with the curling iron, she teased and plucked at it until it framed her face and accentuated her fine features.

Her makeup was as impeccable as the little black dress she'd pulled from the wardrobe to match the stockings and heels.

She needed to let her hair down, find a useful partner on the dancefloor to sweep her off her feet, and take her mind away from the daily reminders of Leila.

Just for the night.

Picking up her favourite perfume, she gave herself a quick spray of it before pulling her jacket on and grabbing her purse.

"Tobi?" She knocked on his door. "I'm going out. Make sure you call Tina."

The door shot open. "You look nice. Got a date?"

"No, I'm just going out."

"Oh, well you look great." He smiled.

"Thank you." She wrinkled her nose. "Can you at least open a window in there? It smells like a hamster snuck into the house."

Tobias grinned. "Will do. I've invited Tina 'round later. I hope that's okay?"

"Of course. The sooner you two start patching things up, the better. I might get my house back the way I like it." She smiled at him. "Tell Tina I said 'hello.' And don't wait up."

"But you'll be home, right?" he asked, as she walked towards the stairs.

Camille turned back and winked. "Who knows? But I won't be reporting in."

"Okay, but at least let me know you're alright."

"Tobias, worry about your own love life, sweetheart. Mine's fine." *At least it will be, when I stop thinking about a certain exotic goddess. Oh God,* she winced. *Really, Camille?*

TWENTY-EIGHT

The Weekend's "Blinding Lights" was blaring from the DJ booth when Camille stepped through the door at Blanca's. *Of course it is.* She closed her eyes and groaned internally, reminded instantly of that night.

"Be a good girl and take it all off for me." She ran her fingertip down Camille's neck. "That little shiver that just ran down your spine...that's how your entire body is going to feel when..."

"When?"

Leila chuckled. "When you grow some balls and show me the better version of yourself."

"Fuck, Leila, that's..."

"What you need," Leila said, pulling back to stare into those eyes again.

"Yes," Camille gasped out.

"So, take it all off and show me," Leila responded. She sat herself down onto the bed and shuffled back until she could lean against the pillows.

"Can I?" She looked around for her bag and reached inside for her phone. "Music, I'd like...I have a playlist."

"For stripping? I'm impressed."

Camille laughed. "No, but...it's...I put it together for an intimate liaison that didn't happen and..."

Leila smiled at her. "Sure, put it on."

She fiddled and then placed the phone on the nearest

surface. Tinny music played quietly, and she grabbed the phone again. "Sorry, volume. I always have it off." With the music louder, she put the phone back down again and took a moment.

"In your own time, Camille," Leila said, recognising the song. "I Feel It Coming" by The Weekend. It was a sexy song, and Leila nodded along as she watched Camille begin to sway and find her rhythm.

Her hips moved first and then her arms. She began to sway. Eyes closing as she felt the music and let it guide her soul with the movements. Her arms raised higher and twirled around one another.

Someone jostled her arm and shook her out of the memory, but the feelings it evoked within her stayed, lingering deep in her soul.

Getting a grip on herself, shoulders back, head up, she walked confidently to the bar and waited. Admiring glances cast her way were ignored. *If they want me tonight, they'll have to grow a pair and become better versions of themselves,* she thought. She wasn't in the mood for making do.

Sadie wasn't serving. Instead, Camille ordered a large gin and tonic from the younger woman behind the bar. They'd never spoken before, other than for Camille to order a drink, but that was fine, she wasn't here to chat with the bar staff tonight.

In all honesty, she liked it there because it was more anonymous. Usually, it was a quieter crowd, and Sadie was often an ear of reason that listened without judgement.

It was halfway through Camille's third drink that everything around her changed. The alcohol was relaxing her. She felt the beat of the music pulse through her, and the urge to dance and just let loose took over.

When a table became free near the dance floor, she headed over and snagged it, draping her coat over the back of a seat and tucking her purse out of sight. She downed what was left of her drink and then danced her way onto the middle of the floor, sliding between writhing bodies all absorbed in the music and their lust for one another.

Camille closed her eyes, and her hips swayed, arms raised, and she lost herself in it all. The anonymous hands that appeared around her waist just added to the sensations, as she backed herself into the warmth of a body pressing up against her.

It didn't matter who.

She enjoyed the way those hands moved around her body. Flat and firm against her stomach, rising just high enough to avoid being indecent and earning themselves a slap.

Another song filtered in, and another body pressed up against her front. For the first time since stepping onto the dancefloor, she opened her eyes and grinned at the woman who'd joined in. Finally she glanced over her shoulder at the woman behind who'd started it all. They were moving together, enjoying the moment, and then everything changed.

Watching from the bar was a pair of familiar eyes; dark, brooding, half closed, glaring. Wearing the same white pantsuit she'd worn in Madeira Leila sipped her cocktail as she stared over at Camille.

And she wasn't alone.

Beside her, clinging to her arm and giggling, was a rather attractive, if not alternative-looking, blonde woman, similar age as Leila, but not as tall.

Camille held Leila's gaze as her own arm raised up and hooked around the back of the head of the woman behind her. Three bodies moving in unison, hips left, then right, and back again.

Leila looked away.

TWENTY-NINE

"Is that her?" Kristen said loudly, leaning into Leila. "She's…wow, I didn't expect her to be so…outgoing?"

"No. It's intriguing to watch her out in the wild."

"I think you woke something inside her for sure."

Leila frowned. "Yes, something she doesn't want to share with me." She turned to face Kristen, seeing a look of concern on her friend's face. "What if she is being honest and she doesn't want me? This is possible, no?"

Kristen glanced furtively over Leila's shoulder at the woman cavorting with two others on the dancefloor.

"I mean…I guess, but your gut instinct is usually spot on. I wouldn't start doubting yourself just yet."

Leila sipped long and hard on her straw, draining the drink to just ice, all crushed and cold at the bottom, much like her heart was feeling right now.

"I'm going to the toilet," she said despondently.

Kristen patted her shoulder. "I'll get another round in."

"Tequila," Leila said, adding a quick, "Please" before she headed off.

Leila kept her head down as she moved quickly between those standing at the bar and those sitting on stools. The bathrooms were down a short corridor, through a doorway, and out of sight.

There was nobody queuing and she was grateful for

that. She went inside and locked herself into a cubicle, putting the lid down and sitting on it. She took a moment to ground herself.

Leila acknowledged her jealousy, disappointment, and the possibility that she'd been wrong all this time, and what kind of a fool did that make her?

She let her mind wander back, to that night when they'd said goodbye, when Camille had asked to make love and then to hold her.

"Go ahead, I am an open book."

"Yes, you are, and I do love that about you, but it's more of a request. Leila, tonight, I want something that I have no right asking of you and I completely understand if you say no—"

"What is it? If I can give you it, I will."

Camille sighed. "Yes, I know you would and that's why it's so difficult to ask."

Leila sat forward and reached for her hand. "Camille, just ask."

"I want to—I would like to experience something with you. I love all the fucking and toying with me and all of that, but I'd like to—" She swallowed quickly and let out a shuddering breath before staring into Leila's eyes and saying, "Make love to me…and then… hold me until we have to leave."

There was more there, she knew it.

Camille wasn't dancing with strangers because she didn't want her. It was because she did, and she was trying to push it away. Yes, that was it, wasn't it?

"Think logically, not with your emotions," she muttered to herself. The way Camille had stared over at her, making a point, had hurt of course, but what else had it said?

"I want you."

Leila sat up, ears pricked. That wasn't her internal monologue responding – that was an actual voice. Someone was speaking aloud, but it sounded so much like…

"Leila?"

She stood up, opened the door, and found Camille leaning back against the four-inch piece of wood between cubicles.

"Camille. What are—"

Unsteady on her feet, Camille twisted around and almost fell against her. "You… I want…you," she slurred, as she righted herself and gripped the edge of the cubicle.

"Oh…that's not what it looked like a moment ago." Leila watched her; beautiful even when a little drunk and sweaty from all that cavorting. She swallowed the jealousy down.

"I just…can't…with you, you now," Camille rambled, but her hand reached up, palm caressing Leila's face. "You're just…you'd want more than…than I can— You're so beautiful." She leaned in, pressing her lips against Leila's. "But you've seen me…raw, untethered…"

There was a small part of Leila that wanted to fight the attraction, and tell Camille that she wasn't a toy, like she'd done in Madeira, but with every movement of that mouth against her own, she couldn't do it.

She wanted it just as much.

Reaching up, she slipped her hand around Camille's neck, pulling her into the cubicle and closing the door just as someone else entered the bathroom.

The small space instantly filled with the scent of Camille's perfume; something different to before, but just as intoxicating.

Her tongue, finding no resistance, slid easily into

Camille's mouth, and the mutual groan of desire only heightened the sensation and encouraged more.

She forgot where they were.

Hands roamed, and with Camille pushed against the wall, Leila reached lower and inched Camille's dress higher, before pushing her thigh between Camille's legs. She groaning again when Camille pressed, tilting her pelvis back and forth, in rhythm with the music that could still be heard through the walls.

"Oh God," Camille gasped, breaking the kiss, her head dropping back against the wall as Leila's lips moved to kiss and nibble the soft skin of her neck.

A loud commotion outside brought Leila to her senses when a group of giggling, chatty women entered the bathroom.

She stepped back and considered Camille...what they'd done...were doing.

Both of them were breathing heavily, locked eyes questioning everything. The mask of fear was back—smothering Camille's features in an instant.

"We shouldn't," Leila said, shaking her head. She licked her lips and enjoyed the taste of Camille on them. "Not with you so tipsy. We should talk—"

Camille gripped the hem of her dress and yanked the material back in place, covering herself. When she stood up again, she sighed.

"You're right, it's...we shouldn't do this...never going to work," she mumbled more to herself than to Leila.

Before Leila could argue, Camille had unlocked the door and stepped out to a rousing, "Whoop whoop!" from someone within the group of women surrounding the mirrors, touching up makeup and hairstyles. The women knew exactly what they'd been doing locked in the toilet together.

"Someone's getting lucky," one of them shouted after Leila as the door was closing.

"Yes, and it's not me," Leila said to herself.

THIRTY

When Leila returned to the bar, she found Kristen with her brows raised. "Well?"

"Well, what?"

Kristen nudged her. "Don't even try to pretend that you and she didn't just—" She pointed to the door and Leila caught the back of Camille, now wearing her jacket, leaving. "Something happened— spill it."

"We kissed."

"What?" Kristen shouted over the music. She then remembered they had drinks and lifted the glasses from the bar, handing one to Leila.

"She came in, she said my name and rambled about how she wants me, but she can't have me because I've seen her raw and untethered?" She shrugged. "I don't know, then next thing we're kissing and getting it on—"

"Why's she leaving?"

"Some women came in, and it was so loud, you know? And then everything stopped, and I said we shouldn't, not while she's tipsy, and we should talk, but she left."

"So, now what?" Kristen asked.

Leila sipped her drink and considered it.

"I don't know, but what I do know is…she will come to me when she's ready to be raw and untethered again." She grinned just thinking about the possibility.

"Okay then, so, are we dancing?"

Leila's grin widened; her mood lightened by the events of the evening with Camille. "I think we should. I have to show you a good time, no?"

"What will Paddy think...me out with all the lesbians?" She laughed and grabbed Leila's hand. "Anyone tries it on, you're my girlfriend, right?"

"Oui, let's go make a scene."

Camille closed the door behind her and leaned against it, listening as the cab drove away, miles now between her and her temptation.

The journey home had at least sobered her up somewhat, but she kicked off her heels just in case she stumbled.

There were low voices coming from the lounge and she remembered Tina was coming over to discuss things with Tobias. She wasn't sure whether to interrupt or not but figured they should know she was back, otherwise, it could potentially get very awkward, couldn't it?

She looked at herself in the hall mirror. The lipstick she'd worn earlier had rubbed off – on the rim of several glasses, and on the lips of Leila. Wiping her face, she felt the emotions build. Her throat constricted, eyes stinging. She didn't cry often, but the urge to do so, right now, was escalating.

What the hell had she been thinking, throwing herself at Leila like that? It was pathetic – needy. She shook her head at her own image.

"Raw and untethered? For fuck's sake," she mumbled to

herself. "Just slit yourself open and let her feast on the innards, why don't you?"

The voices in the lounge got louder as Tina laughed at something, and Tobi joined in.

She composed herself.

"I'm home," she called out, her voice holding.

Opening the door to the living room and popping her head around it, she managed a smile. "Hi Tina, good to see you... I'm going to make some tea and go up to bed... just wanted you to know I was back."

"Hello, Camille," Tina said, standing up and running a hand through her short black hair. She crossed the room to greet her mother-in-law with a hug, just like she always did.

It was all just too much for Camille. Everything was overwhelming her. She felt the tears begin to erupt and blinked them away quickly.

"Oh, are you alright?" Tina looked worried and turned to Tobias.

"Yes, sorry, just—" Camille wiped her eyes gently to avoid mascara smearing her face.

"Come and sit down. Tobi, get your mum a glass," Tina instructed. Estuary Essex, through and through.

"Really, I don't want to interrupt things. You both need to talk and—" She looked at Tina. "You are talking, aren't you?"

Tina nodded. "Yes, we're talking."

"He loves you," Camille said.

"I know he does."

The sound of a glass clinking against a bottle stopped their conversation from going any further.

"Here you go." Tobi handed Camille a glass half-full. "I

brought the other bottle in. That one is empty now."

Tina smiled up at him before returning her attention back to Camille. "So, are you going to tell us what's got you all upset?"

"She's been out," Tobi said. "Was it a date?"

Tina looked at him. "I'm not an idiot, I can see she's been out. Look at her, bloody sensational, and she's not ready for bingo yet, is she?" Tina smiled conspiratorially at Camille. "Was it a date?"

Camille shook her head. "No, no, nothing like that…"

"Cos if it was, and he's misbehaved, it won't be Tobi he has to worry about. It will be me," Tina said seriously, her face stern, one brow raised, ready for battle.

Camille chuckled. "Oh, I'm fully aware of that."

They both laughed, and Tobi baulked. "I could take him."

They both laughed harder.

"I could," he continued. "Nobody messes with my mum…" Tina glared at him. "Or wife," he added quickly.

"You know you can tell us." Tina pressed a little harder.

Biting her lip, Camille considered it. Should she just tell them the whole sorry story? They were open-minded people, after all. *And your son*, she reminded herself very quickly.

Tobias sat down beside her. "Mum, seriously, you're worrying me. Has something happened?"

"Yes." Camille nodded, and Tobias and Tina both stared at each other, wide-eyed, "But it's not what you're thinking. It's nothing…bad."

"What is it?" Tobi asked.

"I'm just… I'm not ready to share right now," Camille

stuttered out. "I don't know what I'm doing about it, and until then, I'd prefer to keep it private."

"So, it's a man? You're seeing someone?"

Camille felt heat rise up her neck.

"No, not quite," she answered quietly, hidden behind the glass, as she sipped the wine and did everything in her power not to grimace at it. Tina's choice, she imagined. Far too sweet. She put the glass down.

"What the bloody hell does that mean?" Tobi continued, looking befuddled.

A knowing smile came over Tina's face. "It means, she's either not seeing anyone, but might like to, or..." The grin widened when she said, "It's not a man."

Tobias scrunched up his face. A look of total confusion now spread and stuck. "That doesn't make any—Oh...oh... Ooooh." Finally working it out, eyes widening, he said, "Mother, have you gone gay?"

"I'm going to bed," Camille announced, instantly sobering. She stood up quickly, too quickly, and realised she was not quite as sober as she had hoped.

"But Mum..." Tobi called out.

She waved him off over her shoulder. "I'll see you in the morning. Fix your own relationship, Tobias."

THIRTY-ONE

Tobi sat stunned.

Tina laughed.

"Are you seriously surprised?" she said to him, and sat back on the couch. "Later-in-life lesbian, they call it."

"Who calls it?" Tobi said, picking up the bottle and topping up his glass before offering it to Tina.

She shrugged. "I saw it on social media. Women of a certain age are abandoning their interest in men and exploring options with women instead."

"Yeah, but…Mum?"

"Why not?"

He squirmed. "Because it's Mum."

"So, what are you saying? Your mum isn't allowed to find a bit of happiness because it doesn't fit with what you think she should do?"

He swigged his drink. "No, of course not."

"Then what?"

"I'm just surprised, that's all. I mean…" He grinned. "Since Dad, she's just not seemed that bothered. I guess I figured this was it."

"Jesus, what, she'd die a lonely old woman cos ya dad sodded off with someone else?"

He shrugged.

"Is that how you see us?" she asked.

"I'm not leaving you for another woman," Tobi argued. "I didn't leave – you asked me to go."

Tina nodded. "Yeah, I did. And has it made any difference?"

"I didn't want to leave, Tina."

"That's not answering the question, Tobi."

He sipped this time. "Mum said it was pretty obvious you didn't want a kid, when you already had one." He looked at her with big blue eyes just like Camille's. "Me."

Tina nodded. "And what do you think about that?"

Tobi sighed. "That she's probably right." He nodded. "And I'm sorry."

"You should be."

"Can I come home?"

Tina shrugged. "Depends, Tobi…are you going to pull your weight?"

"I promise, no more teenager in the house. I can't lose you…us. I've been a selfish sod, I know that. I'm gonna change."

Tina smiled. "Well, then you can come home, when you've changed." She stood up. "In the meantime, I'm going away with the girls for a couple of nights. We can talk again when I get back."

Tobi frowned. "Okay, so, let me come home, and while you're away, I'll prove I can look after the house and keep everything spotless."

She thought about it and then nodded. "Alright, you can come home tomorrow." Tobi grinned. "Don't get too excited. If I come back and there is one speck of dust, we'll be revisiting this."

"There won't be. I'm going to prove to you that I'm the man you married."

THIRTY-TWO

Rosie sat on the kitchen stool and watched Camille move around the kitchen, ignoring the question she'd posed at least a minute ago.

Pot lids clanged, and spoons clanked against the edge of the pots, as vigorous stirring took place.

"I'm not sure spaghetti needs that much attention, until you're swirling it on a fork," Rosie said. She picked up her glass and took a sip.

"The thing is, I know I made an utter fool of myself, okay? I know that," Camille said, finally, at least acknowledging there was a question.

Rosie continued to sip and eye her friend over the rim of the glass.

"And I am well aware I will have to face her on Monday morning, and…" The pot lid clanged once more. Camille turned, looking defeated, with slumped shoulders and a wobbly chin. "What do I say?"

"'I'm sorry' would probably be a good place to start, 'for being an utter tit in the first place and not just falling into your bed.'" She thought for a moment about how that sounded. "Her bed, not mine."

Camille glared at her. "Yes, I got the gist of that. Thank you." She picked up her glass and drank it down. "Why are you so insistent I jump into this lesbian fairytale romance?"

Rosie chuckled. "Because my dear friend, it's the only

time, since before Tom left, that I've actually seen you happy."

"Mum, I'm off." Tobi's voice rang out down the hall, but before she could answer him, he was standing in the kitchen, bags in hand. "I'm heading home. Just wanted to say thanks for…you know, putting up with me, and giving me the kick up the backside I needed."

"You're welcome home anytime, sweetie, you know that," Camille said, rounding the island and moving in to hug her son. "You and Tina will always have a room here. This is your home."

He smiled at her and kissed the top of her head.

"Well, I'd best get moving, or she might think I'm not coming and lock the doors again." He grinned. Turning to Rosie, he said, "Make sure she tells this woman how she feels, won't you? Life's too short."

Rosie laughed loudly, and Camille's mouth gaped.

"Tobias, I'm not dating a woman."

"I'll do my best, Tobes, but you know how stubborn she is," Rosie said, confirming his suspicions and earning a pursed-lipped glare from Camille for her trouble. She didn't care. Someone needed to give Camille a push, but she looked away just to keep from being turned to stone.

"Sorry Mum, but you're not as secretive as you think. Just go for it. What's the worst that can happen?"

And then he was gone, and Rosie turned back to stare at her with a shit-eating, 'told-you-so' grin on her face.

"Yes, what's the worst that can happen?" she asked.

"The worst that can happen is…" Camille pushed her hand into her hair and stood there thinking. "I'll burn under the heat of it. I'll be consumed by her, and how much I want her. And then it will all be over, and everyone will know, and I can't put it back into a box."

"Do you know what I can't understand?" Rosie said, standing to fill her glass, and then Camille's.

"What?"

"When it was that you turned into this negative-thinking idiot." She held Camille's stare and nodded. "Yes, you. You've always been tough as old boots, direct, nothing gets in your way, and here you are, floundering because some woman has stolen your heart."

"I am not flou— She hasn't stolen my—"

"Oh, stop it. Stop lying to yourself, Camille. You practically threw yourself on her."

"Because I was drunk."

"Because alcohol gave you the courage to do it!" Rosie pressed. "You want her. You told her that. When are you going to admit it to yourself?"

THIRTY-THREE

Arriving at the office well before anyone else, Leila snuck into Camille's outer office and left a note for Fatima saying Camille was not to be disturbed.

Then she'd opened the door to the inner sanctum and put down her briefcase and coat. The heating was on, and the room felt toasty. Still a little dark outside, the morning sun was hidden behind huge grey clouds looking angry and fit to burst. She left the blinds closed and walked around Camille's desk, pulling out the chair.

When she checked the time, she almost panicked. Camille would be here any moment, of that she was sure. She'd want to get in and hide away in her office, making sure not to risk bumping into Leila in the corridor.

"I know you too well, Camille," Leila chuckled to herself as she took a seat in the comfortable, ergonomic leather chair, and swung her legs up.

She adjusted the clothes she'd picked specifically for this seduction, deliberately intending to rattle Camille a little more. She wore her mid-thigh black skirt, that had hitched an extra inch when she'd swung her leg up, and had added a matching, two-button blazer, both buttons done up low against her stomach.

There was nothing beneath it.

Visible from the right angle, Camille would just see the curve of her breasts.

She kicked off her heels and flexed her bare feet;

red toenails and suntanned skin made her feel sexy, as she considered the endless possibilities, including Camille telling her to get out.

There was aways that risk, wasn't there?

Before she had time to think any further, she heard the sound of the door handle being grabbed and pressed down, the click as it unlocked, and the door swishing open against the carpet. She turned, head tilted slightly, confident smile on her face, as Camille stepped into the room and stopped dead in her tracks.

Before she could speak, Leila said, "You might want to lock it."

"Why?" Camille asked, the door still open and her hand still on the handle.

Leila stood up, kept her eyes firmly locked on Camille, and watched as her expression changed from one of annoyance to desire in seconds.

Each button had been fumbled open quite easily. Leila let the jacket part with gravity, before she shrugged her shoulders, and let it fall down her arms and back to the floor.

"Because you won't want anyone interrupting this," Leila said, confident, now that she wasn't going to be thrown out. She reached behind for the button and zip, loosening the material, before shimmying out of the skirt.

Proudly, boldly, naked.

"I told you, we're going to find a solution."

"Leila—"

Putting her fingers to her lips, Leila shushed her.

"Lock the door and come here," Leila said firmly, slowly dropping down into Camille's chair once more. "You know where I want you." She smiled, her legs opening to reveal her completely. "And I do not want to be interrupted."

There was a stand-off for all of twenty seconds before Camille turned to face the door, pushed it closed, and slowly turned the lock. The soft click indicated an acceptance.

"Come here," Leila beckoned.

"Leila, we can't—"

"This is not up for discussion, Camille. I've given you everything you asked for, and we both know it isn't what you want, so now...you will give me what I want." She pointed to the spot on the floor between her legs. "Right now."

Camille took a step towards her. "I can't just—"

"*Non*," The finger went up, silencing Camille in an instant. "Time for talking is gone. Now it is me who decides."

"Decides what? My life?" Camille was still closing the space between them.

"If it is how it is meant to be, then yes. If that is what I have to do to fix this, then yes, I will take on the responsibility."

She watched intently as Camille edged slowly around the desk, and when she was within reach, Leila took her hand and pulled her to the spot where she wanted her, enjoying the way Camille couldn't look away.

"You like it. Remember how much you wanted this?" Leila pulled on Camille's hand until she was all but bent over, Camille's fingers nearing the heat of her. "Touch me. Ignite the flame, Camille, don't fight what is inevitable."

Camille pulled her hand away, but only as far as Leila's thigh, resting her palm there, as she lowered slowly to her knees. Her eyes fixed on Leila's nakedness.

"Taste me again," Leila whispered.

Camille looked up at her. "Nobody can know," she said

quietly.

Leila nodded. "For now, nobody needs to know. This is me, and you, nobody else's business." She reached her hand into Camille's hair and tugged. "Show me you remember."

"Leila?"

"Hm?"

"Leila, are you alright?"

Opening her eyes, Leila stared up and found Pamela looking concerned. She sat up quickly and looked around. She wasn't in Camille's office.

"God, I'm so sorry. I must have dozed off." She glanced down quickly, relieved to find she was fully dressed.

"Long weekend, huh?"

"Something like that, yes. I'm sorry, I'll get some coffee."

Pamela smiled. "Probably a good idea."

Leila was about to stand up when there was a light knocking on the open door and they both turned towards it.

"Ms Franklyn?" Pamela squeaked, standing to attention.

"Pamela," Camille said with a small smile in her direction, before her attention turned to Leila. Their gazes held. Heat rose instantly on Leila's face. "I was wondering if I could have a word with Ms Ortez?"

"Yes, of course," Pamela said, smiling and making no attempt to move.

Camille stared at her for a moment before she said, "Maybe you could get a coffee?"

"Right, okay, yes," Pamela replied, looking more than confused, but if she had questions, she didn't verbalise them.

Leila watched the entire scene, a little amused and a

little intrigued. Despite her flushed features, she put the dream to one side and focused on Camille. She stood, magnificent in a red pantsuit, pulled in at the waist, and trousers that dropped long and sleek, tapering at the ankles.

When Pamela was gone, Leila sat back in her chair and let it swing casually back and forth, as she waited to hear what Camille had to say.

"Are you free this evening?"

"Am I free...this evening?" Leila said, repeating back the question, because she wasn't prepared for that invitation so soon.

Camille sighed, her shoulders back, chin raised. "It's a simple question."

Leila nodded. "It is, and yet the answer is not so much, no?"

"The answer is yes, or no?" Camille asked sharply. Her eyes closed as she calmed herself. "My house, seven." She leaned over the desk and picked up a pen, scribbled something down onto sticky note, and handed it to Leila. "My address, if you're free."

And with that, she left the office.

"Oh, I'm free." Leila grinned to herself.

THIRTY-FOUR

Pamela returned to the office carrying two mugs, placed one down on Leila's desk, and then continued over to her own space.

Setting down her mug, she slowly slid into her seat and picked up her pen.

"What was that about?" she asked finally.

Leila tried not to smile. It was obvious to her Pamela would be intrigued, nosy even. In Pamela's mind, she was the link between this office and Camille.

"Hm?" Leila said, playing dumb. She barely looked up from her laptop.

"Ms Franklyn, why... I mean, she usually doesn't come to an office to speak to us. We get summoned, and it would... well, it would be me she summoned, so..."

"Oh, I see." Leila finally looked up at her, lips pressed tightly together. "She just thanked me for bringing her a coffee." It was a small lie, one she was prepared to tell for Camille's sake.

"You brought her coffee, but you didn't get us—"

Leila instantly saw the flaw in her story. This was why she didn't like to hide away from the truth of things. She wasn't very good at it. It had been her downfall as a child. She could never lie to get herself out of trouble. Any time she had tried, she'd been caught out.

"At the weekend, I saw her in town. I was at the front of

the queue and noticed her behind, so, I ordered and paid and let the barista know it was for her—"

"In town? Which coffee shop was it?"

"Sorry, what?"

Pamela blushed. "I mean, if she has a new favourite place, it would be helpful to know. She hates that one downstairs, and I often stop in for a coffee on my way to work, so if it's on my route, I could…get her one."

"Sure, you could definitely do that."

"So, which one was it?"

"Honestly, I don't remember, I was in town. I just stopped in and—"

"Are you trying to one-up me? Is that what this is?" Pamela asked with just a hint of aggression in her voice, eyes narrowing as she stared at Leila.

Leila sat back in her chair. "Do you have a crush on Ms Franklyn?"

Wide eyes opened. Pamela's mouth gasped, "Certainly not, I just…" Her cheeks flushed. "I just appreciate her leadership and her knowledge, and I'd like to—" She slumped. "I just want to stand out and not be overlooked. Every job I've had, I've ended up leaving, because whenever promotions came up, all the 'personalities' got ahead, and I was just… unnoticed."

"I'm not trying to one up you," Leila said.

"Then why are you always bringing her coffee? It doesn't make any sense. You've barely been here a few weeks, and already you seem to have cultivated a relationship with Ms Franklyn where she seeks you out to thank you." Pamela pursed her lips. "She's never done that with anyone."

"I don't know what to say," Leila said, which was as

honest as could be. "All I want to do, is my job. So, let's do such a good effort on this report, nobody can overlook you again, yes?"

Pamela seemed to consider things before she said, "Okay, I guess so."

Leila smiled and made a mental note to be less conspicuous where Pamela was concerned. Because her intention tonight was to find some common ground with Camille that would mean they moved forward, and the last thing she needed was a work-related worry pushing Camille deeper into the closet.

THIRTY-FIVE

"Well, it's about time," Rosie said into the phone. "What are you going to say?"

Camille shifted uncomfortably in her chair and pushed back against the leather, seeking comfort from its softness.

"I'm hoping we can find some common ground to solve any future—"

"Bullshit," Rosie spat out with a chuckle. "You already know what common ground you share, and it involves you both being naked, figuratively and literally."

"Really, Rosie?"

"Yes, really, Camille. Get your head out of your arse."

Camille reached for her coffee; the one Fatima had made her. "I don't even know why we are friends." She sipped the drink while Rosie laughed in her ear.

"Because I don't swallow your crap, and kowtow to you, like those wimps who work for you." She sighed. "Okay, so tell me what solution you have come up with you think is worthy of inviting her to your house…where there is a bed and nobody to get in the way?"

"Tut." Camille rolled her eyes and slumped back again. "I'm not sleeping with her."

"Yes, you will," Rosie stated, rather too firmly.

"No, I—"

"I wouldn't blame you if you did. In fact, I actively

encourage it. You might remember what you're missing."

That's the problem, isn't it? Camille thought. She knew exactly what she was missing. She remembered it all; every damn second of it. The way Leila had so easily penetrated all the walls, and how easily Camille had let them fall...because it was safe, wasn't it? To just once, experience something, without the charade of being someone everyone else needed her to be. Camille ached to feel that way again.

And she'd be a liar if she tried to say the thought of sleeping with Leila again hadn't occurred to her. If Leila made a move, she wasn't sure she could ignore it, or if she wanted to. But that would be selfish, wouldn't it? Sleeping with her and then pushing away?

"Camille, you still there?"

"Oh, yes, sorry, was thinking—"

Rosie laughed again. "Yes, I can imagine. So, what's the solution?"

"I was actually thinking we could just talk. Like immersion therapy, and in time, we can be around one another without the—"

"Chemistry? The need to rip clothes off?"

Camille huffed. "Yes. Happy now?"

"I'll only be happy when you are, and right now, you're not—"

"I am." The higher octave said otherwise.

"You're not, and you're fighting it like a stubborn child, and I know it scares you, and you worry about what might happen if you give in to it, but seriously, this could be something amazing."

"It already is," Camille said quietly.

"What was that?" Rosie said.

Sighing in an over the top and dramatic way, Camille repeated herself. "I said, it already is…well, was…amazing." She expected to hear Rosie gloat, but she didn't. "That's the point, isn't it? I'll fuck it up and then what?"

"You know, you haven't fucked this up yet. You can win this if you just let that wall down again and accept it."

"Maybe she doesn't want to be won."

Rosie snorted. "Oh, fuck off, Cami. She's practically begging you, but with class and decorum."

Camille smiled at that. Was that something she enjoyed? Being chased a little? Maybe.

"What time is she coming over?"

"I said after seven."

"And you're cooking?" Rosie asked.

"I wasn't planning to."

"Well, plan to. The poor girl will be starving."

"She has plenty of time to eat something."

Now it was Rosie who tutted. "Seriously? She'll finish at five, then she has to get home, get changed, work out what she's going to wear. And it will be something spectacular, you know that, right? She's going to go all out to make sure you can't resist her. And then she's going to hop into a cab or drive herself over."

She hated it when Rosie was right all the time.

"Fine, I'll organise something to eat."

THIRTY-SIX

Leila rushed through the door, already unbuttoning her shirt before the door slammed shut. Her bag landed on the floor beside the shoes she kicked off.

"Yes, of course, but what can I do?" she said into the phone.

Kristen laughed. "Make sure everything's shaved and scented?"

"I'm not sleeping with her," Leila said adamantly, shrugging one arm and then the other from the blouse. She stopped in her tracks when Kristen's laugh roared. "I'm not, I swear."

"You're telling me that if she comes on to you, you're saying no?"

"I'm saying, I'm not planning to sleep with her."

The laugh roared again.

"You are not helping the situation," Leila said with a serious tone, as her trousers fell to the floor, and she stepped out of them, leaving them in a pool where they landed.

Underwear followed.

"Sorry, I just…isn't this what you want?"

"Of course." She wandered into the bathroom. "But I'm super confused by this…it's not what I expected." She switched the shower on. "Part of me likes that, you know? That she's a little unreadable at times? But it's…unnerving too. I don't know what she's up to and that leaves me a little…" She leaned against the sink. "I know what I want it to be about, and I'm hopeful, because it makes no sense to invite me to her home just to once more tell me it's a no-go, right? No?"

"You're right, I don't think it's that. Not after she kissed you and all but threw herself on you."

"Yes, so, this is...hopeful? No?"

"It is, but just be wary. I know how much you like her and how much you want this to work, but she sounds a bit like a mixed message and that's not—"

"I know, I know." The steam had built up and she turned to face the mirror, drawing *CF* in the condensation and writing a heart around it. "I'll keep my clothes on, and let her talk, then we will see."

"What are you going to wear?"

"Hm I was thinking the blue dress," she said, knowing Kristen would know exactly what she meant.

"Fuck, she's got no chance if her plan is to resist you."

Leila laughed. The dress would cling to every curve, was mid-thigh, sleeveless, and had a plunging neck and backline.

"I'll wear a jacket over it. I don't want to look like I'm going to a club."

"Make sure your hair is down too. You'll look like an 80s goddess, retro and sexy."

"You're crazy." She turned back to the shower. "I need to get in the shower, but I'll call tomorrow."

"Alright, but if it doesn't go to plan, call me tonight, any time. I don't care if you wake me up."

"Okay, gotta go."

She closed off the call and stepped into the shower, more alert than ever to the possibilities tonight might bring.

THIRTY-SEVEN

The Uber pulled up outside of a three-story terrace house. The walls were painted white and the windows were dark, except for the ones lit up by lamps on the lower floor.

Leila thanked the driver and climbed out of the car.

"Whoever they are...I hope they know how lucky they are," he said, smiling at her through the opened window.

"Me too." She smiled back and watched as he drove away.

She turned and looked at the house Camille called home. It was nice. Who was she kidding? It was more than *nice*.

A low brick wall, with integrated black railings, surrounded the small front garden. Neatly trimmed bushes adorned the area, separating this house from both of her neighbours.

Opening the gate, Leila stepped inside the small garden area and noted the lack of anything needing attention.

Tiny white pebbles covered where any potential grass or flowerbed might have been. Two outside lights lit upwards from beneath the bushes and a wooden bin shed in the corner kept everything in its place. The tiled pathway was swept and immaculate.

It had Camille all over it.

Clearly it was expensive, elegant, and yet, understated; perfectly put together to show a calm and confident exterior.

"But what is the inside like? It is staid or passion? We shall see."

Leila climbed the three steps and made it to the door. Taking a deep breath, she reached up and pressed the doorbell.

It took a full minute - a long time to stand on a doorstep and contemplate whether you'd got the time wrong. The door opened, and Camille appeared.

For a moment, neither of them spoke, each taking a second to absorb their reactions to one another.

Camille wore a plain white t-shirt, tucked into pale blue jeans with slits across both knees. To most people, it would be a casual outfit, but with Camille in it, it looked anything but casual, or cheap.

Camille reacted first. "Leila, please, come in. May I take your jacket?"

Without thinking, Leila's hand moved towards the button, but then she yanked it back. "Eh, no, I am fine with it on."

"Are you sure? It's quite warm." Camille smiled awkwardly. "Unlike outside. Winter just won't leave, will it?"

Leila couldn't disagree. It was very comfortable in the warmth of inside…too comfortable.

"Okay," she agreed, and unbuttoned the jacket, letting it slide off her shoulders and down her arms, until she caught it in her hands just as she heard the faint hitch of Camille's breath. "I guess I was hopeful of that reaction." Leila smiled and handed her the coat.

"I expected nothing less," Camille threw back, with just the hint of the smile lingering at the corners of her lips. "Come through."

Leila followed, feeling a little out of sorts being so close, so intimately invited into the sanctum of Camille's home, and not really knowing for sure why. She tried to keep her mind busy with anything other than questions about what Camille was up to, looking at artwork and decor, taking it all in so she could reflect on it later.

"Drink?"

"Sorry?" Leila said, coming into the kitchen and finding Camille holding out a bottle of lager.

"Or I have wine? Coffee? Juice?"

Leila took the bottle, cold in her hand. "No, beer is fine, thank you."

She watched as Camille raised the bottle, and her lips smothered the top as she drank a long swig from it. Her eyes fixed on Leila's.

Leila put the bottle down and stepped forward. It was time to get answers and stop allowing herself to feel awkward and anxious. She knew what she wanted, and if she couldn't have it, it was best to know now.

"I want to touch you, but I don't want to scare you away," Leila said. She kept her gaze on Camille, and to her credit, Camille didn't look away.

It gave Leila hope.

The bottle moved away from Camille's mouth, her lips parted, and her chest rose and fell, with just the hint of a shudder.

"I invited you here to talk," Camille said.

Leila chuckled. "No, you didn't." She edged closer still.

"No, I didn't," Camille admitted.

"So, tell me…" Leila held her attention. Their eyes locked together.

"You know why."

Leila sighed and shook her head. "Camille, have we not learnt this lesson? Own it. Say what you want."

Camille's eyes scanned Leila's body, from top to bottom and back again, before she said, "I want you to take that dress off."

"Obviously." Leila smiled when Camille's eyes met hers once more. "And then what?"

Camille moistened her lips with a slow sweep of her tongue. "We can go upstairs and—"

"Uh-uh." Leila shook her head again. "No, I mean, and then what? Sex is inevitable, no? But what becomes of us?"

"Oh." This time Camille pressed her lips together, a light pink dusting her face. "I hadn't thought that far. We could— We could have an arrangement."

Leila nodded. "Like a contract?"

"Of sorts," Camille answered.

Leila stepped away, her features changing from playful to serious. "Yet again, I am just the slut, no?"

Camille frowned, reminded again of their time in Madeira. "What? Leila, that's not what I meant."

"Isn't it? You want my body, but that's it? I am just a plaything, something to pick up when you need a release, but too embarrassed to own."

Camille rubbed her face. "I'm not doing this again."

"Oh, we are both agreed on that, my dear." Leila's voice turned icy and Camille stiffened. "If you want this," she ran a hand down her torso, "you're going to have to do better." She turned and walked away, stopping in the doorway. "You let me know when you understand what you're missing out on, and what you could actually have, okay?"

THIRTY-EIGHT

Camille stood still, not moving an inch.

She replayed the last few seconds over in her mind, flinching when the front door slammed shut.

This wasn't how this evening was supposed to have gone. Although, now that she thought about it, she hadn't actually had an idea of how this evening would go, past the sex part.

She reached for the beer Leila hadn't touched and sipped it, mulling over how much of an idiot she felt at that moment.

The worst part? She couldn't disagree with a word Leila had said. What had she expected? That Leila would just happily strip off, give her the night of her life, and then go to work tomorrow as though nothing had happened?

"Idiot," she muttered. "Utter idiotic, selfish, stupid arsed—" She swigged more of the lager and then slammed the bottle down.

Go after her, her brain screamed.

And tell her what? her internal monologue responded. *She's right, you're embarrassed. Afraid to show the world you've met someone as spectacular as she is in case it all goes to shit and you'll have to show them that too?*

"Idiot!" she said out loud once more.

She raced out of the kitchen, sliding her feet into trainers and grabbing her car keys. The door slammed behind her as she ran down the steps and skidded to a halt on the gravel.

"You don't know where she's gone," she angrily said to herself.

Out on the pavement, she looked one way, and then the other – no sign of Leila.

"Damn."

Leila walked with purpose, barefooted. Her heels hung from her fingers as she slid her jacket on and huffed, over and over, at the sheer cheek of it. That's what Kristen would have called it; bare-faced cheek.

Rounding the corner, she pulled out her phone and swiped for the Uber app, glancing around to find a street name.

When she had an address, she ordered the car and waited. Dropping her shoes to the ground, she finally slid them onto her feet.

"Idiot," she muttered. She had been an idiot to think tonight would be some kind of magical, fairytale ending to their love affair, and Camille Franklyn would want more from her than a night of frolicking between the sheets.

You should go back. Make her see. Make her understand. Her internal monologue began to run away with itself, urging her to reconsider walking away so easily.

No, what is the point? She has to learn I am not—

She sighed and found herself wandering back to the corner. She turned, and stared back up the street, towards Camille's house, fighting the urge to go back and knock on her door again.

A car crawling along the road, looking for an address, stopped her from moving. A quick look at the registration number and she realised it was her Uber.

"Saved by the cab," she said to herself, and flagged him

down.

THIRTY-NINE

"Another Monday, another night in here?" Sadie said, when Camille sat herself down on a stool and gave a half-hearted wave.

Camille sighed. "I was hoping for a kind face, a long drink, and a listening ear."

Sadie finished wiping the glass clean and placed it on the bar. Picking out an already open bottle of house white from the fridge, she filled the glass and pushed it towards Camille. "Intriguing, do tell."

Camille took the glass and passed over her card, but Sadie waved it off.

"On the house, you look like you need one."

"Great," Camille chuckled, but didn't disagree. "Leila was in here the other night."

"She's the one you have a thing for but won't do anything about?"

Camille ran a hand over her face and groaned. "Unless I've had too many of these."

"Oh. Now we're talking." Sadie leaned on her elbows and gave Camille her full attention.

"I pounced on her, in the—" She shook her head, because it was not something she was proud of, or something she would usually do. "In the toilets."

Sadie laughed. "Well, we've all done that."

"Have we?"

Sadie nodded. "I'd say it's a high percentage, but do go on."

"Nothing happened, but all weekend, I just…I couldn't stop thinking about her, so, I made a decision." She paused to sip the wine. "This morning, I went to her office and invited her over this evening."

Sadie frowned. "So, why are you here? Did she turn you down?"

"Oh no, she came. Dressed to kill like I knew she would." She stared off into space, remembering it.

Chuckling, Sadie clicked her fingers. "And back in the room."

"Sorry."

"That good, huh?"

Camille breathed deeply and nodded. "So good." She managed to at least chuckle. "She asked me why I'd invited her over, and when I said 'to talk', she called me out. She has this innate way of reading me, like my entire being is written across my skin, in a language only she understands."

"She sounds very perceptive, and I can see why that would be very appealing."

"Hm, hugely."

"So, why are you here and not with her, spending a glorious night between the sheets?"

"Because, as attractive as it is, it's also hugely terrifying to have someone be so easily able to undo you, the way she can with me."

Sadie nodded, but remained silent.

"And because I'm an idiot, who didn't have a plan, other than…you know, and I said I hoped we could have an arrangement, and—"

"She told you to do one?"

"About sums it up, yes."

Sadie reached for another glass and poured herself some wine from the same bottle.

"Can I be frank?" she asked Camille.

"I'd prefer that, yes."

"You're looking at this like a business deal. Something you can arrange on your terms that has a beneficial outcome of sorts for both parties, but with you basically being in control… She's not a commodity."

Camille stiffened. "I don't want to own her."

"Don't you? You want her body, but only if it fits within your comfort zone. You want the excitement she brings, but not if it means showing others you enjoy it. You're letting her think she doesn't matter."

Now it was Camille who remained silent.

"Look, I barely know you, but I know people, and every time, you come in here and sit on that stool and talk about her. Either you're sad, or your face lights up. So that tells me, that whatever you have going on in your life that seems intent on ruining this for you, it's not as important as she possibly is."

"She thinks I treat her like a slut."

Sadie's eyes widened. "And do you?"

"Not intentionally, but I can see why maybe she thinks that way."

"I can see that it hurts you."

"Of course it does. I love—"

Sadie's brow raised. "Go on, say it."

Camille swigged her wine and then sighed. "I can't love someone I barely know, can I?"

"Yes, you can," Sadie nodded. "You can meet someone and know in a heartbeat. It's easy to love someone, to fall in love, to be desiring someone. But you've got to find a way to make it work. That's the tricky part." Another customer came up to the bar and Sadie acknowledged them, standing up, ready to go and serve them. "But first, you've got to accept that's what you want to do."

FORTY

"What did she do?" Kristen said slowly, and if Leila really considered it, a little menacingly.

"What makes you think she did anything?" Leila questioned, always feeling a little defensive when it came to discussing Camille, lately.

She listened as Kristen got herself comfortable. Things rustled and clinked as she moved them from the sofa so she could sit down. Leila smiled as she imagined it.

"You went out, dressed to the nines…you did wear the dress, right?"

"I did, yes," Leila confirmed.

"Right, so hot as fuck, and pretty much offering it on a plate, and it's just gone eight, and you're calling me to say you're home safe. So, either she's turned into an absolute ogre overnight, which I highly doubt, or she did something to piss you off."

Leila sighed. "She didn't do anything, and that's the problem."

"What do you mean?"

Leila sat down in one of the garden chairs. She still had three more days before her sofa was delivered. "She wants me, but she hasn't thought about anything other than that. And yes, it would be easy for me to just sleep with her and enjoy it, but… I want more."

"She's an idiot. I'd be snapping you up in a heartbeat."

Leila smiled.

"So, what now?"

"Now, we wait. I made it clear. I am not her plaything, or a slut. If she wants me, she's going to have to come up with a way for that to work."

"Sorry, babe, I know how much she means to you and how excited you were about tonight."

"I know." Leila sighed again. "But it's a step, right? Movement in some direction at least. And I now know I'm not crazy. There is more there between us. I just have to hope she works it out."

"And if she doesn't?"

"I'm not ready to face that option yet," Leila said quietly. "I'm not giving up yet. We had a similar issue in Madeira, and she apologised, and things were better, so…I'll give her time."

"Just…don't let her break your heart, okay?"

"I won't. In fact, you know what I'm going to do now?" She didn't wait for Kristen to answer, just as Kristen knew she didn't need to respond. "I'm going to take this dress to the bar in town and get myself a drink."

"Ooh…on a school night."

Leila laughed. "Well, one won't hurt, and then I'll come home, but at least I won't have dressed up for nothing. Do you even know how much this makeup costs to apply?"

"Unfortunately, I do. I can't afford to get dressed up for a night down at the pub. Special occasions only!" Kristen joined in the light-hearted moment. "Seriously though, if she hurts you, I'm going to kick her in the flange."

FORTY-ONE

To Leila's surprise, it was Camille who was waiting in her office the following morning when she arrived.

"You're late," Camille said, changing her tone when Leila glared at her. "I mean, I was waiting for you and hoped you'd be in earlier so we could talk."

Leila placed her bag on the desk. "You're in my seat."

"Yes. Very observant. It's quite comfortable," Camille said, in the same way Leila had used those words on her.

"The bus didn't turn up," Leila offered instead of anything flirtatious, but she kept her eyes firmly on Camille. She noticed the little extras which had gone into today's ensemble. Her blouse was open, one button more than usual, the smallest amount of pale blue lace peeking from underneath, and a waft of that new, intoxicating perfume.

Camille sighed and stood up, revealing a pencil skirt with stockings and heels, all of which looked like it would rip off quite easily, should Leila be of a mind to indulge her – which she wasn't.

"So, can we talk?" The way she looked at Leila, under any other circumstance, would have had Leila undressing on the spot.

Instead, Leila shrugged. She took her seat and felt the warmth of it. Camille had waited for a long time. She liked that idea, and probably would have smiled, had she not still been annoyed.

"I mean, you're my boss. If that's what you want to pay me to do this Tuesday morning then…"

Camille reeled back and huffed. "For God's sake, are you going to continue intimating I think of you as a—"

"Morning," Pamela said brightly, as she breezed into the room and then froze. "Ms Franklyn, is everything alright? Mr Connor hasn't—"

"Mr Connor is fine, Pamela, I was..." She forced herself to stop staring at Leila and faced Pamela. "I'd like to have a meeting later, with you both, if you can schedule that in. About three?"

"Oh, um, I actually have a meeting already at three—could we do two?" Pamela was already reaching for her diary.

"No, I have a meeting then. It's fine, I'm sure Leila can answer any questions I have and then fill you in later." She turned to Leila. "Three o'clock, Ms Ortez, my office."

She smirked as she turned, and Leila realised she already knew Pamela would be busy. Without another word, Camille sauntered away, leaving Leila a little frustrated, in more ways than one. It was hot as hell the way Camille could move from wanton woman, to frustrated, and straight into ice queen.

Pamela turned her attention to Leila.

"What did she say before I got here?" she asked urgently. "Are we in trouble? Did she mention anything? Anything at all?"

Resisting the urge to roll her eyes, Leila smiled in that friendly manner she had when it came to dealing with people who itched her annoyance buttons.

"No, she just asked where you were and then we talked small talk until you arrived."

"God, of all the days to be late. She noticed, didn't she?"

"I don't think so." Leila shrugged. "I don't know why you feel so nervous around her. She's just a woman."

Pamela stared at her incredulously. "She's Camille

Franklyn, akin to a financial goddess."

She's a goddess alright, Leila thought.

FORTY-TWO

At three o'clock sharp, Leila passed by Fatima's desk.

"I have an appointment," she said to Fatima when Camille's assistant was about to speak. Not waiting for the response, she gripped the door handle and opened it, pushing it wide enough to step inside.

"Wait, you can't just…"

Fatima appeared in the doorway, looking sorrier than a kid who's been put on the naughty step.

Camille was on the phone, and narrowed her eyes in Leila's direction, before turning her attention to Fatima and acknowledging her with a curt nod that meant Fatima understood instantly that she could leave. She quickly turned and closed the door behind her.

Undeterred, Camille continued with her conversation, turning her chair slightly to remove Leila from her line of vision.

"Yes, I understand that, sweetheart," Camille said.

Leila dropped her files on the desk and stood quietly, arms folded across her chest.

"You know you are," Camille added to the mystery conversation. "I'd love to see you. When are you free?" Camille jotted something down. "Okay, I've got to go, love you."

She closed the call and turned slowly back to where Leila was standing. Eyes scanning the scene, she pressed her tongue into the side of her mouth and ran it along her lower set of teeth before, finally, she said, "You're early."

Leila remained silent but glanced at the clock that said, quite clearly, it was exactly three.

"Look, I don't want things to be awkward between us," Camille tried again.

"Then stop making them awkward," Leila said impassively.

Camille nodded; it was a fair point. "You can sit down."

"I haven't decided if I'm staying yet."

Sitting back in her chair, Camille said, "We have a meeting—"

"No, we have a period of time that you have constructed in order to have a conversation," Leila called her out. "And I'm still waiting."

"For what?"

Leila continued to stare at her.

"An apology?" Camille scoffed. They'd been here before, hadn't they? And Camille knew the outcome the last time and how, inevitably, she'd succumbed and fallen to her knees.

"I should go," Leila said, reaching to pick up her folders and files.

A hand stopped her, arm stretched out across the desk. "No, wait...please."

Her eyes glared at Camille, fiery and impulsive, and fighting the urge to react to the touch.

"I'm sorry." Camille spoke the words sincerely. Unlike last time when Leila had had to all but force them out of her. "I'm not like you, Leila. I haven't had to ever...this isn't a relationship I ever considered I'd be involved in."

To speak now would be foolish, Leila considered, so she remained still, quiet, listening. But it hadn't gone unnoticed this was a relationship, as far as Camille was concerned.

"I won't deny I am attracted to you in ways I've not felt

before, and yes, you were right, it scares me, but more than that, I don't know how to be that person I was in Madeira." She finally let go of Leila's hand and stood up, moving around the desk with ease, until she was standing right in front of Leila. "I want so much to be able to just take your hand, to kiss you again. But outside of the bedroom, away from Madeira, I don't know how to navigate it."

Leila felt her eyes begin to moisten. This was the Camille she knew existed. The one she wanted with every fibre of her being. The one whose walls dropped and allowed herself to be vulnerable.

The urge to touch her became overwhelming, and she couldn't fight against it any longer. Her fingertips burned at the touch.

"I want you. I want this, us. To try at least," Leila confirmed.

"I know, I just…I don't want to disappoint you. I don't know what to do." Camille smiled sadly.

Leila shook her head. "You do know, you just don't trust yourself to do it. And you're worried about what anyone else will say."

"You're right, and wrong. I've never cared about opinion. I've always just done whatever the hell I want but this…it feels very different."

Leila stepped in closer. "Because it's not society's norm, and there will be people who reject you, maybe even people you care about?"

"I don't fear rejection from them. I've never cared what people think, and I know I can get over that part, but it's what I think…I can't get past what I think."

"And what do you think?" Leila reached up, touched Camille's chin and used enough pressure for Camille to look at her. "Tell me what you think."

"That I'm a fraud," she whispered. "That I've either lived

a lie all these years, or this is just...someone else I'm playing at being."

Leila chuckled gently. "Sweetie, you're having imposter syndrome over sex?"

Camille smiled at that. "No, I think I'm quite good there." She touched Leila's cheek. "But outside of that, maybe." She nodded. "I was married to a man, who for the most part was loving and kind, but boring, if I'm honest. We had a couple of years of going to business dinners and parties and then we had the boys, and it was all work and family. And then that ended, and I dated a few men, but even then, it was all so... dull, but you..." She breathed deeply. "I can barely be around you without my lungs feeling like they're burning, or without wanting to get naked and let you fuck me to oblivion, and then I think, is that what it is? Is it just sex?"

Leila shook her head gently.

"I know it isn't," Camille admitted. "I want to go out to dinner with you, or for walks in the park, or whatever it is people do nowadays. I just don't know how to navigate it."

"Ask me."

"What?"

"That's the first thing to do. When you're ready, ask me." Leila moved away from her and felt the pull to rush back to her, but she resisted. It had to come from Camille.

"Can we compromise?"

"In what way?" Leila asked, one foot moving closer again, always pulled back to Camille.

Camille mirrored her movement. "Could we...spend time together...privately, just until I get more comfortable with things and then I promise." One more step. "I will show you off to anyone looking."

"That's a big promise to make, Camille."

Closing the space between them, Camille's lips ghosted

across Leila's. "I know."

"The door isn't locked," Leila reminded her, before her own lips were unable to resist the gentle nudging of their counterparts.

"Nobody will come in," Camille replied, her hands now firmly around Leila's waist. "They wouldn't dare."

Leila smiled. "I did."

"Because you dared," Camille answered, before finally, the teasing, playful nipping, pressed more firmly, and Leila sighed and stopped fighting it.

FORTY-THREE

Kissing in her office had been somewhat a new experience for Camille. Of course, over the years, Tom and various boyfriends had visited, and a chaste kiss 'hello' or 'goodbye' might have been exchanged, but nothing like the kiss she'd shared with Leila yesterday.

Even now, thinking about it made her aroused, and left her feeling almost wanton at the possibilities ahead. Could she really be this person she had caught herself imagining she was?

She had no idea how either of them had had the power, or control, to restrain themselves at the time, or since. And now, she couldn't deny the idea of being fucked over her desk wasn't turning her on more than any other thought she'd had in the last six months.

"Penny for them?" Rosie said, chuckling when Camille's cheeks flushed a light pink. "Or should that be something you don't share?"

Camille smiled and looked away, and at the other diners sitting in pairs.

"I was just thinking whether I could…" She pressed her lips together—could she even admit it aloud and to someone other than Leila? She turned back to Rosie and chided herself for such a question. Her best friend was already on her side, no matter what. "I think I want to date Leila."

"Well, halle-fucking-lujah," Rosie laughed. "Finally, the Ice Queen has melted." She raised her glass.

Camille grinned. "I wouldn't go that far."

"So, what did the delightful Leila do, this boring Wednesday, to warrant such a change of mind?"

"She just exists, and I realise, despite all of my efforts otherwise, I can't ignore that." She sipped from her glass of water. "But..."

"Uh oh."

Camille shook her head. "It's not bad, well, no…it's fine, I think. We've talked, and I've asked for time, to get used to 'us', and so I can get my head around this…" She chuckled. "Leila called it 'imposter syndrome', which is probably the best way to explain it."

"You feel like a fraud?"

"Strangely, yes. And it was pointed out to me that maybe I've been treating her like a business endeavour, which is truly awful, and I realised it leaves me feeling something I haven't felt before…"

"And that is?"

"Shame." She blew out her cheeks and then signalled the waiter. "I've never felt that before." As he approached, she said, "Can I get a glass of Merlot?"

"Of course." He almost bowed as he backed away.

When he was out of earshot again, Rosie said, "So, what do you think this shame is about?"

"I don't know, but every time I work out one part of my reticence to be with her, I find something else pops up. I guess maybe I have a subconscious and internalised homophobia, and an absolute fear of failure."

"Okay…I've never known you to be homophobic before," Rosie said.

Camille shrugged. "Well, I've never been gay before."

They'd had a similar conversation back in Madeira, when Camille had been very clear she wasn't saying she was gay, but now…

"So, are we now saying you are gay?"

"We are not saying anything, I am saying…" She paused while the waiter placed her drink down. "I'm saying that… I think it's a strong possibility, which makes no sense to me. How can I have been attracted to men all these years, and now I'm not?"

Now it was Rosie's turn to shrug. "I don't know. But does it matter?"

"Maybe not, I don't know, but what I do know, is that I am not ready to stroll out of the closet wrapped in rainbows and wearing a strap-on."

Rosie roared with laughter. "Please send me a photo when you do."

"I'm not sure we are that close of friends, Rosie," Camille laughed.

"Seriously though, do you think it's possible you're just trying to find reasons to avoid the inevitable?"

"That's possible too," Camille admitted with a sigh. "I know I'm not homophobic. I just—" She glanced at her phone as it beeped. The serious face turned into a smile as she lifted it from the table and swiped the screen.

"Please tell me you've finally used her number?" Rosie grinned as she watched Camille read the text, and once more, her cheeks blushed.

"We've been texting," Camille confessed. She swallowed hard, and then put the phone screen down, pressing her lips together to keep them from saying something they shouldn't.

"That good, huh?" Rosie enquired.

Nodding slowly, Camille said, "I think she might be the death of me."

"Ah, but what a happy death it will be." Rosie raised her glass once more, and this time, Camille met it halfway to gently clink. "Cheers! To younger lovers and lots of hot sex."

FORTY-FOUR

Leila lay back in the bath and laughed to herself. The image she'd sent Camille several minutes ago was relatively decent, if not provocative, for a dull Wednesday evening by herself.

It would definitely get her attention. The blue ticks indicated she'd seen it.

Naked legs, one bent at the knee, both covered in bubbles, with just the hint of bare stomach. The angle of the phone's camera, resting on her chest, might have been tilted just enough to give an illusion of whatever Camille's imagination wanted to conjure up, which was only what she deserved, following the text she'd sent Leila earlier.

She re-read it, aware she would continue reading it, over and over, whenever she needed that little spark of interest in her alone time.

Camille: You make me so aroused. Just kissing you like that causes a reaction in me that requires your attention. I want your hands on my body, your tongue in my mouth, or… if I'm honest, licking my clit. I fantasise about it when I use my fingers to come.

"Jesus, Camille, you have no idea." Leila laughed again and slid her hand down her wet skin, under the water, between her legs, to touch the very place she knew would welcome it.

She was barely into it when a loud rapping on the door made her jump, almost out of her skin. Sitting up, she listened as the knocking continued.

Urgent.

Climbing from the water, she pulled a towel around her and edged her way, into the hallway, towards the door.

"Who is it?" she asked, unaware of anyone who would be visiting her this late at night. Kristen would have called.

"It's me," Camille's voice came from the other side.

Leila grinned, unlocked the door, and opened it quickly. "What are you—"

Camille leered salaciously. "Oh good, I was in time," she said, before lurching forward, taking Leila's face in her palms as she kicked the door closed. "Can I?"

"You have all the permissions you ne—"

Her words were cut off as Camille pressed forward and found Leila's mouth with her own, kissing her hard, her tongue instantly activated.

Leila found herself pushed against the wall, all sense of anything logical leaving her mind and body instantly, as she became consumed by Camille's ambush.

Only when the need to breathe became too much did Camille break away, barely an inch apart, hot breath on her face, eyes locked in.

"I want you," Camille gasped.

"Uh huh, I can see that," Leila chuckled.

Any concerns Leila may have had, dissipated. They couldn't keep saying no to this. It was happening organically, and that was the best way.

She watched as Camille finally realised there was just a towel between them. Her eyes lowered and searched every part of Leila. It felt indecent, and turned her on even more than the kiss had. Being scrutinised by Camille Franklyn was definitely up there in her list of favourite things.

Slowly, Leila let it fall to the floor, watching every minuscule reaction flush across Camille's face, but when Camille reached out to touch, Leila said, *"Non..."*

Camille's eyes flashed annoyance as they moved away from Leila's naked breasts, back up to focus on her eyes.

Questioning.

"Take that off," Leila instructed, pointing to Camille's jacket. "And then those." Her eyes lowered away from Camille's, to stare at the jeans. "And then…" She stepped forward to speak into Camille's ear. "We will see just how aroused you are for me."

FORTY-FIVE

Camille watched the naked backside, and then the trailing towel, disappear into a room a little further down the hall. The only sound was her own jacket landing in a crumpled heap on the floor, and her breath catching in her lungs, as she tried to control the urgent need to strip bare, literally and figuratively.

This was it, wasn't it?

The moment she stepped into her new true self again and allowed Leila to see her, all of her; not just the nakedness, but the depths of her wants and needs.

No backing out. She had to embrace it all, or risk losing it all.

She felt frozen to the spot.

With no idea how long she'd stood there, it was only Leila's voice that broke her from her thoughts.

"Are you going to keep running, Camille?" Still naked, Leila casually walked back down the hallway and stood in front of her.

"Probably, yes," Camille answered honestly, but she didn't move away. "I'm here, aren't I?" She softened, as though preparing herself.

"You are, yes." Leila smiled.

They were less than a foot apart, still reachable, but

Leila held back, and it was maybe the hardest thing she'd ever done.

She wanted to launch herself towards Camille, physically and mentally; to tell her how she was falling for her, and how much she wanted her, but that would be a mistake.

"I—"

"You?" Leila's smile grew, a playful twinkle in her eyes, as she watched Camille search for words. "You came here, remember?"

For a second, Camille closed her eyes, but when they opened again, she smiled back. "I'm unable to ignore you."

"Well, that's kind of good for me, no?" The smiling continued.

"It's dangerous, that's what it is," Camille responded, a sense of urgency in her voice, as though Leila must be a complete fool to not understand why, even though she wanted this, it was so nerve-wracking for her.

Leila scoffed. "It's passion. Wild. Intense even. But dangerous?" Her eyes narrowed at Camille, and the smile lingered, and this time, she risked reaching out a hand, just her fingertips barely touching. "No. Not dangerous."

"For you maybe, for me, it's…this is—"

Leila stepped closer. "You…came…here," she said again, a little more quietly.

Her other hand rose, fingertips reaching until she was touching skin with both hands, connecting them like an electrical circuit, allowing the current to flow from one to the other.

Camille's bare arm bore flesh that puckered like a cool breeze had blown over it, but in reality, burned to the touch.

"I want to know you, Camille, every part of you, raw and

untethered." She whispered the words drunken Camille had used. "Will you let me?"

Camille sagged. "I don't think I can stop you."

Leila grinned, stepped back, and looked her over.

"So, why are you still wearing clothes and not naked in my bed?"

"Sorry, I just had—" She laughed at herself. "I get all brave and then—"

"It's going to take time, I know. And this is why you need this space to get...comfortable, no?"

Camille nodded. "You always read me so well."

"Hm." Leila danced a finger along Camille's clavicle. "Well, I was reading something else earlier...a certain text message?" The fingers danced lower, and then her palm flattened out, as she said, "I think you said, you want my hands on your body..."

"Your tongue in my mouth, yes," Camille answered for her. She took a deep breath. "I do want you."

"I know."

Camille reached for the hem of her t-shirt and pulled it up and over her head, unbuttoning her jeans, as Leila now leaned with one naked shoulder against the wall, and watched.

She was thankful she'd showered and changed after work before meeting Rosie. The underwear choice was clearly a winner.

Lilac lace – matching, of course.

"Leave that on," Leila suggested, her finger pointing. "Yes, leave that...mm." She stepped forward. "Let's go." She took Camille's hand and walked backwards down the last part of the hallway, leading her into a small bedroom with a double bed and furniture that matched. "I've missed you."

"You saw me this afternoon."

"No." Leila shook her head. "I have missed *you*." And Camille understood she meant: sex, intimacy. She'd missed *them*.

"Me too. Nobody else has—"

Leila pressed a finger to her lips and glared. "Do not tell me about anyone else."

"Okay, sorry, I just figured you'd—"

"No. Not one since you." Leila stepped closer, their bodies touching, thigh to thigh, stomach to stomach, breast to breast. "Not one. I was…I am…consumed by you and only you."

Leila smiled, as she realised that admission had just triggered something in Camille – something that turned her on. She grasped Leila's wrist and pulled her hand between her own legs.

"Wet?" Camille asked, as they kept their eyes on one another. She watched the fire burn between them. "You make me like that."

Leila growled, "Get on the bed."

FORTY-SIX

Camille got comfortable.

Her head rested easy on a pillow, arms upstretched beneath it, her knees bent and together until Leila knelt on the mattress, and instinctively, they fell open and welcomed her lover to come closer.

"So eager." Leila smiled, leaning over her and pulling a pillow free. "Lift," she demanded, and tapped Camille's hip.

When Camille thrust up, Leila slid the pillow beneath her.

"What do we need that for?" she asked, just as Leila climbed back off the bed.

With a wicked grin, Leila inched away, dropping down to her knees to reach under the bed and pull out a small box. It was nothing fancy, just one of those cardboard ones that had been covered in a thin material and had a matching lid.

Camille leaned over the edge to watch, fascinated with anything this woman might do next.

Lifting the lid, Leila grinned up at Camille, before she reached inside and moved a few things out of the way.

"Do you remember in Madeira, you asked me for something…" She glanced up quickly. "And I didn't have it?"

Remembering the day, Camille smiled slowly, as Leila's hand lifted, holding a thin leather belt-like contraption and a phallic toy with a disc shape on the end.

"Oui?"

Camille bit her lower lip and considered it for all of two seconds. "Yes. Absolutely." She scrambled to sit upright and watch, as Leila held it up to work out which way around it went on.

"Now, you will have to be patient, because I am, by no means, an expert with this, okay?" Leila said in a slightly warning tone, a little vulnerable, something Camille had never heard from her before.

"You don't have to—"

"I know. I want to. Pleasing you is…I like it." She lifted one leg through a hoop. "But not many of my previous lovers were into it, so…" She shrugged the loop up her leg and then reached behind for the part that was un-looped, and soon to be looped around her other thigh and waist.

"I don't know what I actually expected, but this isn't it." Camille chuckled.

Leila frowned. "You don't like it?"

"Oh, I'm all about exploring it. It's just not what—actually, I don't know what I imagined it would look like." She reached out and took the phallus in her hand, testing the weight and feel of it. "Sturdy."

Leila laughed. "Hm-hm, trust me, I won't be needing to get my breath back and wait until it goes hard again." She took it from Camille's hands and expertly slotted it into place, laughing as it jiggled around. "Can you believe men want to be taken seriously with one of these bobbing around?"

Camille grinned as she took hold of it in her hand once more and pulled Leila forward.

"Just…" Camille's tongue slid across her lower lip. "I really think you…I want you inside me."

Leila nodded. "There's nothing I want more right now. To be connected so…intimately. So, if you could…" She shooed her comically to move her back up the bed.

With one knee on the mattress, ready to follow Camille, her lover said a sudden, "Wait."

Leila stepped back off the bed and frowned.

"What's wrong?" she asked, fearing a sudden bout of running again from Camille.

Instead, Camille moved as gracefully as she could, until she was off the bed and standing beside Leila. "I had a little fantasy, the day I asked you about it, back in Madeira."

Amused now, Leila said, "Okay, go on."

Without another word, Camille turned back to the mattress, pulled the pillow over and bent at the waist, her arms out flat, on either side of the pillow, as she lay on top of it.

"From behind?" Leila said, already sliding the lace down her thighs. "Alright, are you still—"

"Yes, soaked," Camille said. Unclipping her bra, she raised up quickly and dropped it to the floor. "Fuck me, like you mean it."

FORTY-SEVEN

Men were always so eager. Eager to get naked, eager to get hard, and eager to fuck her quickly, get off, and then collapse as though they'd just accomplished something monumental Camille should be telling her girlfriends about for years to come.

In their dreams.

For decades, she had settled for that. Tolerated it, because that was just how it was, and she was lucky enough to be getting any kind of sexual intimacy at all.

But this, with Leila, was nothing of the sort.

She'd widened her stance, readied herself for it, but it didn't come. There was no pushing and grabbing and thrusting. Instead, she felt the delicate brush of lips against the small of her back. Soft palms, smoothing over her skin, from her backside, up her spine. Into her hair, gripping just enough to tug at the follicles, before releasing and slinking away, never breaking contact, teasing her nerve endings and heightening her senses.

"You know…" Leila's voice, her accent, it all added to the sensuality of it. "I like when you're compliant."

Camille whimpered.

"When you're a good girl, you know that?"

Camille couldn't find her voice, swallowing harder, to liberate her tongue enough to mumble something that let Leila know she heard and understood.

Her body jerked as Leila leaned over her. The phallus rubbed softly between the cheeks of her backside.

"You like that, don't you?" Leila continued. "Letting yourself comply, and be led."

God, she could read her like a book.

Camille nodded – her face almost squashed against the mattress, as Leila's weight pressed against her again.

Hands squeezed beneath to cup her breasts. Leila's lips kissed her shoulder. Her hips moved just enough to remind Camille what was coming.

"I want to hear you. To watch your fingers grip the bedsheets."

"Yes," Camille finally uttered, groaning when Leila lifted, and air filled the space between them.

She listened and heard the sound of something familiar, but she couldn't place it. Camille tossed a quick glance over her shoulder and watched, as Leila squeezed something liquid into her hand and smiled at her.

"There's wet, and then there's..." She held the bottle up. *Liquid Silk.*

Camille sighed.

She wanted Leila close. To feel her skin against skin. Relaxing, she tried to focus, once more, forehead resting against the pillow.

Soft hands took hold of her again, and she arched into it, needing more. And then she felt it: the nudged between her legs. The tip pressed against her for entrance and slid into her, in one smooth move of Leila's hips and just the right amount of pressure.

The gratification that surged through her body in that moment was like nothing she'd felt before in this position.

Camille grunted her approval. She pushed back, wanting to feel more of it, or Leila, inside of her, but she couldn't move. A firm hand pressed down on her back; another gripped her right hip.

Leila had full control of her pleasure now, and Camille was content to let her have it and wanted her to take it. To deny her or please her – it was all Leila's choice now.

Slow thrusts.

The angle.

Pressure holding her in place.

All of it excited her more than she'd ever imagined would be possible.

Hearing herself make sounds she'd never heard before, it was all so surreal. Guttural – literally from the depths of her – and a place she'd never connected with, before now.

"Fuck, yes. Harder." She heard herself speak in a way that suggested she would beg, not demand. "Please…so good."

The pressure on her back eased, replaced by hands on both hips. Her flesh squeezed between strong fingers, as now she was pushed and pulled, her body jerking with every delicious thrust, the speed not changing. Still a slow, a focused movement, just more intense now. Skin hit skin in a rhythmic, slap, slap, slap.

She could feel it forming, her muscles spasming, contracting, releasing, contracting. From the corner of her eye, she saw her fingers gripping the sheet, and she almost laughed at the way Leila knew her every move before she made it.

Camille pushed up with her hands. Half upright on one palm, she reached for Leila's hand, brought it away from her hip, and pushed it against her breast. The movement brought Leila closer, bent over Camille's back.

A rhythm of "Uh, uh, uh, uh," spilled out from her. "Faster."

Leila complied.

Both hands moved to cover both breasts now, curved over her. Camille held herself up on her palms, like a dog on heat, the angle of the thrust changing just slightly.

Camille closed her eyes and let the pleasure take her somewhere...Leila's voice drifted away, as she encouraged and cajoled Camille to let it all go.

All that mattered was reaching the summit. The muscles in her arm shook, and she fell forward onto her elbows, Leila falling on top of her.

"Let me hear you," was the last thing Camille heard before her body erupted into climax. Jerking and twisting, writhing, lustful and wanton, she cried out something unintelligible. She went limp, and she flopped against the pillow, the weight of Leila on top of her, inside her.

Everything just...Leila.

FORTY-EIGHT

Leila lay on her side, head resting on one elbow, staring at the naked body now lying alongside her. Sated and relaxed, she breathed deeply and smiled, as she considered the way Camille had feasted on her moments earlier.

That wasn't the only adjective she could think of to fit what it was – a devouring, all-consuming banquet of lips and tongue on her pussy. Her clit throbbed again, just thinking about it.

"I take it, by the way you're smiling, that that wasn't too much?" Camille asked, playfully grinning at her.

"Hm, intense, powerful. Utterly delicious...never *too* much." Her hand reached forward and touched Camille's stomach. "Maybe I didn't quite anticipate just how much you missed eating—"

"You," Camille said. "Eating you."

Leila's face broke out into a grin. "And now, tomorrow, I have to walk around as though that never happened."

Camille sat up, glancing at the clock. "Sweetheart, I can barely walk. Do you think it will be simple for me too?"

"You could just announce it at the next meeting," Leila grinned.

"When I'm ready, maybe I will, but right now, work needs to remain a space where I can—"

Leila touched Camille's cheek. "I know. I'm okay with it...for now." She winked.

"I don't know how to navigate this," Camille said. They lay wrapped up in one another, spent and not quite exhausted. It wouldn't be long before that moment faced them both.

"What do you mean?" Leila asked, leaning up on one elbow.

"This...it's not just sex now, is it?"

Leila smiled down at her. "No, it isn't."

"So, I don't know—"

"How to navigate it, I heard you." She kissed her slowly. "And I'll help you."

"I'm not sure your idea of help will *help*." Camille smirked playfully.

"Oh, and you know what my idea is?" Leila climbed on top of her and pressed down, rubbing her clit firmly against the softness of Camille's stomach.

"I have a good—"

Leila leaned forward and pressed a finger to her lips, and then she let it slide down to lift her chin.

"I'm going to sit on your face, and you're going to make me come. That is your punishment for being so assumptious."

Camille's eyes widened. "I can be more *presumptuous*."

"Are you correcting my English?" Leila laughed as she moved higher. What she didn't expect was for Camille to hold her hips and twist them until she was now on top, lying between Leila's legs.

"I'm being serious."

"So am I." Leila stroked her face and sighed. "We go slowly."

"Define slowly?" Camille asked, rolling off and lying on her back again so they could talk.

Leila turned onto her side, resting her hand on Camille's still naked torso, her fingertips lightly moving. "For a start, this is between us. Nobody else needs to know right now."

Camille sat up, pushed a pillow behind her and pulled the sheet over them both. "In Madeira, you wanted everyone to see you. What's changed?"

Mirroring her movement, Leila sat up and crossed her legs like a child sitting on the floor, the sheet falling away.

"There...it was just you and I. I didn't care about strangers and their opinions. I just wanted...I wanted you to see me for more than a fling. To pretend for a few days that this beautiful, successful woman saw something in me she wanted to show off." She shook her head and sighed. "I don't hide in this world. I refuse to be small, but I understand now, that I can't force that on others, that I have to meet you where you are, and we travel the path together."

"Thank you. Work is just—" She shrugged before she leaned closer, and pressed a kiss to Leila's lips. "Speaking of which, I need to go."

"No, you can stay." Leila sulked a little.

"As much as that face does turn me on a little, no, I cannot. And you need to get some sleep."

As if on cue, Leila yawned.

"Can I see you at the weekend?" Camille asked, standing up and searching for her underwear.

Leila rolled onto her back and watched as Camille slowly redressed. "That would be nice. What would you like to do?"

Camille smirked. "This?" She sat down on the edge of the bed in her underwear and leaned closer. "And I was thinking maybe dinner? I could cook, or bring something here." She glanced around the room again. "Here, I think."

"That would be lovely."

"And I will be home...alone..." Camille walked her fingers along Leila's thigh. "Pretty much for the rest of the week."

"Are you inviting me over, or are we playing a game?" Leila asked seriously.

Camille huffed and sat up. "I'm trying to be playful and show you that I want to see you."

Leila smiled. "Okay, I can do playful, just as long as you remember I like it when you're explicit about what you want and need."

The quiet whimper was audible enough.

"Understood," Camille said, as she stood up again. "I think my clothes are in the hall, so..."

Leila climbed from the bed and walked around it, to the back of the door, where she retrieved a silk dressing gown and slid it on.

She slipped out of the door and returned a moment later carrying the pile of clothes, holding them out for Camille to take.

"Thank you," Camille said, taking them from her. She seemed to hesitate for a moment. "To be clear, I don't want to leave. I'm doing so because it's the practical thing to do with tomorrow being a workday." She pulled her t-shirt on first.

"Of course." Leila's lips curled upwards, just enough. "I don't have to like it."

"Maybe at the weekend, I can stay overnight?"

"The option is there should you want to take it, but there is no pressure. We agreed to take things slowly and my petulance can be ignored."

Zipping her jeans, Camille said, "Your petulance might be a little of what I enjoy about you."

"Then I should do my best to avoid you all day tomorrow while I petulantly wander around, turned on, and unable to satisfy my urge to come into your office and—"

Camille placed her finger to Leila's lips. "Hold that thought. The time will come when I shall want exactly that."

"Don't tease me."

"Why not? You've been teasing me since you arrived." Camille smiled. "Don't think I didn't notice."

"Oh, I know you noticed. I also know you enjoy it."

"I'm not sure 'enjoy' is the word I'd use." She lifted her jacket and shrugged it on. "I would really appreciate if you could avoid teasing me at work when other people are around."

Leila leaned in and kissed her. "I'll do my best."

FORTY-NINE

Leila closed the door behind her, but didn't quite push it completely closed, as she listened to the sound of Camille's heels tap away into the distance.

Camille's footsteps stopped at the lifts. A sharp ding a few moments later and then the last steps before the doors slid closed and silence took over. That was when Leila pressed firmly, until the lock clicked into place, and she turned and walked barefoot down the hall.

Back to the bedroom where just moments ago, Camille had been naked between her sheets.

Leila leaned against the doorframe and studied the room: sheets tossed around where they'd been thrown back. Sex toys on the floor. The strap-on pointing up towards the ceiling like a triumphant arm raised after scoring a goal.

She laughed to herself as she moved around the room, picking up the toys to wash quickly.

It was all falling into place, wasn't it? Camille's turnaround had been quicker than she'd anticipated, but she wouldn't complain. There would be backward steps, she was sure of it, but still, this evening had been a pretty good indication of things to come.

Camille's perfume lingered in the room. Those sheets would carry the scent too, she imagined...hoped.

She slid the robe off, hung it on the back of the door again, and headed for the bathroom.

She needed a shower.

The bath water was still in the tub, so she emptied it. Sluicing warm water around it to clean out the last remnants of bubbles, she rinsed clean the toys, while the shower heated up a little.

Catching sight of herself in the mirror before it steamed up, she noticed the way her face had settled into a happy place.

She gave a little squeal and clapped her hands together.

"Oh my God." She laughed as she stepped into the shower. She could indulge in her enjoyment for just a little while, couldn't she? "Maybe dreams do come true."

For the second time that night, Leila wrapped a towel around herself. This time, there was no knock at the door. She wandered into the kitchen and poured a glass of water, taking it with her back to the bedroom. She dried off quickly and pulled a sleep shirt on.

It was feeling chilly in the room now that the heating had switched off, and her body had come back down to earth, somewhat.

Picking up her phone to set an alarm, she noticed a new message, and smiled as the screen came to life and Camille's name flashed up.

Camille: Home. Thank you for indulging me this evening. I am aware I am a walking bag of mixed messages lately, I want to fix that.

Camille: P.S. I can still feel you…

Leila noted the time when Camille had sent the messages and when she was last online. It was only minutes ago.

Leila: We will fix it together.

Leila: P.S. I encourage sweet dreams.

She climbed under the covers and got comfortable, breathing in the scent of Camille, and their lovemaking. Though, she could hardly call it that. Frenzied and intense, maybe.

Her phone beeped.

Camille: I'm not sure I'll sleep. All I can think of is… everything.

Leila: Then focus only on the positive things.

Camille: I will try. Goodnight x

Leila replied with a single kiss before closing the phone and placing it back onto the bedside cabinet. She snuggled down and switched the light off.

Lying in the darkness, she could almost pretend Camille was there with her.

FIFTY

Regardless of being tired, Camille rose with a spring in her step she hadn't anticipated. Expecting to be exhausted with the workout, lack of sleep, and the overstimulation of all of her senses, she'd assumed today would be an avoid-all-at-all-costs kind of day.

But she was happy.

A feeling, she realised, she hadn't felt in a long while, despite telling herself to the contrary. But then she realised, that was a lie. She'd been happy just a few months ago – in Madeira.

She showered, dressed, and even managed to warm a croissant before leaving the house and driving herself to the office, singing along to the radio.

Her phone beeped and the message appeared on the screen on the dashboard.

Leila.

Camille pressed the button on the steering wheel that would have the robotic voice read it out to her, and then offer her the opportunity to respond.

Leila: Good morning. I hope you are feeling refreshed and satisfied this morning. Coffee? X

"Would you like to reply?"

Camille smiled. "Yes." She paused until it was ready and then she said, "I would love a coffee, and to see you, but I think maybe that is a bad idea. Because I need to be focused for meetings all morning, and I can't do that if you've distracted me. Kiss."

She drove on, the radio playing again as she hummed along.

Leila: I will make sure it is delivered by someone unappealing then. Enjoy your day, beautiful. X

Camille laughed. "Beautiful? The little charmer."

She didn't respond. Instead, she focused on driving and bringing her libido back into a normal range – not something she'd had to ever deal with at work before. There had been staff members she'd found attractive in the past, but never enough to risk letting them take her bed.

Imagine it. She laughed.

At least they'd all been closer to her own age. That was something she still hadn't quite gotten her head around. In bed with Leila, it didn't matter. She was mature, smart, and fun; all the things anyone looked for in a partner.

A partner? She hadn't really processed that part yet, either, but she couldn't deny it was what she had expressed she wanted.

She pulled the car into her space and switched off the engine. Twelve years; that was the difference in age between them. Was that really such a big deal? *She's going to be forty soon. That makes it pretty much okay, doesn't it? Is it even questionable?*

Looking at herself in the rear-view mirror, she exhaled. She didn't look fifty-two, did she? She didn't look forty either, but then neither did Leila. Maybe that was why the age gap felt so big. She poked at her face. A few lines here and there, and some grey hairs, making themselves known with each visit to the salon. But still, she didn't look old, not like her mother had at this age.

"Stop questioning everything and just let yourself enjoy it," she said to herself, before realising she was being watched by a confused-looking Pamela, who clearly wasn't sure if she was being spoken to.

Camille smiled at her, and almost laughed at the expression on Pamela's face, as it morphed between one of shock, excitement, and then panic.

A deer in the headlights.

"Good morning, Pamela," Camille said, as she pushed the door open and stepped out of the car.

"Ms Franklyn, good morning. I was just heading to… coffee?"

Camille thought of Leila arranging that already.

"Thank you for the offer, but I think I'm good." She checked her watch. "And you have a meeting this morning with Mr Connor's group again, correct?"

"I do, yes." Pamela nodded furiously. "I'll be… Yes, maybe I'll leave the coffee and—"

Camille sighed. Was there nobody, other than Leila, with a backbone in this company? All were great at their jobs; she couldn't complain about that.

"For the love of God, Pamela, get a coffee. You are not beholden to my whim every moment of the day." Camille walked off in the direction of the building, leaving Pamela to decide if today was the day she might actually make a decision not based on what she thought Camille wanted.

FIFTY-ONE

Camille smiled brighter when she entered her office and found the coffee cup from her favourite coffee shop on her desk, sat on top of a piece of paper to stop it marking the wood.

She lifted the cup and laughed as she realised what Leila had done. Beneath where the cup had sat was a perfect ring, drawn with a blue ink pen. Leila had used the circumference of the cup to draw around, and then inside the circle, hidden from any potential prying eyes, she'd written: Tomorrow night? I'll come to you. Lx

Her phone buzzed. Meeting at 8:00 a.m. Maddox account, New York, Connor update.

She slid the sheet of paper into her drawer, picked up her coffee, and headed for the meeting room.

Leila walked casually along the corridor beside Pamela. She felt her heart race as Camille stepped out of her office and glanced at them both. She felt sure that just for a second, Camille smiled, but then her piercing blue eyes focused on something else.

"I see you grew some balls, Pamela," Camille said, before striding off in the direction they were all headed.

Leila turned to Pamela. "What was that about?"

Blushing profusely, Pamela held her coffee aloft. "I think she's referring to my getting coffee."

Leila frowned. That made no sense, but she didn't push it. Instead, she smiled to herself when, up ahead, Camille lifted her own cup to take a sip.

They were only a handful of steps behind, but when they entered the room, Camille was already seated, back ramrod straight in her chair, eyes watching like a hawk, as each member of staff required to be there arrived.

All of them, on time, and prepared.

"Good, we're all here," Camille began. Her eyes glanced briefly in Leila's direction before they settled on the other side of the room.

A week ago, Leila would have enjoyed making her squirm. Now though, there was no need, was there? Certainly not, if last night was anything to go by.

"Ms Ortez, are you with us, or daydreaming about something you'd like to share with the room?" Camille's voice was somewhat icy, and yet, the slight upturn of her lips suggested she knew exactly what Leila was thinking about.

"Sorry, I was just thinking about a position I need to fully attend to later."

"I see. Well, right now, I'd like your full attention on me. Am I clear?" Camille said, daring her to say otherwise.

Not that she would.

She was being given permission to openly admire. Camille's way of proving, just a little, she wanted this; wanted her.

Even if it was still too soon to throw herself, full force, out of the closet. And a little confusing after the whole 'please don't tease me at work' speech last night. But Leila accepted that unexpectedly, Camille would flip and flop as she worked through what she was comfortable with, and Leila would have to find a way to deal with it.

Something was definitely switching in Camille Franklyn, wasn't it?

"Of course, my apologies," Leila said, realising the tables had just been turned, and it was she who was now squirming a little. *Well played, Camille,* she thought, as she turned in her chair and stared directly at her lover.

"So, Pamela. Bring me up to speed with the Connor situation." Camille let her eyes settle on Leila as she spoke to Pamela.

"Uh, yes." Pamela stood up. "Everything is running smoothly. We've made several suggestions of where we feel money can be saved, while moving into a more cohesive structure Connor Holdings can work with without a further —"

"So, you can finish that off and free up Ms Ortez, yes?" Camille interrupted.

Pamela swivelled her attention to Leila, who shrugged. She had no idea what Camille was going to suggest, but she was equally intrigued.

"Yes, I guess that would be—"

"Good," Camille said, instantly stopping Pamela in her tracks. She turned back to Leila. "I need someone to oversee a new account that's coming onboard. I want you to liaise with Jack Maddox and his team. I have a meeting with him later to find out what they are expecting going forward, with Franklyn Financials at the helm, and then you will take over. I will then expect a report on my desk by the end of next week."

Leila jotted everything down.

Looking up at Camille, she couldn't hide the smile. "And you'll handle the initial—"

"Of course, I'll email it over. As soon as we are done here, I have a meeting with him." With that, she stood up and picked up her things from the desk. "Any other business?" she asked, and when nobody spoke up, "Then don't let me keep you. Time is money, as they say."

She didn't stop to talk with anyone, leaving the office in a cloud of subtle perfume and an air of icy disregard, and Leila could not deny just how hot it was.

"So, you've been here all of five minutes and you've already been given a star account option?" Pamela stood, arms crossed, and looking a lot more than a little put out.

"I don't even know who this Jack Maddox is. It could be a complete—"

"Jack Maddox is one of the biggest names in local business. His account has been at the top of the 'get list' for over two years, and you stroll in here, and it's just yours?"

"I really don't think—"

"I do. I think something very fishy is going on and I will get to the bottom of it," Pamela warned.

Glancing over her shoulder, Leila saw something more concerning. Camille stood in the doorway, eyes wide as she listened to Pamela.

"Honestly, if you were a man, I'd think you were sleeping with her."

Camille turned and bolted out.

"And much more of this, and I will speak to Vincent about your language. I am here because I have a CV that warranted the job, and if Ms Franklyn has asked me to do a job, I'm going to do it, regardless of what you, or anyone else, thinks is happening." Leila snatched up her files and phone. "And maybe, if you actually stopped pussyfooting around her, and just did your job to the best of your abilities, you'd probably find her more interested in moving you forward." She took two steps and then stopped, shoulder-to shoulder with

Pamela. "Grow a pair."

FIFTY-TWO

Leila wanted to waltz right into Camille's office, hold her, and tell her everything was fine.

But she didn't.

That would be the last thing Camille needed right now. To be confronted by the very thing she panicked most about, and they were nowhere near to telling anyone. This was just a flippant remark, made by a jealous co-worker in the heat of the moment, but it was near the mark, and that stung too deeply.

"Leila, wait up," Pamela called after her.

She came to a stop but refused to turn around. She forced Pamela to walk around and face her.

"I'm sorry. You're right, that was uncalled for and absolutely out of order on my part. I would never suggest that, even if you were a man. I just lost my—"

"Integrity?" Leila snarked. "Because I have mine. I don't earn jobs by sleeping with the boss." She added a curt, "Thank you."

"No, of course not. I'm sorry, I just... I've worked so bloody hard to get her attention and, finally, she handed me the Connor report and I figured I was on my way, especially when I was given an assistant. You know?" Pamela looked contrite, at least. "And we've done such a fantastic job, I just assumed I would be the one she praised with a shot at Maddox."

"Stand up to her," Leila said quietly. "Don't be an arse,

but don't let her push you around. Stop letting her boss you about. When you know you're right, call her on it."

"I couldn't do that, she's—"

"She wants people with the balls to do whatever it takes, and that includes putting her in her place," Leila insisted.

Pamela frowned. "How do you know all that?"

Leila shrugged. "I just read people well." She took Pamela by the elbow and guided her to the side of the corridor, away from listening ears. "Go in there and tell her why you're the best person for the Maddox gig."

If Pamela's eyes could bug any further, they'd have popped right out of their sockets.

"Look, you want it. I don't care." She shrugged again. "So, go in there, and explain why she's wrong, and that you are the better fit for this."

"What if she says no or sacks me?"

"She's not going to fire you. You're one of her best staff members. She's going to listen, and then make the best business decision, and that will be aided by the fact you grew a pair and forced the issue." When Pamela didn't say anything, Leila pulled her around and pushed her towards Camille's office. "Go on."

"I can't—"

"You don't get anywhere by being timid. You want to be like her?"

Pamela nodded.

"Then be like her!"

Something about those words clicked with Pamela. She seemed to grow an inch taller, puffing her chest out as she nodded. "You're right." And then she turned and marched towards Camille's office.

FIFTY-THREE

Fatima pressed the 'call through' button to Camille's office, and when Camille answered, she said, "Ms Franklyn, Pamela Naysmith would like a quick—"

"Send her in," Camille said curtly. She did not have time for impromptu meetings. Still, she was intrigued to hear what Ms Mousey wanted, especially having overheard the conversation with Leila. She'd process that afterward, but right now, she was in work mode.

A moment later the door crept open and Pamela appeared, only she didn't look quite so timid.

"Make it quick, I have an important phone call in five minutes," Camille said as abruptly as anyone would expect.

"Yes, thank you for seeing me at such short notice. I just wanted—"

Camille sat back and stared at her with the icy glare she saved for these kinds of conversations. She found it got rid of them a lot more quickly than if she placated them.

For once though, it didn't appear to be having the effect she usually witnessed. Pamela stepped forward, right up to the edge of her desk.

"I wanted to say I think it would be a mistake for Leila to take on the Maddox account, if there is to be one. She's very adept, and I am sure, that over time, she will make a perfect lead on any business Franklyn Financials wanted to work with, but right now, I believe I'm the best candidate. I understand who Jack Maddox is, what his business is about, and I already have a plan written up ready, as I anticipated it might be a deal we would get to consider. And so—"

Camille raised her hand. *Well, well,* she thought. *Someone finally found a spine.*

"Do you think Ms Ortez is competent to complete the Connor deal without you?"

Pamela nodded. "I do, yes. Like I said, she's very adept at what she does—"

"Fine." Camille picked up her pen and began making a note. "Tell Ms Ortez you're taking over the Maddox file and she's to complete the Connor deal."

If Pamela was surprised, she held it together well.

"Thank you, I won't let you down." She turned to head towards the door.

"Pamela?" Camille said, not looking up.

"Yes, Ms Franklyn."

Now Camille stopped writing and gave Pamela her attention. "In future, I want to hear what you have to say at the meeting, not ten minutes after. Speak up." She picked up her pen again. "That will be all."

Only now did Pamela allow herself a small grin. She opened the door and stepped out, doing a quick fist pump, much to Fatima's amusement. "Sorry," she mouthed to the receptionist, and headed for the last door and out into the corridor.

"Well?" Leila said, waiting for her outside.

"She said you're to finish the Connor account and I am to take over the Maddox file." She couldn't hold in the urge to grin any longer. "You were right. I walked in, pleaded my case, and she didn't even question it."

"See, I told you. Be like her."

Pamela nodded.

"Without the iciness, though, no?" Leila laughed.

FIFTY-FOUR

Jack Maddox was a man of wealth, power, and entitlement; at least, that was what the grapevine said. Camille didn't like the grapevine gossip, per se, but it did often have an element of truth behind it, which gave her a heads-up on who she might be dealing with.

He certainly looked the part: smart suit, clean shirt, cufflinks - not buttons. He didn't wear a tie, but a casual, button-undone style that worked for him, as he lounged in the seat opposite her.

"So, Jack…what can Franklyn Financials help you with?"

"Initially, I'm looking for investors. I want to expand the company and, in all honesty, I don't want to use my money to do it." He smiled, and she could imagine that in his day, he was a charmer.

He was still attractive now, despite the balding head and slight paunch that was developing. A month ago, and he might have held her interest for all of two minutes, because what he said next fully ended that.

"I've recently become a father again." He pulled a face that said, 'I know.' "The joys, apparently, of having a younger partner, but it's given me food for thought about the company, and where I see it headed and my part in it all. I've four other children, all adults, who show absolutely no interest in taking it on, and I feel like…" He sighed. "I should take a leaf out of my ex-wife's book and start enjoying the life I have." He laughed. "Before I keel over."

Camille smiled. "Your ex-wife has it all figured, does she?"

Jack nodded. "God, yes. Married to my eldest daughter… that's a story for another time. Obviously, Claudia isn't Scarlett's mother," he added in quickly.

But Camille wasn't listening. She'd gotten stuck on the fact that his ex-wife was married to a woman.

"Really? You're going to drop that little bombshell and not explain it?" she urged.

Sitting forward, legs spread, elbows on knees, he grinned. "I was a naughty boy in my heyday. Scarlett was conceived before I married Claudia. We then had three kids, as you do." He sat back again, relaxed, and clearly comfortable telling the story. "Then we got divorced because Claudia finally saw sense and kicked me to the kerb…" The grin returned. A naughty schoolboy. "She met Scarlett in a bar, one thing led to another, and, turned out, Scarlett went to uni with our eldest Diana too. Strange how the universe works, isn't it?"

"Yes…it is," Camille said slowly as she processed it all. "And they didn't mind? This big change in their mother's life?"

"I think the young'uns nowadays are quite receptive to it, encourage it even. It's why I tend to employ a younger staff now. They view the world differently to how we did."

"So, you didn't mind, Claudia? Swinging the other way and with someone so much…" She tried to calculate roughly. "Younger?"

"I guess my ego took a little dent, but honestly, I only have to look at them together to know she's made the best choice for herself."

Camille remained silent, and Jack studied her for a moment, but if he thought anything, he didn't say it aloud. The smile said enough. And she wasn't going to spill her guts and tell him all about Leila, but she couldn't deny she felt something settle more calmly in her.

Perhaps sensing her unease, he said, "So, what I want to do is find the right investors, and then, eventually, put a management plan in place so I can take a back seat and semi-retire."

Camille nodded. "I think we can definitely help you achieve that." She picked up the phone and dialled a number. "Can you come to my office?"

"I've heard good things about you," Jack said.

"I'm not surprised," Camille answered honestly. "We work hard to make sure we are the best at what we do."

"I think you actually worked with Claudia's firm."

Camille thought for a moment. She was sure she didn't know any Claudias.

"Oh, not her, I mean, she doesn't own the company." He laughed. "No, the big hotel group over in Bath Street, she works for them, goes all over the world setting up new hotels. Remarkable really, but yes, I think you helped them set up their financial investors."

"We did, yes." Camille nodded but said nothing further. Integrity meant she wouldn't discuss another business's dealings.

"Maybe you should have a chat with her sometime." His suggestion was gentle but implied anything but work.

"I don't know that that would be appropriate."

Jack was about to speak again when a knock on the door stopped him. He turned slightly, and watched as a thin woman came in, looking all expectantly at Camille.

"Ms Naysmith, this is Jack Maddox. Jack, Pamela Naysmith. She's going to be heading up your account on our behalf. Anything you need, or any questions, Pamela is who you'll need to liaise with." She watched Pamela as she said, "Ms Naysmith is held in high regard at Franklyn Financials. I have every faith that Maddox will be in very safe hands."

It was quite endearing, the way in which Pamela seemed to flourish with a little validation. Camille made a mental note. Maybe Leila was right about giving the staff more of an 'arm-around-the-shoulder' approach.

"Absolutely. I have several ideas already planned out I can run through with you and get your opinion on, so we can see if your vision tallies with what we believe we can achieve," Pamela said confidently.

FIFTY-FIVE

Her feet were killing her, and she had a headache coming on. She'd barely set foot through the door before Leila was knocking to be let in. Camille's heart raced though, and she felt herself lifted at the prospect of time with Leila, out of the office, again.

That said something, didn't it?

When Camille opened the door, and Leila stepped inside, there was instant concern on her face.

"What's wrong?" Leila questioned, moving in closer to place the back of her hand against Camille's cheek and forehead. "Are you coming down with something? You look… exhausted."

"I have to admit, I do feel a little ropey," Camille said, accepting a hug. "Have you eaten?"

"No, but you're in no fit state to be cooking for me. Sit down," Leila instructed, slipping her jacket off. She hung it on the back of the stool and then pulled it out, insistent that Camille take the weight off. "Now, first…" She came around the stool to look at Camille once more. Her gaze stopped on her feet. "Shoes."

Leila bent down, and gently took one calf in her hand, lifting Camille's leg to ease the shoe off. Placing the expensive item on the floor, she returned to smooth her hand over Camille's foot, softly pressing and prodding into muscles, and places that made Camille instantly relax.

She groaned. "God, that's so good."

Leila repeated everything with the other leg and foot before standing. Camille watched her lover attend to her. She'd never allowed anyone else to do that.

To be so attentive.

"Right, do you have a headache?" Leila's voice broke through her thoughts.

Camille nodded, and then wished she hadn't as she made a grab for it. "Yes and getting worse. There are some painkillers in that cupboard." She pointed, and Leila made her way around the island. She stopped to wash her hands, before she poured some water into a glass and retrieved the tablets from amongst the multitude of medicines and vitamins.

"Okay, take these, and drink that while I search for something to eat."

Camille did as she was told, too off-colour to argue. She continued to watch Leila moving around her kitchen with ease, as though she lived there.

That thought didn't settle how she'd imagined it would. The idea of anyone ever living with her again had never quite sat right, until now.

Is this what it would be like? she asked herself, as Leila began to hum. She bent over to delve into the fridge and came out with packets of continental meats and cheeses, pressed to her chest and held tightly, like a child who'd just won prizes in a smash and grab.

She placed her haul onto the countertop.

"How hungry are you?" Leila questioned without looking back, her nose already back in the fridge to see what other delights it might be concealing.

"I'm not starving, but I'd like something relatively decent," Camille admitted. Even that, admitting she was hungry and willing to let Leila provide food for her, wasn't her usual response to being unwell, was it? Tom wouldn't have even asked. A bowl of lukewarm soup would have been placed in front of her, and she'd have had to put on a smile and force her gratitude he'd managed to wield the tin opener and press the start button on the microwave. The boys would have let her starve. So, this was…different.

Leila stood up, turned, and smiled at her. "I'll make us a nice platter. We can nibble while we watch a film."

There was no question. It was a statement. They would eat while watching a film, whether Camille wanted to or not.

She wanted very much to. To just do something mundane and normal, with her lover beside her. Yes, she wanted that a lot, actually.

"Can I help?" Camille at least asked, though she already knew the answer would be a 'no.'

"*Non*, you sit there or go sit in the lounge with your feet up." She stopped what she was saying and looked more closely at Camille. "Actually, get changed into something more comfortable. The office is closed."

"And what about you? You've come all dressed for an evening of—" She was about to say lovemaking but now felt a little vulnerable about that. Maybe it was more… debauchery? Either way, cooking and looking after the sick were not on the agenda. "Did you bring a change of clothing?"

Leila looked down at herself and the carefully put-together outfit that was chosen with a very specific outcome, to be removed as soon as she'd arrived. The short skirt and barely-there camisole under a woollen jacket was not the kind of outfit one wore to the office the following day.

"Would you have let me stay the night?" she asked, with just a hint of playfulness.

"Probably not," Camille admitted. It was a workday in

the morning, albeit a Friday and almost the weekend, and it was still important to maintain some level of normal in her life.

"Precisely, so no, I did not bring any change of clothing."

"Well, you can borrow something of mine, if you'd like?"

Leila grinned. "I would like."

"Okay, I'll go and grab a quick shower and get changed, and then…come up whenever. Just root through my wardrobe. I'm sure you'll find something that fits." She was about to walk out when she stopped and said, "You look beautiful, by the way. Don't think that I didn't see, because I did."

"Thank you, I am glad you noticed."

"When you're around me, you're all that I notice."

FIFTY-SIX

By the time Camille came back downstairs, Leila had snuck up, rooted through as requested, and found herself some jogging bottoms that she'd had to roll the legs up. And a T-shirt that was at least one size bigger, but only made it even more comfortable for lounging around in.

Bare of foot, she padded around the kitchen, putting last pieces together on a large plate, and almost jumped when she turned around to find Camille watching from the doorway.

"Bloody hell," she laughed, her accent even more pronounced with the minor swearing. "You scared the bejeezus out of me."

"I'm sorry, you just looked so…cute in my clothes. I've never had that before," Camille acknowledged and then sneezed. "Oh."

"Oh indeed. I think you are coming down with something." Leila picked up the plate. "Come on."

She passed Camille and led her to lounge, which she'd also scoped out while Camille was otherwise engaged. Drinks were already on the coffee table, and a blanket that had been thrown over the back of one of the high wingback armchairs was now on the sofa.

"Sit, get comfortable," Leila insisted. She put the plate down onto the table and reached for a glass of something that looked quite undrinkable.

"What is that?"

"Lemon juice, honey, hot water, ginger, and turmeric." Leila urged her to take it, which she did. "Drink it, you'll feel better."

Camille pulled a face. "I'm not sure I believe you." She sneezed again. "God, I cannot be ill."

"Why not?" Leila waited for her to sit down before shaking the blanket out and covering her with it, tucking it in around the back. "You're not Superwoman."

"Who says I'm not?" Camille smiled, watching her intently as she went about taking care of her.

Leila squeezed into the space beside Camille, before patting her lap for Camille to rest her feet. Once more taking one foot in hand, she began to massage.

"Sometimes, you just have to give in and let others take the reins for a bit. You haven't learnt this by now?" Leila pressed her thumb into the soft pad just below the big toe, and Camille released a gentle moan as her eyes closed. "See, too much tension." Leila continued to work the area.

"Where did you learn to do that?" Camille asked, still with her eyes shut, enjoying the feeling.

"I am sure you're aware I know all sorts of ways to relax your body, Camille. They don't all have to result in an orgasm."

"No, but those are so very much appreciated." Camille's eyes opened slowly, and she pursed her lips into a smile. "You told Pamela to grow a pair, didn't you?"

Now it was Leila's turn to smile knowingly. "I might have suggested she do that, yes."

"I was quite surprised when she turned up in my office. I didn't think she had it in her."

Leila's fingers moved lower, towards the arch. "She's good at what she does, and she just wants to impress you, to be like you."

Camille scoffed.

"Yes, exactly. So, I simply told her to do that then. That if she were more like you, she wouldn't be scared to speak up."

Camille nodded. "God, that's good, right there."

Leila smiled, pleased with herself, and pressed the spot a little harder. "When was the last time you allowed anyone to take care of you?"

"I'm not sure I've ever allowed it. Nor was it offered often. The boys will buy gifts and flowers occasionally, I'll get a phone call once a week from Marcus, and Tobi pops in. Tom wasn't really one for physical touch, unless—"

"Unless it got him off?"

"Usually, yes," Camille agreed with a sigh. "So, you get used to just getting on with things, don't you?"

"I guess. I like being taken care of, and taking care... I find it an intimate moment to share. Not sexual, but intimate, loving, you know?" Gently, she placed that foot down before lifting the other.

"I'm beginning to understand that, yes." Camille held her gaze. "If I didn't feel quite so unwell..." As if on cue, she sneezed again. "I hate having a cold. It's just so unproductive."

Leila smiled. "You can still work, if you insist. Just do it from home."

"That would be very..." She braced herself as another sneeze threatened and then exploded. Sagging, Camille said, "I really hate being ill."

Placing her foot down, Leila shifted out from underneath her and crawled up the sofa and into the space between Camille and the cushions until she was able to slide an arm beneath Camille's neck and pull her close.

Kissing the top of her head and enjoying the smell of her shampoo, Leila said, "Nobody likes being ill. But not everybody has a Leila they can snuggle up with."

FIFTY-SEVEN

A cold chill slowly brought Camille awake.

Unable to breathe clearly through her now bunged-up nose, and aching like hell, she groaned and tried to move, except her right side felt heavy and stuck.

The quiet snuffling reminded her instantly that she was on the sofa still, and she was not alone. The TV had switched itself off and Leila was asleep beside her.

Lifting her left arm, and through squinted eyes, she focused on her watch and the time. Three in the morning. No wonder it was cold and dark, though moonlight illuminated enough to just about see. The cooler night air, and the fact that the blanket was now pulled up around Leila's shoulders, was the reason she was cold.

"Leila," she croaked. Her throat was dry and sore when she swallowed. "God."

"Hmm." Leila moved, her fingers tightening their grip on Camille's top. "Is he there yet?" she mumbled, before her words dipped back into incoherent.

Camille chuckled, before coughing so hard that this time, it woke Leila up.

"Huh, what?" she said, sitting half upright and blinking rapidly. "What time is it?"

"Three," Camille said, and sat up herself to cough some more.

"You sound awful."

"I feel awful." She reached for the glass of water Leila had gotten for her earlier.

"Okay, probably time for some medicine," Leila announced.

"Time you went home," Camille croaked with a smile over her shoulder.

"Tut." Leila moved and climbed off the sofa. "I'm going nowhere, except to the kitchen to find something that will help you sleep, and feel better."

Camille didn't have the energy to argue and allowed herself to be pulled up and onto her feet. She didn't complain when a kiss pecked upon her lips either, and her backside was slapped as Leila insisted she went to bed.

If she were honest, she was enjoying it.

Being Mum had meant she was always the one to look after everyone else. Now though, here with Leila; it felt different.

She wasn't trying to take control. She was simply being nice, and loving, and Camille wanted it. Even in her bunged-up, headachy state, she knew she wanted more of this.

"Come on, let's get this lurgy to bed," Leila cajoled, and pulled her hand to make her shuffle along behind her.

At the foot of the stairs, Camille held back.

"Are you alright?" Leila said, instantly concerned. A soft, warm palm reaching up to touch her cheek gently felt comforting.

"Will you stay with me?" Camille asked. "I know I said you couldn't stay, and you said you weren't leaving, but...*I* want you to stay. *I'm* asking you to stay."

Leila gazed up at her. And Camille understood, in that moment alone, that she was being loved right now.

"Yes," Leila said without hesitation. "Now, go on up, and I'll bring everything."

Leila watched as Camille made an exaggerated effort of climbing the stairs, sniffing and coughing every couple of steps, groaning and complaining.

"You don't have to watch," Camille said without looking back. She could feel those eyes on her.

Leila laughed. "Oh, but it's such an impressive sight."

"You won't be saying that in the morning when I look like Rudolph and sound like a twenty-a-day smoker." She turned on the half-landing.

"I might find it quite sexy." Leila winked.

Camille gripped the stair rail and lifted one foot to the next step.

"If ever there was a moment where I wanted you more than right now…damn you, lurgy."

"I'll be up in a moment."

"Alright, I'll…" She didn't say anything else as another coughing fit took hold. One step at a time, and then she was on the cusp of her bedroom, and the lure of a warm bed pulled her through the door.

Shivering as she switched the kitchen light on, Leila made her way quickly to the fridge. One lemon and a chunk of ginger. She made light work of squeezing and chopping into a pan. Hot water followed, and she boiled it all up gently. When it was warm, she poured it through a sieve, into a cup, and added honey.

It was missing one thing though, she remembered: a

shot of rum, or whiskey, or even brandy.

She wandered back into the lounge and looked around at the cupboards, trying to work out which one hid the booze every house in the UK seemed to have.

Photos lined the edge of one, and she stopped to look at them all. Images of a younger, just as beautiful, Camille, smiling at the camera, with two boys beside her, all of them ageing and growing as she moved from one picture to the next.

"I wish I'd known you back then," she said, smiling along with one particular image of Camille in an evening gown, looking absolutely stunning. "Alcohol," she reminded herself, and crouched down to open the cupboard door. "Ah ha." She grabbed a bottle of brandy.

Expensive brandy.

"She's worth it." She grinned and turned away to complete her task.

FIFTY-EIGHT

Inside Camille's boudoir, Leila found her sitting upright, against a wall of pillows. The duvet was pulled up tight around her chest, arms poking out over the top, but clad in blue-and-white striped pyjamas.

Her head lolled back against the pillows, eyes closed, as she breathed through her mouth in gasping breaths interspersed with sniffing.

"Here, drink this down," Leila said, holding out the warm mug for her to take. "It's not too hot."

"Thank you." Camille took the cup with one hand, and Leila's hand with the other. "You don't have to stay. I don't want you coming down with it too."

"I think if I'm going to get it, then I've already got it," Leila said, sliding the jogging bottoms off. She pulled the cover back and smiled. "Is it weird that I've never seen you wearing pyjamas?"

Camille swallowed the drink down in one. "No weirder than me seeing you in my clothes."

With her legs pulled up and under the duvet, Leila twisted around to face Camille. "I do look cute in your clothes."

"Yes, you do." Camille smiled.

"Are you warm enough?"

"Yes, thank you. Especially after drinking this...how much brandy is in it?"

"Enough." Leila chuckled and shrugged. "You need to

sweat the germs out."

"Sounds so…" A sneeze. "Attractive."

Camille groaned and reached for a tissue, dabbing at her nose and shoving the tissue up her sleeve for later.

She opened the small drawer and dug about until she found a packet of mints. She popped one out of the wrapper and into her mouth, sucking it.

"I like it that you're allowing me to see you in such a—"

"Mess?" Camille said, before launching into another coughing fit.

When she was finished, and flopped back against the pillows, already exhausted, Leila said, "Vulnerable position. I think when you did that in Madeira was when I really began to fall for you."

Camille shook her head slowly. "What did I do in Madeira?"

Leila reached out, her fingertips touching Camille's chin and turning her face towards her. Sleepy, cold filled eyes smiled at her.

"That last night when you asked me to make love to you, and then hold you…I saw then that you were being you, just for the night, letting all the walls fall for a few hours…raw and untethered is a good description."

"I didn't think I'd see you again."

"I know." Leila's eyes flashed playfully. "And yet, here we are."

"Here we are." Camille smiled. "I want to be that person with you," she admitted. "I want to let my walls down. I'm just…not there yet. Not enough. Not what you deserve."

"I know. But we're closer to it than we were, right?"

"I guess so, yes." Camille started to laugh and then morphed into a cough. "God, this is frustrating."

"It's time for sleep," Leila said.

Camille nodded, blew her nose, and sunk a little further down the pillows, but remained mostly upright.

"Goodnight, *ma cherie*," Leila whispered.

"*Bonne nuit.*" Camille sighed as Leila snuggled against her, and despite feeling unwell, she'd never felt better in her life.

FIFTY-NINE

Pamela was calling Leila's phone as she rushed through reception, annoyed when she got stuck at the electronic gates. She pressed her pass over and over, but it didn't open.

Muttering under her breath, the same security guard who'd been there on her first day smiled and pressed a button that allowed her in.

"Thank you," she said, out of breath and harried.

She'd thought she'd set an alarm before falling asleep again, but if she did, it didn't go off. Her natural body clock woke her at just after seven.

Camille was asleep, finally, and Leila was exhausted. All she wanted to do was roll over, snuggle in, and go back to sleep, but a nagging voice in her head shouted, 'get up.'

She'd dragged Camille's joggers back on, kissed her forehead, and run down the stairs, grabbing her bag, and waited outside until the Uber arrived a few minutes later.

Getting home, she'd begun stripping as soon as her front door closed.

Now, it was almost 8.30 a.m., and Pamela had already rung once. This was the second call. Leila didn't answer it. Thrusting the phone back into her bag, she would pretend she had no idea because it was on silent.

The lift pinged and she pushed her way through a group of people.

"Sorry," she shouted over her shoulder, and just about

managed to reach the lift as the doors started to close.

Sully pressed the 'open-door' button quickly and she slid inside.

"Thanks." She leaned against the side wall, catching her breath.

"Late?" he asked with a grin. He held two coffee cups in a cardboard tray in his other hand.

"Yes." She nodded, but didn't give him any reason as to why. Nobody would know she'd spent the night with Camille.

"Buses, eh?" he said, trying to keep the conversation going.

"Always something to hold us up, right?" She smiled just as the lift pinged again and the doors opened.

"After you," he said, and she stepped out and right into the path of Pamela.

"Where the hell have you been?" Pamela said, clearly channelling her inner Camille a little too well. "We have a meeting in ten minutes."

"I have a meeting. You are not on the Connor account now, and I have it all in hand. Don't worry," Leila reassured her as they walked towards their office. "I have everything prepared."

"Good, because—"

"Pamela," Leila said, a little more frustrated than she'd intended. "We're all good. There will be no issues, Mr Connor will be happy, and the account will remain within the FF portfolio. But right now, I need to get a coffee, so, can we do this…whatever it is, later?"

Pamela huffed. "Ms Franklyn hasn't turned up. Fatima is worried about her because she isn't answering her phone."

"I see. Well, I am sure Cam— Ms Franklyn is fine. She looked peaky yesterday, didn't you think?" Leila put the thought into her head. "She definitely sneezed a few times."

"Did she?"

"Hm-hm. Anyway, I need to get going. I'll find you after the meeting, alright?" She didn't wait for a response.

Coffee.

Meeting.

Home.

That was her intention for the day. And then she would pack a small bag and head back over to Camille's and play nurse for the next two days.

SIXTY

It was almost twelve hours later when Leila arrived at Camille's again. The Uber dropped her, the bag of Chinese takeout, and a holdall of clothes right outside, and she all but bounded up the steps and rang the bell.

When she saw the figure through the glass walking towards her, she began to smile. And then the door opened and the woman looking at her wasn't Camille.

"Oh, uh…I was—"

"Camille, there's a very beautiful woman on the doorstep. Shall I let her in?" The voice was pure London or Essex. Leila wasn't expert enough to know the difference between the two. "Come in." She smirked as Leila stepped past her. "You must be her."

"Her?"

Leila could hear Camille coughing and glanced at this woman for permission to enter further. She got it with an amused raise of her brow and jut of her chin.

Unsure what the woman was talking about, or who she even was, Leila walked into the lounge and found Camille laid out under blankets and looking very sorry for herself.

"Leila," she croaked.

"Ah, so she has a name," the woman said, following Leila in. "Tina," she said, holding a hand out. "I have the dubious distinction of being married to Camille's youngest son, Tobias."

"Oh, well, it's lovely to meet you," Leila said confidently, as she took the hand. "I brought dinner, but if—"

"Thank you, I'm actually starving," Camille said between sniffs.

Tina raised a brow. "Why didn't you say that? I'd have made you a sandwich or something."

"Because I didn't want a sandwich, and I knew Leila was coming back, so I hoped she'd have the foresight to bring snacks at least."

Leila smiled. "Chinese, and snacks."

"See, so you can tell Tobias that I'm not dying, I'm being perfectly well looked after."

"By your new...friend?" Tina pushed, smirking again at Leila. *She knows. Totally knows*, thought Leila, but she would neither confirm nor deny anything until Camille answered.

"If I say she's someone special, will you sod off?"

Tina laughed. "Only if it's true."

"Fine. It's true. I'm in a relationship with Leila, and we'd like to have dinner without a third wheel," Camille said, and Leila had to admit, she was impressed by the announcement. Unexpected as it was, it sent a warm, fuzzy glow racing around her heart. Were they really doing this, already? This easily?

"Okie dokie. Have fun." Tina laughed and turned on her heel, saying over her shoulder, "I'll fill Tobi in on the development."

Camille's eyes moved slowly away from Tina, towards Leila, her gaze holding with Leila as she said, "Okay?"

"Yes," Leila said with a smile. "Now, Chow Mein, rice, or a little of everything?"

Camille fell back against the cushions. "Give me all the

food, please."

"Starve a fever, feed a cold," Leila sang out, as she left the room with the bag of food.

SIXTY-ONE

"I'm sure this tastes lovely," Camille said, sniffing again. "I'm so bunged-up I can only use my memory to know what it should taste like and enjoy it."

"I picked up something from the chemist. We have to put it in boiling water and then you breathe it in with the towel over your head." Leila twirled a fork into noodles, forgoing chopsticks in an effort to just eat.

As she'd plated up and smelt the delicious aromas, she'd realised just how hungry she was too.

"Thank you," Camille offered, chewing mostly with her mouth open just so she could breathe. "This really wasn't the way I saw…" *Cough.* "…our relationship developing."

"Oh, you thought just lots of sex and that would be enough?" Leila smiled at her and held out the bag of prawn crackers.

Camille shook her head and Leila shrugged, delving into the bag to pluck one out and bite into it. 'Crunch and crumbs,' that was what Kristen called them.

"I mean, sex is pretty good." Camille smiled back.

"It is," Leila said, her smile matching Camille's. "You wanna know something?"

"I find myself wanting to know everything."

Leila placed her plate down onto the coffee table and turned to Camille.

"When we met, in Madeira, I was there because I was

getting over a broken heart. My friend, Kristen, suggested I get away from it all and just enjoy some time to heal. And then I saw you."

It was cute the way Camille's cheeks flushed at that.

"I had it in my head that a holiday fling would be just the thing. What is it they say? 'Get under someone to get over them?'"

"I think that's the old adage, yes."

Leila nodded. "But, honestly, that's not me. I'm not someone who just jumps into bed with another. I do need to actually feel something. Chemistry is one thing, but I don't know how to explain it, I just know whether someone is for me." She leaned forward. "I saw you and I couldn't take my eyes off of you. You were mesmerising to me."

"It's funny," Camille croaked. "Men have spoken like that about me, and I've never believed a word of it, but you…I look at you. The way you look at me, and I know, I feel, all of it."

"Good."

Camille squeezed her knee. "Please, go on, I feel like this wasn't the point of this story."

Leila laughed. "Very perceptive. The way you offered yourself to me; brave, but vulnerable. It allowed me to be me, too. To drop all of my walls and pretences. My heart was broken because she didn't want me… not the real me. My confidence, my ability to read her, it was all too much. But you…you embraced it. Enjoyed it."

"I love that you read me. That I don't have to ask, even though you make me." Camille sniggered.

"When I got home. I realised I was more heartbroken losing you, than I'd ever been about her."

Camille frowned. "I'm sorry, I wasn't able to be—"

"It's okay. You were honest and you never led me on to believe anything different to what you offered. You gave and took only what you said you would, and for that, I respected you, but...I missed you. I missed not having that in my life any longer, knowing I'd be going home to a life where you didn't exist in it."

"When you speak like that, I realise how much I really do like romance." Camille laughed and coughed. "Sorry, not the most romantic, am I?"

"I think the fact you keep pointing out all the ways in which you're not being romantic, coupled with the way you were in Madeira, tells me that 'romantic' is exactly who you are."

"Maybe...I know when I first met Tom, I was romantic. At least, I thought I was, but then life took over and I didn't have time for it." She smiled sadly. "I've always blamed Tom for our marriage failing, but I think I played my part too. Don't get me wrong, he left me to it. Let me take on the parenting, the home, and running a business."

"It's no wonder that romance went by the wayside?"

"Yes, I guess it did. When I looked up from my book and found you staring at me across the pool, I realised nobody had looked at me that way for a long time. Oh, I've had men leer and stare, but you...you penetrated me. Your stare went to my core, like you could see me."

"I do." Leila smiled.

"Even in my worse state," Camille laughed.

"*Especially* in your worse state." Leila leaned forward. "I'd take you in any state."

SIXTY-TWO

Leila pottered in the kitchen. The sun shining through that morning was bright and warm, as she loaded the previous night's dishes into the washer and searched cupboards for cleaning sprays and cloths.

Music played from the speaker, and she danced around in her underwear and the same baggy T-shirt of Camille's she'd worn to sleep in these past two nights.

She filled the kettle and set it to boil.

When she spun around, she almost had a heart attack when she found a man standing there grinning at her.

"You must be Leila," he said, and then his head tilted to one side as he considered something. "Oh, you're *her*." He pointed, and Leila had no idea what he was talking about, or who he was. "Sorry, oh God, how rude…I'm not a murderer." He laughed and held out a hand. "I'm Tobi… Tobias. Camille's son."

Leila felt her heart rate come down a notch and she tentatively reached out and shook his hand. "Yes, I'm Leila."

"An accent, wow."

Leila smiled, unsure how to react.

"Sorry, God I sound like a dork. Sorry, you're just not… I've seen you before. When Mum and I were at dinner, she drifted off, staring out the window, and when I turned to look, it was you."

"Oh, I—" She felt the heat rise up her neck. She remembered that night too; when she was jealous about who

Camille was dining with.

"So, how is the invalid? Still dying on the couch?"

"Actually, she's in bed. I was just going to make her some breakfast. Have you eaten?"

"Ah, yes, all good in that department." He rubbed his tummy. "I'll just pop up and say 'hi.'" He smiled and stepped back. "It was great to meet you."

"Indeed," she replied, a little amused by him and his reaction to her. *Just like most men*, she thought, and shrugged as he wandered off.

Camille could hear voices downstairs, but didn't have the strength to get up and find out who. For all she knew, it was the TV or radio, and what a monumental effort that would be to find out.

She knew who it was the minute she heard the thudding footsteps racing up the stairs.

"Mum?" Tobias called out, more to let her know he was coming in than to find out where she was.

"In here," she answered anyway.

His face appeared at the door instantly. "Oh, you look glorious." He grinned and entered the room, sitting himself down on the edge of the bed. "Tina said you looked rough but…"

"Thank you, sweetie, I feel so much better already," Camille snarked gently at him.

Oblivious, he held up a paper bag. "Here, I bought you some of those chocolates you like." He patted her leg. "So, that's Leila?"

"Yes," she said slowly, taking the chocolates and placing them on the bedside table. She'd enjoy those when she could actually taste something again.

"She's…"

"Yes, she is." Camille smiled. "And yes, I am happy, and yes, she is important to me, and yes, we are sleeping together."

Tobi's face flushed. "Well, duh, who wouldn't be sleeping with someone like that."

Camille punched his arm.

"Ow." He rubbed at the spot, just like he did when he was a child and Marcus had poked him.

"Let me be very clear about something. I appreciate that this is all new, and maybe a little bit unlike whatever you think I might be, but there will be no crass remarks about Leila, or our relationship, do you understand?"

Tobi smiled, taking her hand. "Mum, all we want is for you to be happy."

"Good, because I am. And I'm terrified about it, so the very least you can do is be supportive."

Tobi frowned. "What are you terrified about?"

Camille blew her nose. "Everything. Have you seen her?"

Tobi laughed. "Yes, she's stunning. Have you seen you? I know where I got my good looks from."

Camille smiled at him. "Charmer. But seriously, she's younger… What happens when I don't look like this? What happens when I'm a dragon at work and she's on the end of it? What happens when—"

"Mum, what happens if you just enjoy it?"

"I don't know. I've never been able to just enjoy it."

"Not even with Dad?"

Camille sniffed and pulled another tissue free. "Your dad was…so long ago, in terms of romance. Yes, right at the beginning it was, I suppose, what anyone would hope for. I married him, didn't I?" She laughed. "But then life happened, you boys came along, bills and responsibility, and then the business. Romance was put on a back burner that fizzled out. And I'm in my fifties, and about to embark on something so very different to what anyone else has known me as." But even as she said it, she couldn't remember a time when this didn't feel like the most natural thing she'd ever done. Other than her kids, of course.

"Fuck 'em." Tobi laughed. "Seriously Mum, when have you ever cared what anyone thought? Just fuck 'em."

"You really don't care?"

He shook his head. "I really don't, and neither does Marcus. I told him." He winced, suddenly realising that might not have been his decision to make, but he laughed and added, "He said it might make you more interesting."

"Cheeky sod," Camille chuckled. "Thank you, I feel better with both of you onside."

"Not that it would have made an inkling of difference if you've set your mind on it."

"True, but I'd have been sad about it."

SIXTY-THREE

It was Sunday night, and Camille snuggled up with Leila on the sofa for another evening of not watching a film that played quietly in the background.

She was still snuffling, but not quite so bunged-up now following the head-over-bowl breathing thing Leila had come up with. Her cough was still there, but mainly as night fell, which was annoying.

"If you wanted to go home and get a decent night's sleep, I wouldn't blame you," Camille said.

Leila lay between her legs, flat out on Camille's torso with her head on her chest. Her fingertips moved gently, gripping and releasing the material beneath them.

"Do you want me to go?" she answered without moving.

"No," Camille found herself saying. "I'm aware that my coughing must have disturbed your sleep, it has mine, but I've been napping on and off, while you've been—"

"Working. I finished off my reports and sent them in to Pamela. And then I emailed Vince and explained that I needed a day's annual leave."

"Oh, you did?"

"Hm-hm." When Camille didn't speak again, Leila raised her head and said, "Is that okay with you?"

"As your boss, I would probably grant your leave, under the circumstances." Camille smiled.

"And as my lover?"

"As my lover, I'd probably be quite happy you're bunking off to spend the day with me."

"You know, I like that...being your lover." Leila leaned up and kissed her gently.

"I don't," Camille admitted.

"Oh." Leila's face crumpled into a frown. "I don't under—"

Placing a finger to her lips, Camille smiled. "It just feels too...casual. Don't you think?"

"Oh," Leila said with more excitement, one brow rising as her lip curled. "Well, when you put it that way, yes, I suppose it does. So, what would you prefer?"

"I'm not sure. I'm not there yet, but I'm moving that way."

Leila settled back down into the same position she'd been in. "Let me know when you know."

"Aren't you concerned what people will think of you?"

Slowly, Leila sat up again. "What do you mean?"

"One day I'm going to walk into the office and not care who knows about us."

"Yes, this is good, no?"

"And then you'll face the possibility that some might think you slept with me to get the job, or you got the job because you were sleeping with me."

"I see." She shrugged. "Let them."

Camille laughed. "That's it? Let them?"

"Yes, why do I care? I have the job, and I have the boss... why is their opinion of any concern?" She smiled.

"And it's that simple, is it?"

"Well, they had their chance and never took it."

"You really are something else." Camille continued to laugh until coughing brought an end to it and she shook her head, still smiling. "I think we should go to bed."

"At last, this film bored me an hour ago," Leila said, jumping up and holding out her hand. "Come on, let's get rid of this lurgy so I can start ravishing you again."

SIXTY-FOUR

"Do you think you'd be up to getting some fresh air today?" Leila asked, looking out of the window at the world passing them by. "You've been cooped up all weekend. It might actually do you some good to get up and move around a bit."

Camille unwrapped a cough sweet and popped it into her mouth, sucking it as she considered the idea.

"I guess we could. As long as it wasn't something too ambitious. Anything that gets me out of breath just brings on a coughing fit."

Leila chuckled. "Oh, I'm saving ambitious for when the coughing stops, and the bedroom beckons. I was thinking we could go into town for a coffee, maybe do a little shopping?"

"I'd love that, but could we maybe go to Bath Street, or Amberfield?"

"You don't want people to see us together?"

"I don't want to be accused of skiving off to be with you." She sniffed. "Ooh I think my nose is clearing." Looking at Leila she added, "There are some nice cafés and the bar along the river. We could go for a walk."

"I think that sounds lovely." Leila smiled. "It's not raining, so you just need to wrap up against the cold."

"I'm already wrapped up," Camille laughed. She had on a turtleneck jumper and woollen trousers. "Thank goodness it hasn't snowed again like it did over Christmas. A good coat and I'll be fine."

"I missed that, though we had some snow in Nottingham. I'm not sure I was born for snow."

"I quite like it if I don't have to actually work. Skiing is fun, but driving in it? No, thank you."

"Right, let's get moving then," Leila announced, jumping to her feet and holding out her hand to pull Camille to hers, before she dashed off to the hall and returned with coats.

She held Camille's up so she could shrug her arms in, then twisted her around and zipped it right up to under her chin. Holding the collars, Leila said, "You need a hat and scarf. We're taking no chances."

Camille stared into her eyes. "I can't wait until you can kiss me again."

"I can't wait for that either." Leila pulled a woolly hat down over Camille's head. "I'm falling in love with you, you know that, right?"

"The feeling is mutual, you know that, right?" Camille reached for the scarf and slid it around Leila's neck. "Just so we're very clear about that."

"We're clear." Leila grinned. When Camille turned, Leila slapped her backside. "Come on, let's go."

"That's twice you've done that," Camille laughed. "Do not get into the habit and do it in the office."

"I wouldn't dare." Leila winked as Camille opened the door.

"Yes, you would."

"Yes, I would."

SIXTY-FIVE

The riverbank in Amberfield was busy enough for a Monday afternoon. People ambled along or mingled to chat.

"It must be nice not having to be anywhere, and just stand around talking to friends," Camille said as they passed by a small group.

They strolled with arms linked, and Camille had stopped flinching a while ago whenever people looked at them and smiled. Now, it all felt quite comfortable, and she questioned why she'd ever worried about it in the first place. Was it really this easy?

"Maybe, I mean, don't they get bored?" Leila said, wrinkling her nose at the idea.

"They look kind of happy," Camille laughed. "Would you get bored?"

Leila nodded. "I think I'd need something to do, yes."

"Like what?" Camille pulled her closer and whispered, "Tell me all your dreams."

"All of them? In public?" Leila continued to chuckle. "Maybe when we get home, but the decent ones, I dunno… travel more, I suppose." She glanced up at Camille. "Start my own company?"

"Oh, and here I was thinking Frankyn Financials was your dream job." She smiled.

"It is…my dream job working for someone else, but you know…" She shrugged nonchalantly. "One day I'd like to be you and boss them all around."

Camille laughed hard. "Well, maybe I'll retire and join these, to stand around talking and leave you to run the company."

"This sounds like a serious proposal, Camille." Leila winked playfully. "Be careful, I might take it seriously."

Camille brought them to a halt. "I'm taking you and me seriously." She glanced around quickly, before leaning in and kissing Leila on the lips. Just a peck, but it was more than enough to say what she meant. "There's a café over there. Shall we get something for lunch?"

"Yes. I'd like that, and I liked the kiss, and the words. Affirmative action is always appreciated." She giggled and took Camille's hand as they turned and walked towards Aston's.

"This looks nice," Leila said, as they pushed the door opened and entered into the warmth. "Have you been before?"

Camille shook her head. "No, I've only recently been exploring this area." Her cheeks flushed, and not just because it was cold out.

"Oh, the gay bar," Leila said quietly.

"Yes, that," Camille said, a little flustered, becoming even more so when she looked up and noticed Sadie sitting in the corner with three other women and smiling at her. It took just another second and her hand came up and waved.

"You know them?" Leila asked.

"Not really. That's Sadie. She runs said bar." Camille waved back and smiled, blushing further when she understood Sadie's expression to mean, 'is that her?'

"Well, the only free table is that one." Leila pointed to the table right next to Sadie and her group. "Shall we?"

Not waiting for an answer, and still holding Camille's hand, Leila led them to the table and smiled politely at the women as she removed her coat and slung it over the back of a spare chair.

"Hi. Fancy seeing you here," Sadie said when Camille was in earshot. Turning to Leila, she said, "And you must be Leila."

Leila chuckled at that. "Yes, how do—" And then she realised Camille had been talking about them to a listening ear. "It's nice to meet you, Sadie."

"Camille, Leila, this is Natalie, my partner, and our friends, Claudia and Scarlett."

The names reverberated in Camille's brain. What were the odds? The chances that two women, one slightly older than the other, clearly a couple by the way they sat together, would be called Claudia and Scarlett, and not be related to Jack Maddox?

"Hello, nice to meet you," Camille finally said. "We were just taking some air. I've been unwell and..." She turned to Leila. "Leila's been looking after me."

"And doing a fine job, I'd say." Sadie grinned, clearly enjoying the opportunity to see Camille out in the wild and with her lady love in tow.

"What can I get you?" A woman's voice from behind made Camille jump.

"Oh, sorry, wasn't expecting—" Camille laughed at herself.

"The hot chocolate is to die for," Claudia said with a cheerful wink.

351

When Leila nodded, Camille ordered two hot chocolates and finally removed her coat and sat down.

"So, Camille tells me you run the bar?" Leila said to Sadie. Striking up conversation seemed easy for her. She felt Camille's resistance and discreetly took her hand, squeezing reassuringly.

"I do," Sadie answered proudly. "It was actually where we met." She smiled at Natalie, who nodded in agreement.

"Yes, twenty-five years ago," Natalie added. "Can you believe that?"

"That's amazing, and—" Leila narrowed her eyes at Claudia and Scarlett. "You met there too?"

"Oh, no, we met in Art, in town, but we're big fans of Blanca's now. A little more sedate for us," Claudia chimed in. "What about you?"

Camille felt like the earth was opening up and about to swallow her whole, the heat rushing up her neck and firing out of the tips of her ears. But, as she felt her hand squeezed, and looked at the smiling faces of women just like her, smiling back and interested, she felt a sudden sense of peace.

"We met on holiday, actually," she found herself saying. "A wild and passionate fling that was supposed to end there, but…" She turned to Leila, who was looking at her as though she might be the only person on the planet. "Apparently the universe had other ideas."

"Gotta love the universe," Natalie said, raising her mug.

SIXTY-SIX

By the time they'd finished lunch and chatted more with the group, Sadie had invited them over to the bar. A behind-closed-doors event that would be for just them, and a couple of Natalie's other friends, who were on their way to join them.

Camille had surprised herself with how eager she was to go, and even had to persuade Leila, who thought she might be overdoing it.

It didn't take much for Leila to agree, however. How could she not? This was everything she had wanted. Camille publicly showing her off, openly being her authentic self around other people, and new friends in the making for both of them, but especially for Leila. She was new in town and knowing nobody, except for her co-workers, and Chloe the waitress in her local restaurant.

It was the ideal and most perfect opportunity, wasn't it?

They all walked as a group, arm in arm with their significant others, along the embankment and over the bridge towards Blanca's. It was fun, and engaging, and Camille didn't think once about what anyone else was thinking, until they passed a group of lads, one on a bike, the others walking. The one on the bike cycled closer and shouted, "Dykes!"

Camille cringed internally and felt her entire body stiffen.

Instantly, Sadie called back, "Sweetheart, dikes are what little boys put their finger in. You'll never find where a lesbian sticks her tongue. Home to mummy, sweet cheeks, before you come inside, and your friends understand just how queer you are."

"Oh Sadie, don't be so mean." Natalie laughed as the boy cycled away with his friends laughing at him.

"That wasn't mean." Sadie laughed. "That was playful."

Camille felt her arm tighten. "You okay?" Leila asked.

"Is that something you deal with a lot?" Camille asked her.

"No, not really, but now and then an idiot shows themselves," Leila admitted. "I can't say it's not something you won't face from time to time."

Camille looked at the group, all laughing at what Sadie had said, carrying on as though nothing had happened.

"It doesn't bother you?"

"Of course it bothers me, but what can we do? Sadie dealt with it her way, you'll find your way, and we live our lives despite these idiots. In fact, we live them to spite them," Leila corrected herself.

"I don't know that I want to just deal with it," Camille said, and Leila prepared herself to hear the worst—that she couldn't do this. It wasn't something she wanted. But instead, Camille said, "I might have kicked his back wheel out if he'd gotten any closer."

Leila laughed. "That's my girl."

"So, how do you all know one another?" Camille asked, when another couple had joined the group and wine was flowing. Gabby and Nora were another pair with a definite age-gap. Camille was beginning to wonder if Rosie was right, and this was now quite the done thing.

It was Sadie who spoke. "They're all part of the big lesbian business group."

"You know full well that isn't what it's called," Natalie laughed.

"It is to us." Sadie giggled, Scarlett and Nora joining in.

Claudia leaned forward, "We're all members of the Bath Street LGBTQ business group. It's the LBG for short. We meet up monthly and talk about—"

"They get drunk mostly," Nora chipped in.

"You should join us," Natalie said to Camille, at which point Sadie stood up and groaned, followed by Scarlett and Nora.

"Oh no, they've started the recruitment phase. Come on gang, let's skedaddle while they rope her in. I've got a fabulous cocktail to try out on you all."

"I'm not drinking," Nora said as they walked away.

"I'll make it alcohol-free then," Sadie answered, before shouting back, "Leila, come on."

Leila glanced at Camille. She seemed content enough, and so she got up too.

"I'm just at the bar, okay." She kissed the top of Camille's head and squeezed her shoulder.

When she was out of earshot, the other women all made that face that said, 'aw,' and Camille blushed again.

"So, you two are absolutely gorgeous together," Natalie said.

Camille couldn't hide the smile. "Honestly, I'm still getting used to it. This is my first—"

"Yes, we can see that," Gabby laughed. "But it suits you."

"Yes, I think it does. It's just all so new, and if I'm honest, a little scary," Camille admitted.

Claudia reached out and patted her knee. "I know exactly how you feel. That was me not that long ago, terrified everyone else would judge and comment, but the reality is, most people don't care."

"Are you all late bloomers?" Camille asked.

Natalie laughed and shook her head. "Not me. Gay my whole life."

"It took me getting married and then falling for a girl half my age to realise," Gabby answered.

"And I was into my fifties when I met Scarlett. There really isn't a time frame on it," Claudia finished.

"Thank you," Camille said. "Honestly, I can't tell you how much I needed to meet you and to hear your stories. Last week, I was still fighting this. Even though I'd accepted I wanted her in my life, I couldn't quite envision how to navigate it. And then I got ill, and she virtually moved in, and now, meeting all of you and being able to see how normal it all is… it's freeing."

"Mm, younger women," Gabby laughed. "Not to be sniffed at."

SIXTY-SEVEN

Stepping inside Camille's home that evening, a little flushed from the wine and cocktails, but full of laughter and the pizza that had been ordered in, Camille and Leila slipped off coats and shoes.

As they were about to walk down the hall, Camille stopped and quickly reached for Leila, tugging her back towards her to stare into the large mirror.

"What are we doing?" Leila asked, a little amused and confused.

"Something Natalie said." Camille put her arm around Leila's neck, and leaned in closely behind her, their faces cheek to cheek. "We look good together."

Leila grinned at their reflection. "We do."

"I never quite realised before just how much we fit together. Not just in bed, or how we are with each other, but physically too, we look good together."

"You look happy."

Camille bit her ear gently. "I am. Being around you makes me happy, and being around people like me, makes me happy."

Leila turned just a little. "Are you feeling better?"

"Yes, why?"

Now, Leila turned some more, until they were almost face to face.

"Because I want to fuck you so much right now and if I can't, then I'm going to have to let you watch me fuck myself," she admitted with a devilish grin.

"I think, in that case...I'm going to insist on both of those things." Camille pressed her lips together just as tightly as her thighs clenched, and her clit throbbed.

"Fine. Where?" Leila said, all cocksure and confident about it, already pulling off her jumper as she walked towards the stairs.

Camille chewed her lip and considered the question.

"Bedroom. I want to be comfortable," Camille said, before racing past her and up the stairs. At the top, she had a sudden coughing fit, but waved Leila off. "I'm fine."

"If you get out of breath and cough running up the stairs, then—" Leila laughed, as she scooted past her. Dropping her jeans at the bedroom door, she kicked them off. "Don't die on me."

"I've still got life in me yet, don't you worry." Camille followed her into the room and pulled her sweater and T-shirt off as she clambered onto the bed and grappled with Leila until they both fell onto the mattress, kissing.

Taking Leila's hand, Camille brought it down between them and eased it into the space between Leila's legs.

"Show me." Staring into her eyes, Camille pushed up on her palms. "On your knees, facing me, leaving your underwear on."

Scurrying out from under her, Leila moved to the end of the bed. She waited for Camille to adjust her position and get comfortable against the pillows, and then she rose up onto her knees and let them slide apart, just enough to balance her.

Her hand slid down her torso, palm flattened against her skin, until her fingers met lace and slid inside.

"Slowly," Camille instructed. "There's no need to rush this."

"Hm, you say that now." Her fingertips touched her clit, and she mewled quietly, moving in tight circles. Already so turned on by the day's events, she knew it would be a task to keep it going for long.

It turned her on even more to watch the way Camille's eyes drifted down from her face to her hidden fingers.

"I'm so wet," she admitted, teasing Camille a little. And when Camille suddenly moved and began inching her way towards her, Leila thought she'd already won.

But what happened next surprised her, in a very good way.

Without a word, Camille mirrored her stance. On her knees, six inches apart, her hands reached out and rested on Leila's hips, warm skin that, as it moved lower, hooked the material of her underwear and pulled the lace lower to rest just below the cheeks of her backside, her pussy and fingers clearly visible.

And then she retreated, back to her spot against the pillows.

"Much better." She smiled, not taking her eyes from Leila's movements. "Slowly," she reminded, when Leila began to speed up.

"Babe, I need to…" Leila said before Camille cut her off.

"When I say you can."

The arousal that flooded through Leila in that moment was nothing short of circuit-breaking. She felt every muscle contract.

"Please," she asked again, desperate to get herself off and release the climax that was sitting there, just waiting to be unleashed.

"Not yet...you look so...delicious, all dishevelled and wanton. You're making me so wet just watching you," Camille taunted. "You want me to be wet for you, don't you?"

"You know...I...do." Leila's head thrashed side to side. She needed to...her eyes fixed on Camille, and when Camille looked up and connected with her, she only needed one command: one word.

"Come."

SIXTY-EIGHT

Leila lay on the bed, face down, exhausted.

Sweat chilled her skin, her heart rate still rapid, breathing finally slowing from the gasping, moaning, and pleading she'd been subjected to for the last hour.

When she thought about that, she laughed.

"So, I don't know what brought that on..." she said, pushing up and rolling over.

Camille grinned like the proverbial Cheshire Cat.

"I think something changed today," Leila finished.

"I think I finally understood that what we have, how I feel, and what we're doing together, is perfectly normal, and it doesn't matter whether I've thought of it before, or not."

She moved closer and snuggled into Leila, bringing the duvet up and over them both.

"Speaking with Claudia, and Gabby. Seeing them with Scarlett and Nora, it gave me a sense of... I don't know, peace? I looked at them and saw two couples in love, and then I looked over at you and—"

Raising up on her elbow to look into Leila's eyes, she smiled. "It made me realise...I love you." Her free hand stroked Leila's face. "And I don't care if that's something anyone else struggles with. I'm not going. I want you. I want you in my life, and I want us to be together."

Leila swallowed.

"I—" She bit her lip, not wanting to say the wrong thing right now. "You have caught me by surprise. I honestly didn't expect you to be here so quickly, and—if I'm honest, I almost can't believe it."

"Believe it," Camille urged, taking her hand and raising it to her lips. "Please, believe it."

"I said almost…" Leila smiled. "I fell in love with you a long time ago. I want everything you want." They kissed tenderly. "Oh, and that…what we just did, I don't know where she came from, but can she stay?"

Camille laughed and rolled them over until she was on top and gazing down at Leila.

"She's here for as long as you are."

"Oh, forever then?" Leila smiled.

"I hope so. Because you have unleashed and untethered me, and for that, you are going to have to pay the price."

"I think I can afford that." She placed her hands flat against Camille's naked chest.

"Really?" Camille's brow raised. "Because a moment ago you begged and pleaded for it to be enough."

"I did, yes, but that was before I decided it's my turn to be on top…and I have something in my bag that's going to have you begging and pleading."

Camille pushed up until she was straddling Leila's thighs.

"You brought it with you, even though I was unwell?"

Leila heaved upwards to meet her.

"I was optimistic you'd make a swift recovery, and look, I was right." She smirked and licked her lip. "And I'm not satisfied with just the taste of you. So, do you want to keep sitting there and I just use..." She waggled her fingers. "Or would you prefer that I get it, and let you ride me while I keep you on the edge?"

Camille's mouth moved side to side as she contemplated her options.

"I like it when you torment me." Camille climbed off to allow Leila to get up.

"I know...I'm very good at it." Leila winked and padded barefoot and naked around the bed to where her bag was casually tossed into the bottom of a wardrobe.

Retrieving the strap-on, she turned back to Camille.

"Assume the position."

"Oh, sweetheart," Camille said, putting an arm around her neck and pulling her towards the bed. "I'm going to be on top."

"Of course you are," Leila laughed.

EPILOGUE

Camille walked out of the lift and into the foyer of the office. Heads turned in her direction as they all heard the footsteps, or were nudged by a colleague.

The Ice Queen had returned.

"Welcome back." Fatima smiled when Camille entered the outer office and placed her bag down onto the desk to remove her coat. "How was the conference?"

"Boring. All okay here?" she asked, with an arch of her brow that said she was prepared to hear the worst, although she already knew everything was fine. Leila had caught her up most nights.

Fatima grinned. "Actually, yes, all is good. Ms Naysmith managed quite well in your absence."

"Excellent. Maybe I'll book a holiday and let her continue with pretending to be me." She smiled, pulling off her gloves.

Laughing, Fatima got up and grabbed empty mugs. "I'm not sure she's ever going to be that good, but she did okay. Coffee?"

"Yes, in about thirty minutes, I'll need it for my meeting." She smiled. "Oh, make it twenty…I want to speak to you in my office." When the look of alarm spread across her assistant's face, she smiled again. "Nothing to worry about. I just want you in the loop on something."

"Sounds intriguing."

She waited for Fatima to leave before entering her own office.

"Took your time," Leila said, smiling at her from behind the desk where she'd been waiting, feet up. "I was beginning to think you'd decided to stay at the conference." Her feet landed gracefully on the floor, and she stood.

"Now, why would I do that?" Camille grinned, crossing the room to meet her. "Did you miss me?"

"No, I had Pamela here to glare at me and keep me in line, though, I do have to say, that with her in charge, there are a lot of perks I miss out on."

Their mouths met; hot, but slow and tender. Tongues met that had been denied for long enough.

"Well, I'm back now." Camille tapped Leila's nose. "I'll make sure my glaring is on point."

"Please do...did you lock the door?" Leila asked, not waiting for the answer as she crossed the room and turned the lock slowly. "So, now it's just us..." Leila turned to stare at her with a look that couldn't be mistaken for anything else.

Camille didn't need any further instructions.

With Leila's eyes trained on her, she reached behind and unbuttoned her skirt. The only sound in the room was the small zipper as it moved downwards, and the figure-hugging cloth loosened enough to fall to the floor.

"We have twenty minutes," she said smugly. "And I came prepared." She couldn't hide the smirk as Leila's eyes scanned downwards and widened when they found underwear lacking.

"I like this new, bold, Camille." Leila smiled as she closed the space between them. "You do remember what you promised me before you left, don't you, darling?"

Her head tilted towards Camille but retreated as she passed by. She lifted her skirt, slid her own underwear off and re-took Camille's office chair, getting herself comfortable before she leant towards the desk and tapped it.

"Oh, I remember. It's all I've thought about these past nights." Camille stepped out from the puddle of Ralph Lauren and kicked off her heels. "But I don't see—"

Leila grinned, pulled the desk drawer open and then dipped into it, lifting the strap-on and belt with ease. "First, I get what I want."

Camille's eyes lit up as she squeezed into the space and knelt between Leila's knees.

"You do know that what you want isn't a hardship for me, right? It's just extended foreplay." Camille began to chuckle, until Leila reached out. One hand behind Camille's head, she scooted forward on the chair all in one smooth movement.

"Be a good girl, and—"

Anything else Leila had to say was lost in a stream of obscenity and moans. The sweeping tongue, sucking lips, and nipping teeth had her over the edge in no time.

Camille placed gentle kisses along her inner thigh. She needed more, but they didn't have time; not if she was to keep her promise and bring Camille's fantasy to life. Who was she kidding? It was her fantasy too.

Pushing the chair back, she urged Camille upright, reaching into the drawer. "I just need to put this on and then—"

Camille bent over the desk, readying herself, but Leila had other plans.

"*Non*, turn around. I need to see you."

When Camille turned, Leila reached for her blouse,

their mouths meeting as she nimbly unbuttoned it. The kiss grew in intensity. She tasted herself as she moved in closer, Camille's legs wrapping around her the moment Leila was inside.

"God, yes," Camille gasped, her head thrown backward. Her hand moved to support herself, pushing her day planner out of the way, the pen cup toppling and spilling its contents. "God, I've missed us," she said, uncaring about the mess.

Leila's hands held her firmly, eyes locked on one another. She knew the fantasy by heart.

"Can you imagine what they'd all think if they knew you were getting fucked at your desk by your lesbian lover?" she said, her hips pulsing to the rhythm she knew Camille liked best. "The ice queen? ...all hot, and wet and..."

"Uh-huh...keep talking." Camille tightened her legs around Leila's waist, directing the movement.

"Maybe Pamela thinks about it," Leila said, pushing the blouse off of Camille's shoulders. She kissed the skin there, licking her collarbone all the way up her neck to her ear. "You're so fucking hot."

"Fuck," Camille said, ramming her fist into her mouth.

"You like that?"

Camille mewled. The times she'd imagined this over the last few weeks, never having the courage to see it through, till now.

Lifting her hand, Camille threw both arms around Leila's shoulders and held tight, her own hips thrusting to meet Leila's.

"Harder." She squeaked and grunted when her instruction was followed instantly. "Fu—ck."

It was obvious to Leila that Camille had never been this

turned on in her life, not the way she was whenever Leila worked out her needs and led her towards it, systematically breaking down every single barrier and obstacle Camille had put in front of them.

"Want to come," Camille gasped, her knuckles white, gripping the edge of the desk now. She felt the hand on her head, fingers winding into her hair and tugging, as Leila kissed her neck.

"Come," Leila demanded, with one hard, fast, thrust after another, until Camille pressed her head against her lover, and muffled cries of ecstasy rang out.

"Yes…yes…Uh."

Camille slumped, limp and pliable. Soft kisses smattered her skin as she caught her breath. Her legs unhooked, feet back on the ground.

Finally, Leila stepped back, already unbuckling. Camille heard the soft thud as it landed on the floor and heard herself laugh.

"That was…" The smile said it all as Leila leaned in to kiss her. "Incredible."

"It was…" Leila grinned and adjusted her clothing. She bent down and picked up the strap-on, opened the drawer and dropped it in. "You can deal, no?"

"I need to freshen up. So, yes, I will deal." Camille checked her watch. "I need to take a call in a moment."

"I am aware of your schedule." Leila moved around the desk and retrieved Camille's skirt. "You have a thirty-minute window this afternoon."

Camille raised a playful brow. "I'm sure I can oblige." She took the skirt offered and redressed. "Do I look okay?"

"You look stunning, darling."

There was a knock on the door, which made them both stop and stare for a second, before Camille laughed. "Are you coming over later?" she asked, ignoring the door.

"I might," Leila teased, palms against the desk as she leaned over it to where Camille now sat. "Do you want me to… come?"

"Yes." Camille smirked. "I'd like that very much." She tidied her desk and re-potted the pens, sliding her diary across to where it usually sat. She reached into her bag and found her perfume, giving the area a quick spray, just in case.

The knock on the door was a little louder this time, and Leila quickly crossed the room to unlock it, stepping away before Camille sat down in her chair and they looked like two colleagues discussing work.

"Come," Camille said, not taking her eyes from Leila and registering the way, just that one word now, could have her lover liquify in front of her.

"Your coffee…" Fatima stopped and looked at Leila. "Oh, sorry, I didn't realise you were in a meeting." She placed Camille's coffee on the desk.

"It's fine. Actually, Ms Ortez is what I wanted to talk with you about." Leila crossed the room and closed the door, while Camille indicated to Fatima to take a seat. "You are my most trusted employee, and as such, I must ask a favour."

"Okay." Fatima giggled nervously.

Camille glanced at Leila. A month ago, she wouldn't have been able to imagine herself saying what she said next.

"The thing is, Ms Ortez and I are in a relationship, and as much as I don't believe it is anyone else's business, I do appreciate that eventually word will get out and office gossip will run wild."

"I see, yes. People do like to talk," Fatima nodded. "So,

you want me to run interference, put them off the scent?"

"No. I want you to spread the rumour." She steepled her fingers and looked Fatima directly in the eye. "Get it out in the open, over and done with. Let them have their five minutes of sniggering and gossiping, and then I'll call a meeting and make a really big deal about growing the fuck up."

Leila grinned. They'd already discussed this over the phone the previous night, but seeing Leila's delight at being acknowledged would be a sight that would stick with her for the rest of her life. Finally, she understood it, and wanted it for herself too.

"Well, I can certainly get that ball rolling." Fatima grinned. "It will be fun to actually start a rumour."

"Indeed. I appreciate that you're usually the last one to gossip and I am very aware my personal life is protected by you in your office."

"What would you like me to say exactly?"

Leila stepped forward. "Maybe something simple like, you came into the office and caught us kissing."

Camille smiled at the thought. "And obviously, as of now, Ms Ortez has access to my office without an appointment."

"Okay, well, let me be the first to offer you both congratulations and I hope you both find all the happiness together."

"Thank you," Camille said.

"I will do my best to act shocked when I leave here, and whoever asks first, I will…confide in." She winked.

Camille laughed. "An Oscar-worthy performance it will need to be."

She watched as Fatima left the room, the door closing

quietly behind her.

"So, that should give us about five more minutes before you are the talk of the office," Camille said, taking a deep breath. The wheels were in motion.

"And you."

"They won't dare talk about me yet. It will all be about you," Camille laughed. "They will have all weekend to come up with all kinds of scenarios, and on Monday, I'll bring it all to a head."

"Fabulous. So, dinner tonight and then home to yours or…"

Camille tilted her head. "Let's skip dinner. I need to feel your touch in an extended visit. Can you order pizza?

"I can do that." Leila checked her watch and then moved towards the door. "By the way, I booked the flights and the hotel. Madeira won't know what's hit it."

"Hm." Camille relaxed back in her chair. "I can't wait."

The door closed and Camille considered how different her life was now. Everything felt… complete, like all the voids had been filled with something light and fun.

She had new friends, a new attitude towards work and those who worked for her, and best of all, she had happiness. All of it stemmed from that one glance across a pool on a hot day, miles away from here. That one moment, when she'd taken a chance, and found a part of herself that was now hot to the touch— a spark, ignited.

All because she dared to love again. Because she couldn't ignore the taste of her a moment longer.

A sharp knock on the door, confidently hit, interrupted before Fatima had the chance to press the call button.

"Sorry, it's Pamela. She's insisting on speaking with

you."

"Thank you," Camille responded to Fatima before she gave a commanding, "Yes."

The door opened and Pamela stepped inside, all bold and confident. It would appear Leila hadn't just affected Camille, but everyone around her.

"Well, don't expect me to go easy on her just because you're screwing." Pamela smiled. "The entire time?"

"No…yes…kind of." Camille grinned. "It's complicated. The rumour mill already activated, I see?"

"Honestly, half the staff have had a bet on it the minute Sully discovered Leila was gay." She sat down in the chair opposite.

"Interesting." Camille frowned. "I didn't realise I was giving off quite so many gay vibes."

Pamela laughed. "Jesus, the Ice Queen act absolutely spurs on the gay vibes… You do realise every woman in this office has a crush on you, right?"

"Every woman?" Camille's brow raised, and she watched Pamela blush as she realised the trap she'd just walked into.

Finally, there was someone Camille could respect, and hand things over to when she wanted to swan off and enjoy the finer things in life.

"I need to discuss the Maddox account, and it can't wait," Pamela said, quickly changing the subject. But she grinned, and Camille understood this was a working relationship she was going to enjoy from now on.

Camille smiled. "So, tell me what the issue is. You've got three minutes."

The End

If you enjoyed this book or any other of Claire's books, then please consider leaving a review.

Many thanks!

You can find Claire on all Social Media Platforms, however, if you wish to engage, then here is the best place to head to:

Patreon (Free)

Claire Highton-Stevenson | Making hearts flutter with every turn of the page | Patreon

Keep up to date and get all the information when Claire's next book is released and subscribe to:

Claire's Newsletter here

www.itsclastevofficial.co.uk

Printed in Great Britain
by Amazon